KID
NORMAL
AND THE
ROGUE
HEROES

Also by Greg James and Chris Smith

KID NORMAL

KID
NORMAL
AND THE
ROGUE
HEROES

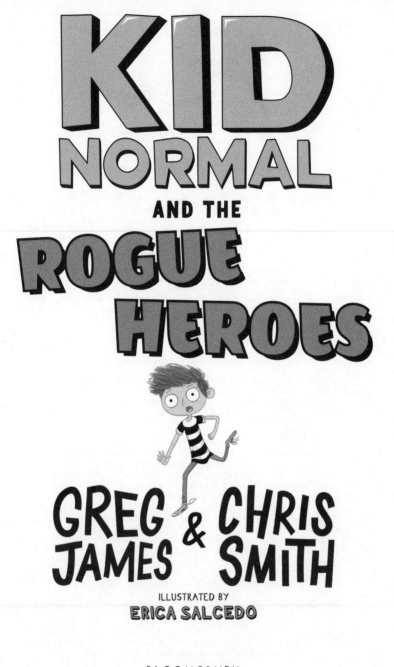

GREG JAMES & CHRIS SMITH

ILLUSTRATED BY
ERICA SALCEDO

BLOOMSBURY
CHILDREN'S BOOKS
NEW YORK   LONDON   OXFORD   NEW DELHI   SYDNEY

BLOOMSBURY CHILDREN'S BOOKS
Bloomsbury Publishing Inc., part of Bloomsbury Publishing Plc
1385 Broadway, New York, NY 10018

BLOOMSBURY, BLOOMSBURY CHILDREN'S BOOKS, and the Diana logo
are trademarks of Bloomsbury Publishing Plc

First published in Great Britain in March 2018 by Bloomsbury Publishing Plc
Published in the United States of America in September 2019
by Bloomsbury Children's Books

Bloomsbury books may be purchased for business or promotional use.
For information on bulk purchases please contact Macmillan Corporate and Premium
Sales Department at specialmarkets@macmillan.com

Library of Congress Cataloging-in-Publication Data
Names: James, Greg (Radio personality), author. | Smith, Chris
(Radio personality), author. | Salcedo, Erica, illustrator.
Title: Kid Normal and the rogue heroes / by Greg James and Chris Smith ;
illustrated by Erica Salcedo.
Description: New York : Bloomsbury, 2019.
Summary: Murph Cooper and the Super Zeroes are looking forward to a quiet second
year at The School—where children with superpowers learn to develop and control their
abilities—until a supervillain in a top-secret prison demands to see Kid Normal.
Identifiers: LCCN 2018047046 (print) | LCCN 2018056185 (e-book)
ISBN 978-1-5476-0098-4 (hardcover) • ISBN 978-1-5476-0103-5 (e-book)
Subjects: | CYAC: Superheroes—Fiction. | Supervillains—Fiction. |
Ability—Fiction. | Schools—Fiction. | Humorous stories.
Classification: LCC PZ7.1.J38487 Kl 2019 (print) | LCC PZ7.1.J38487 (e-book) |
DDC [Fic]—dc23
LC record available at https://lccn.loc.gov/2018047046

Printed and bound in the U.S.A. by Berryville Graphics Inc., Berryville, Virginia
2 4 6 8 10 9 7 5 3 1

All papers used by Bloomsbury Publishing Plc are natural, recyclable products made
from wood grown in well-managed forests. The manufacturing processes conform
to the environmental regulations of the country of origin.

To find out more about our authors and books visit www.bloomsbury.com
and sign up for our newsletters.

KidNormal.com

To Sylvia Bushell

1920–2017

A true hero

One for sorrow,
Two for joy,
Three for a girl,
And four for a boy.
Five for silver,
Six for gold,
Seven for a secret
never to be told.

1

The Treasures of Amasis

Running a team of crime-fighting superheroes is a complicated business, especially when you're not allowed to tell your mom.

And it's even worse, thought Murph Cooper as he glanced at his watch, *when you're supposed to be home by half past eight.*

Murph's mom had made him promise to be back in time for a special end-of-the-summer-vacation takeout dinner, but it was already seven forty and he hadn't even started to save the day yet.

"Showtime," said Murph, turning to the rest of his team. "Let's move."

The five members of the Super Zeroes crunched up the gravel driveway in front of them. Up ahead was an impressive stone building with a large sign hanging from one brass handle of its entrance doors.

The sign read: **Museum Shut.**

Murph beckoned his team over to one side of the path, where they crouched down behind an enormous ornamental fountain.

"This is the place," he hissed over the trickling of the water.

"So, what are we up against this time?" asked Mary Perkins, the late afternoon sunlight reflecting off her bright yellow raincoat. "I suppose it's too much to hope that the HALO unit has actually given us some useful information, for once?"

Murph pulled what looked like a cell phone out of his pocket and stared at the green-tinted screen. Text scrolled across the top:

ROBBERY IN PROGRESS . . . NEUTRALIZE.

Beneath this was a map marking the museum's location with a blinking lightning-bolt symbol—and just next to it, a tiny winged letter Z showed their own position. This handset was known as a HALO unit, and it was the Super Zeroes' only connection to the Heroes' Alliance. It had been handed to Murph months earlier by the head of the Alliance, Miss Flint, on the day they'd become the youngest heroes ever to join that legendary but notoriously mysterious organization.

Murph thought back to that day. None of them had known what to expect. What actually happens once you become a superhero? Is there a special shop where you pick up your costume? Do you get issued a cool utility belt and a selection of gadgets? Does a wizened old butler come and live at your house to give you advice when the whole hero-ing lark gets a bit too much for you emotionally?

Murph now knew the answers to all these questions, and they were—in no particular order—no, no, and no.

In fact, from what he could tell, the world of Heroes seemed to have changed a great deal since the "Golden Age" of a few decades ago. These days, Heroes operated in the shadows, for fear of being exposed and causing panic in a world that was scared of anything seen as too different or hard to understand. So their missions were carried out in secret, using only the most basic information from the Alliance. No adoring crowds, no newspaper headlines, and most definitely no costumes. But still, on a few occasions this summer, the HALO unit had flashed its small green light to indicate that the Alliance had a job for the Super Zeroes, and, costumes or no costumes, Murph's heart always did a little skip like a mischievous lamb at the sight.

"Just says there's a robbery in progress," he told Mary, looking at the closed front doors. "But we can't go in that way—whoever's in there would see us right away."

It was a humid day, and Murph eased his sticky T-shirt away from his sweaty back as he cast his gaze about for another way in. High up in one honey-colored stone wall, a window had been left slightly open. Below it was a wide window ledge and the blinking red light of a security camera.

"Nellie," whispered Murph, "we need to take out that camera."

The figure at the back of the group silently stuck up a thumb. Nellie Lee, who was wearing her usual ripped jeans and baggy sweater despite the heat, slipped out from behind the fountain. Darting from

4

shrub to shrub to avoid the camera's line of sight, she scuttled over to the wall, holding her hand out, palm upward, as she went.

The clouds above the museum began to grow darker. There was a rumble of thunder, and all at once a lightning bolt forked down and hit the camera, which fell to the ground in a shower of sparks. Another smaller bolt of electricity branched off and down. It seemed to disappear into Nellie's hand, which glowed with dancing blue fire.

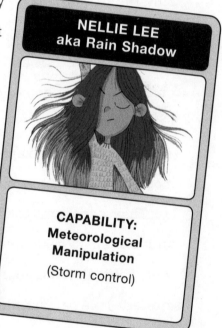

NELLIE LEE
aka Rain Shadow

CAPABILITY:
Meteorological
Manipulation
(Storm control)

Nellie made a swift chopping motion with her glowing hand and mimed wearing binoculars to signal to her friends the words "Camera's out." That doesn't make much sense written down, but get your hands out and have a go and you'll see what we mean.

"Good work, Nellie," said Murph, as the others ran

over to join her. "Right, time to get inside." He turned to Mary. "Would you do the honors?"

Mary nodded, producing a small, folded-up yellow umbrella from her raincoat pocket and pressing the button on the handle.

"Hang on!" she said.

"Oh no, what's wrong? What's the holdup?" asked Billy Talbot, who was prone to being the voice of doom at times like this.

Mary looked at him in exasperation. "No, *hang on*. As in, you're going to need to grab on . . . ," she explained patiently.

Billy gave her the universally recognized stretchy-mouthed face that means "Oops, sorry."

They each grasped the handle of the umbrella and began to rise into the air like . . . well, it's quite difficult to compare it to anything really. They looked like a bunch of flying child-grapes. They looked like five kid-shaped fish on a hook. Most of all, they looked like five children hanging on to an airborne umbrella.

Mary steered them toward the window ledge.

6

"Right, so what do we reckon they're here to steal?" asked Murph as they rose. He was still quite new to the town and until now hadn't realized it even had a museum. "What's the most valuable stuff here?"

The others shrugged.

"I heard there's a whole display about the history of cheese graters or something," whispered Billy.

"My dad said the woodwind gallery is really fascinating," said the final member of the Super Zeroes, Hilda Baker, her red curls tickling Murph's nose as she spoke. "Apparently they've got the region's oldest bassoon," she added excitedly.

Murph grimaced. "I don't think anyone's going to want to steal that," he retorted. "Sounds like you'd be doing everyone a favor if you did. Well, we'll just have to get in there and take a look."

The five Super Zeroes squeezed onto the ledge on

the third floor and one by one dropped through the open window and into a dimly lit room. It was lined with glass cases filled with hats.

That's right: in a museum that did indeed contain a display devoted to cheese graters, they had been unlucky enough to drop straight into the Hat Room, the least interesting exhibit in the whole place, and possibly on earth.

"Worst. Museum. Ever," said Murph softly, reading the label on the nearest display case.

This hat was worn by Sir Thomas Wimpole on the day his second-cousin-once-removed married the fourteenth duke of Carlisle. It is a fine example of late Regency hatsmanship, fashioned from finest Canadian otter skin with mouse fur trimmings. For goodness' sake, Murph, why are you still reading that ridiculous hat label?

Murph realized that last part wasn't written down. It was just Mary whispering in his ear.

"Sorry," he said, "but who in their right mind would want to steal anything from this museum?"

"The thieves aren't here for the hats—" Mary began.

"Nah, 'course not. Who'd be wearing a hat in this weather anyway?" Billy broke in. "Your head would get all sweaty."

"No, I mean the hats aren't worth stealing but—" Mary tried again.

"What about this lovely one?" cried Hilda. She had her nose pressed up against another large case. "It's divine, look! A genuine 1920s horse hat! It's even got holes for its little ears." Billy and Nellie headed Hilda's way. Even Mary was beginning to look a bit interested.

Another complicated aspect of running a team of crime-fighting superheroes, thought Murph, *is to not let them get sidetracked by weird hats.*

"Can we focus, please?" he said through gritted teeth. "Mary was about to say something important."

"Oh yes," said Mary. "I was saying that whoever's robbing this museum is here . . . for *those*." She pointed to a brightly colored poster near the doorway.

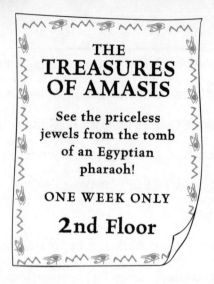

THE
**TREASURES
OF AMASIS**

See the priceless
jewels from the tomb
of an Egyptian
pharaoh!

ONE WEEK ONLY

2nd Floor

The Zeroes looked at one another, all raising their eyebrows and going **"Oooohhhh"** at the same time in an impressive display of coordinated realizing. Mary nodded smugly.

The five crept through the doorway, Hilda giving one last longing look back toward the horse hat.

The landing was in darkness, but at its end a large stone staircase led to the second floor, and they could hear a faint clinking and clumping coming from down there—definitely the sounds of people up to no good.

Murph's attention was caught by a glowing red panel on the wall turning green. `ALARM SYSTEM DISABLED`, it read.

Murph beckoned the Super Zeroes toward the

top of the stairs. As they craned their necks over the banister they could make out soft voices and the light from a flashlight moving on the floor below. They could just hear a woman's voice crooning, "Come to Aunty, my pretties . . ."

Murph felt a thrill of fear, like someone had tickled his back with an ice cream sandwich. What weird kind of a thief described themselves as "Aunty?"

He made a zipping motion across his mouth for silence and beckoned his team of Heroes onward, down the dark staircase . . .

Penelope Travers owned one of the finest collections of Egyptian antiquities in the country. Well, legally speaking, she didn't actually own it, because most of it had been stolen. But she certainly *had* a large collection of Egyptian antiquities back home at her family mansion, and tonight she was planning to add to it.

The burglar's eyes sparkled as she padded around, gloating over the glinting treasures that filled the museum's glass cases. "Have you disabled the alarm, Hugo?" she snapped.

"Yes, Aunty," a smartly dressed young man said, cringing. He had been busily tapping at a panel on the wall. "We're ready to rock and roll."

"Don't use that ridiculous expression," barked Penelope, wagging a ring-encrusted finger in his general direction. "Now, where's my other nephew? Come over here, you great lumbering brute of a boy."

A third figure galumphed into view. It was a hugely thick-set youth, whose belly was fighting against his shirt and very, very nearly winning.

"Have you got the bags, Rupert?" she asked.

"Yup," he replied, not being a great one for banter.

"Then it's time to add some more pretties to my little collection," breathed Penelope Travers. "And I think we'll start with pusskins over there."

She heaved herself over to a plinth in the center of the room, on top of which stood a gleaming golden statue of a cat with green jeweled eyes. "Come to Aunty!" she coaxed, reaching out a clammy hand.

But at that moment she was distracted by a strange noise. It sounded, impossibly, like the clip-clopping of a tiny horse's hooves. The would-be cat burglar peered over her shoulder, but could see nothing through the gloom.

When she turned back, the golden cat was gone.

"Where is it?" shrieked Penelope, scrabbling at the plinth and looking around frantically, as if the treasure had wandered off like a real cat and would be somewhere close by, licking its bottom.

She thought she caught a glint of yellow toward the back of the room, and her eyes narrowed. "There's someone over there. **Ru-PERT! Get them!**"

"My pleasure, Aunty," grunted Rupert. He lumbered over to the enormous golden sarcophagus at the back of the gallery. Its label read:

The Mummy of the Pharaoh Amasis
DO NOT TOUCH

"I can't see anyone, Aunty. Just a mummy," called Rupert.

"Look for them, then!" came Penelope's bossy voice from behind the cabinets. "They must be hiding somewhere."

Rupert edged toward the upright tomb, reaching out a hand to open the lid and see if anyone was lurking inside.

"Come to Papa, mummy," he murmured to himself, proving why he should stick to banter-free conversation.

Suddenly, the sarcophagus burst open. Ancient bandages flew everywhere like streamers at the most bizarre party ever, and Rupert screamed in pure terror as the preserved remains of the pharaoh Amasis shot out of the coffin and ballooned toward him.

He turned and ran, shoving his aunt out of the way as he pelted out of the room and away down the stairs.

Behind the tomb, Billy looked across at Murph, who was hiding in the shadow of a nearby sphinx, and gave him a large thumbs-up with a large thumb.

BILLY TALBOT
aka Balloon Boy

CAPABILITY:
Corporeal Inflation
(Ballooning of parts of himself or nearby objects—sometimes without meaning to)

Penelope Travers's other nephew, Hugo, had watched in horror as his beefier brother had fled. He was just starting to sidestep toward the door when his aunt stopped him.

"Not so fast," she barked. "I didn't come all this way to leave without these pretties. **Get back there and snag me something shiny! NOW!**"

Hugo was scared of inflating mummies, but he was even more scared of shouting aunties. He edged tentatively forward, hoping to swipe something and get out quickly. His eyes rested on a brightly polished metal jug standing on its own on top of a display cabinet. He made a grab for it, but as he did, another hand shot out from behind the cabinet and touched the jug at the same time. Its metal surface was immediately covered with tiny, criss-crossing blue lines of electricity. Hugo's body jerked and danced as the electrical power of Nellie's stored lightning raced all the way through him. He snatched his hand away and careered off down the stairs after his brother.

"Useless boys," harrumphed Penelope to herself, straightening her shoulders. "Well, as the old saying goes: if you want something stolen, steal it yourself."

She clumped to the nearest cabinet, which held a display of animal statues: crocodiles, cats, snakes, and, at the very front, two tiny horses.

"Stop right there!" came a voice from behind her. Penelope spun around.

Framed in the doorway, standing with hands on hips in the internationally recognized Hero stance, was a young boy. His hair was tousled and his jeans scruffy, but he was looking at her confidently and coolly.

"And just who are you supposed to be? Officer Pip-squeak?" crowed the thief arrogantly.

"I don't really know what that means," said Murph. "But your little shopping trip's over."

"Oh, I don't think it is." Penelope was playing for time. "In fact, I'm going to gather up these ancient statues and walk right out of here. And there's nothing you can do about it."

She reached into the cabinet and grabbed the horses before making a run for the door.

Just as she got to the top of the stairs, she decided to stop for a little gloat. Now that she knew the source of all this chaos had been one puny boy, she was confident she'd be back at her mansion in time for tea, ancient Egyptian horse statues in hand.

"Come on, then, pretty horsey," she fluted, holding one statue up to her face. "Let's gallop away from this funny little boy."

Penelope just had time to register that it really was a *very* realistic statue before the horse lunged forward and bit her firmly on the nose. She screamed and flung the tiny horse away from her.

"Careful!" came a shout from behind a bookcase.

HILDA BAKER
aka Equana

CAPABILITY:
Classified as "Anomalous"
(Can summon two tiny horses from thin air)

Hilda ran out and dashed to the horse, which was lying on the stone floor.

"Artax, are you okay?" she whispered. The little horse whinnied in a comforting way. Hilda glared at Penelope furiously. ***"Nobody* hurts my horses!"**

At that moment Penelope realized that she was still holding the second horse. She squealed as it pirouetted neatly, kicked her squarely in the chin, and sent her toppling all the way down the stairs, her arms flailing and her face wobbling like Jell-O on top of a washing machine.

All five Super Zeroes came together at the top of the stairs to gaze down at the now-unconscious burglar.

"Good work, Hilda," Mary said as she drifted down from the ceiling. She was clutching her umbrella in one hand and the golden cat statue in the other. "And nice work with the exploding mummy, Billy."

Billy grinned. "It was Murph's idea," he admitted.

"Our best ideas usually are," said Mary. They all turned to their leader.

Murph blushed and lifted the HALO unit to his

MURPH COOPER
aka Kid Normal

CAPABILITY:
None
(Leader of the Super Zeroes)

mouth. "Alliance, come in. Super Zeroes here. Museum suspects neutralized. Please advise CAMU." Signing off, Murph looked around to his friends in satisfaction at a job well done.

"Copy that, Super Zeroes," came a calm voice from the handset. "Police will be in attendance shortly. Clear the scene and keep out of sight. Good work."

As the screen went blank, Murph looked at his watch. It was 8:25.

"Myaaargh! I'm gonna be late for dinner!"

Mary smiled and flumphed her umbrella at him. "Need a lift home?"

Outside the museum, Penelope Travers was being pushed into the back of a police van.

"But there were children," she was gibbering.

"At least two children. One of them may have been electric. And one of them had horses! Tiny horses! One bit me!"

"Yeah, absolutely, hon, we'll look into that right away," mocked the police officer, who some weeks later would be awarded a medal for capturing one of the country's most notorious cat burglars. "We'll get the tiny horse detectives on the case, don't you worry. For now, though, get in the back of the van."

He helped a still-complaining Penelope into the van, not noticing the flash of yellow that took off from a high window ledge and disappeared into the low cloud.

Murph could see drops of dew sparkling on Mary's hair and woolen scarf as the two of them cleared the clouds and began skimming across town. One of her hands was holding tight to her umbrella—the other was wrapped around his waist. Away to the west, the sinking sun was just beginning to gild the edges of the clouds with pink. It looked like a giant plate of mashed potatoes that had been dusted with a delicate frosting of strawberry-flavored sugar—which sounds disgusting but actually looked very pretty.

It made Murph feel slightly uncomfortable, though. Ever since Mary had rescued him from certain death-by-pavement by grabbing onto his hand and flying him out of danger a few months ago, it was as if his awkwardness dial turned itself up a few notches whenever they were alone together. And now, floating in silence above rosy-white puffs of cloud, it was in danger of going all the way up to eleven.

To break the tension, he asked, "So, um, how's your new umbrella working out? I thought you said that you didn't really need one to help you fly any more."

"Oh, well, it still seems easier with the umbrella. Helps me focus, if that makes any sense," Mary replied airily.

It made no sense at all to Murph, but he was so glad the silence had been broken that he gave a nervous, neighing laugh for no real reason.

Mary looked at him knowingly. "Anyway, enough chit-chat. You're late as it is." And with that, they descended into the strawberry-dusted clouds.

At eight thirty precisely, Murph's mom marched to the door of their house and looked angrily down the street.

"Murph!" she shouted into the evening air.

"Yes?" fluted an innocent-sounding voice from behind her. She spun around to see her youngest son tripping down the stairs like a carefree pixie who has been at home for literally hours.

"Er . . . Oh. I didn't hear you come in," she said, confused. "Anyway—come on, it's last-night-of-vacation takeout. Get right in before your brother has all the spring rolls."

"Save some for me, Andy, you greedy great elephant!" yelled Murph, pelting for the kitchen.

Not a bad evening's work, he thought to himself. *Robbery averted—and home in time for lemon chicken. Maybe this Hero business isn't that complicated after all.*

He could not have been more wrong.

A LONG WAY AWAY, a man in black sat on the cold stone floor of his cell and listened.

Eyes closed, head cocked, he tuned his super-sensitive hearing like a radio, scanning the world above him. He listened to words being uttered miles and miles away and sifted them like river sludge, searching calmly for the nuggets of gold that he could use to forge a plan of escape.

For years he had listened and heard nothing of use. But now, at long last, something had changed. He had scented it in the salty air, like the turning of a distant tide.

It was time. Time to take up his work once again.

The man in black opened his cruel eyes. With one pale, spindly hand he reached out and grasped a small stone.

Looking for all the world like an ancient, stooped bird in his tattered black clothes, he hunched over and used the stone to write on the granite floor. It made a hideous screeching—but there was no one except him to hear. Nobody else had been into this cell for thirty years.

But that was about to change.

He stopped only when he was surrounded by letters—large, uneven, white.

He heard the whine of a camera as it focused in on the message, relaying it to a screen somewhere in the world above.

The message on the stone read:

I Am Ready To Talk. BrIng Kid noRmaL to ME.

2

Mr. Flash's Emotional Antelope

Mr. Iain Flash was woken at 5 a.m. on the first day of school by a lovely fluffy little wren sitting upon a dew-dappled twig outside his bedroom window. It was tweeting a delicate song, as if to welcome the beautiful start of a fresh new day.

"SHUUUUUUUUUT UUUUUUP!" screamed Mr. Flash directly into its innocent little face.

The wren fell to the ground, stunned. (Although we should point out for all bird lovers that it made a full recovery.)

Mr. Flash stalked angrily back toward his bed, stubbing his toe on a huge dumbbell on the way. He looked in the mirror and preened his large ginger mustache with a special mustache comb, then

began his morning exercises. First, he performed fifty push-ups and fifty jumping jacks, and then he stomped down the stairs for his early-morning run.

He slammed the front door behind him and squinted angrily at the rising sun, as if it were personally trying to annoy him by shining in his eyes. Then, abruptly, he seemed to disappear as he sprinted off down the road, leaving a cloud of fine dust in his wake.

Mr. Flash was a teacher at Murph's school. In fact, Mr. Flash was Murph's least favorite teacher, because he never missed an opportunity to bully Murph about the fact that he had no superpower—or Capability, as they were known in the secret world that Murph had stumbled into. Mr. Flash's own Cape was incredible speed, as he was currently demonstrating with his morning sprint.

Five minutes later, Mr. Flash appeared back outside the front door, beet red and sweating.

The wren, which was by now feeling much better, peered nervously at him around the corner of the house. He didn't dare say anything until the teacher had vanished inside, but then he gave a tiny **peep**— which is actually a very rude word, but luckily you don't speak Wren. Or if you do, please do not repeat it at home because we'll get in loads of trouble. Which would be a **peeping** nightmare.

Inside, in the spotless kitchen, Mr. Flash stomped around grabbing ingredients as he mixed himself an enormous protein shake to the following recipe:

Mr. Flash's Morning Shake

5 raw eggs

8 bananas

1 pint of milk

A handful of flaxseeds (which he privately nicknames Flash seeds)

1/2 pound raw minced steak

1 red onion

Half an avocado

Again, this is something that you should not try at home. It's disgusting. But Mr. Flash scarfed it down. When he'd finished, he wiped his mouth with the back of his hand and let out a burp that both sounded and smelled like a young bull elephant.

Mr. Flash was looking forward to the first day back at school. His subject was Capability Training, or CT. It was his job to help students develop their Capes and control them. Often this involved shouting at them—and this was the part of the job that he really loved.

After their first year at The School, students were split into two classes. Mr. Flash took charge of what he proudly called "the A Stream"—those students who had powerful, useful Capes and might one day be suitable to join the Heroes' Alliance. Popping a couple of slices of bread into the toaster and flicking the kettle on, the teacher curled his ginger mustache in satisfaction as he thought about how happy he was not to have to teach the other class—or, as he called them, "the remnants."

Kids with weird Capes? What a waste of space. Tiny horses? Blowing your hands up like balloons? Hah.

But as he began arranging cutlery on a large tray, his thoughts turned to his least favorite students, who, you may have worked out, were Murph and the rest of the Super Zeroes. When Nektar, a crazy man-wasp, had attacked The School last year, Murph and his friends had saved the day while everyone else had either been captured or made into a mind-controlled slave. And yet, far from being grateful, Mr. Flash couldn't bear this. In fact, he was as far from grateful as you could imagine. If Grateful was a small town just outside Sydney, Australia, Mr. Flash was very much located somewhere near Birmingham, England.

To make it worse, thanks to their actions the Super Zeroes had actually been recruited to the Heroes' Alliance—an incredibly rare privilege.

Totally nuts; what on earth were they thinking? fumed Mr. Flash as he angrily made a mug of tea. It's hard to make tea angrily, but he managed it.

When the breakfast tray was assembled, he popped back outside. The wren was sniffing a flower at the edge of the lawn.

"MOOOOVE, YOU LITTLE BROWN . . . HEN, or whatever you're supposed to be!" Mr. Flash bellowed at it.

The wren raised one of its eyebrows sarcastically and flapped off as Mr. Flash picked the flower and carried it carefully back into the kitchen, placing it in a small vase on the tray.

"Iain! Where's my breakfast?" screeched a voice from above suddenly.

"Coming, Mother!" answered Mr. Flash. With a

final snort of fury at the thought of the Super Zeroes, he lifted the tray and climbed the stairs.

At eight o'clock sharp, Mr. Flash appeared in the front yard of the school after running the eight miles from his house in just under three minutes, not only breaking the land speed record but successfully avoiding detection from any passersby. He was a little surprised to find the head teacher of The School, Mr. Souperman, waiting for him outside the main entrance wearing an expensive jacket and a rather strained smile.

"Morning, Mr. Flash," said Mr. Souperman, his teeth and oiled hair both glinting heroically.

"What are you doing here?" replied Mr. Flash rudely.

The headmaster's smile became slightly more strained. If you'd been close enough, you'd have heard it make a small creaking sound.

"Well," he began, gesturing for Mr. Flash to walk with him as he turned and started to pace across The School's deserted front yard, "I just wanted to have a chat before school resumes. Nothing major, nothing to worry about."

Here's some advice that will help you out in the workplace later in life: when your boss tells you there's nothing to worry about, you should *immediately* start worrying and possibly even accept the fact that your life is about to be ruined. Mr. Flash was instantly on his guard, like an antelope scenting the waft of hungry lions on a soft African breeze.

"I've been very, very impressed with your teaching over the past year . . . ," continued Mr. Souperman.

When your boss tells you not to worry and then immediately compliments you, this is an even larger sign that your world is about to implode.

"And with that in mind," the headmaster went on, "we're having a little shake-up."

Mr. Flash now felt like an antelope who had just gotten its foot stuck in a mudhole while being chased by eight hungry lions.

"But I'm . . . I'm still the CT teacher?" he blustered, mustache flapping with anxiety.

"Oh, yes, yes, yes, of course," Mr. Souperman soothed him. "Yes, yes, yes, yes indeed." He was overdoing it now. "It was your class that I wanted to talk to you about. The A Stream."

Mr. Flash's emotional antelope was now feeling the first bite of a lion's tooth in his antelopean bottom. He was fiercely protective of his A Stream students, and resented anyone trying to interfere. Which, he correctly anticipated, was exactly what Mr. Souperman was about to do.

"I know you've always been, ahem, *insistent* about selecting students for the A Stream yourself, based on the P-CAT test," continued the headmaster. He was referring to the Practical Capability Aptitude Test, the fearsome assault course for first-year students, which was the highlight of Mr. Flash's year. "But I think the events of last term have shown us that the P-CAT is not necessarily the right way to identify those students with Alliance potential. After all, the Super Zeroes have just become the youngest students ever admitted to the Heroes' Alliance, and *their* P-CAT results would have been abysmal . . . if the test hadn't been interrupted by that, ahem, wasp fellow."

Mr. Flash made a noise like a vacuum cleaner full of whipped cream being accidentally set to "blow."

"THEM?" he spat disgustedly. "That bunch of . . . of . . . half-baked . . . baked beans? They'll never be Heroes! They—"

"They already *are* Heroes," Mr. Souperman interrupted him. "And it's not our business to question the decisions of the Alliance."

Mr. Flash looked like he wanted to make it very much his business—with a fully furnished office and a website and everything—but the headmaster silenced his next burst of bile with a warning eyebrow. Mr. Flash's head went a color that a paint catalog would describe as "crimson inferno."

"The Super Zeroes will be joining the A Stream this year, **and that's final,"** Mr. Souperman concluded, before shoving his way through the double doors at the front of the school and vanishing off into the gloom, feeling all managerial.

Mr. Flash slumped back against the wall, with his emotional antelope now spread over a twenty-yard radius and being picked at by vultures. This year could not have gotten off to a worse start.

3

Veterans Day

The beginning of the school year is like the start of a roller coaster: once things get going, they tend to move very fast. One moment you're clambering into a carriage in the sunshine at the top of the ride, with grass-stained knees and wearing a summery T-shirt. Then, moments later, you're hurtling past pumpkins and fireworks, and before you've even digested your candy apple, you're trundling to a halt at Christmas and your nose is freezing.

And Murph was looking forward to every bit of it, he realized as he zipped along the sidewalk to begin his second year at The School, still full of spring rolls, chicken chow mein, and excitement.

What a difference a year makes, he thought.

A year ago he was getting teased for being the only kid at school without a Cape, but now he was one of the youngest people ever to be made a member of the Heroes' Alliance. If that didn't prove that he belonged at The School as much as anybody, he didn't know what did. Finally, after putting up with all the whispering and teasing, he might be about to get a little bit of respect.

"HEY! HURRY IT UP, YOU USELESS LITTLE MAGGOT. STOP MAGGOTING AROUND LIKE A . . . LIKE A . . . A MAGGOT!" bellowed an enormous and all-too-familiar voice.

Mr. Flash had decided to soothe his wounded pride with a bit of really high-quality shouting, and his least-favorite student had appeared at just the right time. Murph faked a spurt of speed by doing that waddle that looks a bit like you're running but in reality isn't actually any faster than walking.

"COME ON! GET IN HERE! The party can really get started now Kid Normal's arrived!" roared Mr. Flash as Murph run-walked past him with his head down. "Though what you're doing here at all I've still got absolutely no idea," he concluded in a fake whisper that was perfectly audible to everyone within a ten-yard radius.

As Murph followed the press of students toward the main hall, Mr. Flash's jibe hung around in his brain like a mean-spirited daddy longlegs, bothering his newfound confidence with its unnecessarily dangly limbs and dampening his spirits. Soon he began to be uncomfortably aware of people looking at him: he noticed expressions of interest, puzzlement, and, from one or two of the older kids, real hostility. Being a Hero didn't bring automatic respect, Murph was quickly realizing. Instead, it brought a large helping of disbelief with a jumbo-size side order of jealousy. He was relieved when Hilda fell into step beside him.

"Look at all the new little people," she said as they came upon a tangle of wide-eyed new students blocking the hallway. "I can't believe that was us a year ago. We're so grown-up now. Grown-up *and* Heroes!"

Hilda had always been fascinated by the world of Heroes. Of the five of them, she was by far the proudest to be a member of the Alliance, albeit a little disappointed that she wasn't allowed to wear a special costume. Murph suspected (correctly) that she had secretly designed one anyway, and was just waiting for an excuse to wear it in public.

The main hall was already filling up, but he could see Billy and Mary waving from a row near the back. Billy had ballooned a hand to save them both seats.

"Keep one for Nellie too," Mary reminded them as they sat down. "Has anyone seen her?"

They scanned the room as the rest of the school swirled around them. The older kids greeted one another confidently and swapped summer stories, while the new students were milling around hesitantly toward the front of the room amid a faint smell of nervous gas. One of them was so anxious he accidentally activated his Cape; his neck suddenly extended to twenty times its normal length so that his head shot into the air like a jack-in-the-box.

"I'm sorry! I didn't mean to do it!" squeaked the head as it bobbed among the light fixtures. Billy looked up at him pityingly as laughter rose around the hall; he knew all too well what it felt like to be laughed at for his own unpredictable Cape.

"Oh dear," said Mary, smiling. "Poor little mite. Let's hope he winds his neck in before Mr. Souperman gets here."

Neck Boy did indeed succeed in reverting to a more traditional shape, just in time for Mrs. Fletcher, the school librarian, to call for silence in her own unique way.

"PAAAAAAAAAAARP!"

Mrs. Fletcher's Capability was the power to transform her head into a large foghorn.

A hush fell on the hall as the last few stragglers rushed in and took their seats. Among them was Nellie, who slipped around the corner like a shy snake and slid into place beside Murph, wiping her hands on her jeans. They seemed to be covered in oil stains.

"Where have you been hiding?"

Murph whispered to her. But Nellie, who was not given to long speeches at the best of times, only squeaked briefly and shook her long, green-tipped hair at him.

At that moment, Mr. Souperman strode purposefully into the hall, waving an unnecessary hand for silence. (His hand in general wasn't unnecessary—he found it useful on an almost daily basis. But the wave wasn't necessary, because Mrs. Fletcher had already silenced the room. Look, we're getting bogged down here. Let's close these parentheses and move on, shall we?)

Mr. Souperman climbed the steps to the stage at the front of the hall and faced his students.

"Welcome in," he began, before correcting himself. "Welcome here . . . back here. Welcome back in here. Good morning."

Mr. Souperman could get a bit flustered speaking in front of large crowds from time to time, and it appeared that today was no exception. But he rallied valiantly and went on in dramatic hushed tones: "It is the start of a new school year."

It's amazing how many speeches start with something really obvious, thought Murph to himself. *He might as well have stood up and said, "Well, here we all are, then, in the hall."*

Mr. Souperman had paused, as if to find exactly the right words with which to continue. "Well, here we all are, then," he said eventually, "in the hall. Ready to begin another exciting journey. But for you new students, this will all seem a little strange and overwhelming. So let me say a few words of reassurance. You have been admitted to this school because you are . . . special."

Mr. Souperman gazed intently at the youngest students as he continued. **"The world can be a dangerous place for people like us.** But here at The School we will teach you to control your Capabilities, so you can keep them secret and live in safety."

Murph heard Mr. Flash **harrumph** scornfully from his seat along one wall.

"Or, if you are exceptionally skilled," continued the headmaster, "we will give you the tools you need to take on the duties of a Hero. You will rise to the top . . . of the glass. Like cream. This school is the milk—no, wait—the school is the glass. We put the milk in . . . you are the milk. But some of you . . . are the cream. And I . . . in some ways, I am the cow."

He paused and furrowed his brow, his public-speaking jitters having apparently resurfaced once again.

"What on earth is he talking about?" muttered Mary.

"Anyway—we're getting sidetracked with milk," said Mr. Souperman.

"Time to *moo*-ve it along?" said Billy, more loudly than he'd intended.

"What was that?" asked the headmaster, looking over toward them.

Billy's right foot inflated in consternation, sending his shoe flying off. It bounced off the wall and landed near Mr. Flash. The CT teacher glared balefully in their direction.

"As I was saying," continued the headmaster, "those of you who are truly world class will have the chance to take this vow."

He indicated an impressive stone tablet that hung proudly above the stage:

THE HEROES' VOW
I promise to save without glory,
To help without thanks,
And to fight without fear.
I promise to keep our secrets,
Uphold our vow,
And learn what it means
To be a true Hero.

"Ooh, it gives me the shivers every time," said Hilda excitedly, and then she blushed furiously upon noticing that most of the hall was now staring in their direction. Mr. Souperman was pointing at them.

"Last spring, five of our students stood on this very stage and became the youngest people ever to say those words, and—" Mr. Souperman had begun dramatically, but this time Mr. Flash interrupted him with a **harrumph** the size of a hippo's sneeze, and it seemed to bring the headmaster down to earth with a bump.

"Yes, well," Mr. Souperman blustered, "I wouldn't want any of you to get too excited about that. Those were exceptional and . . . highly surprising circumstances. We certainly don't expect anything quite as dramatic to happen this year."

At these words, the daddy longlegs of doubt returned to bother Murph's brain. He felt even more deflated now—as did Billy, apparently, as his foot sank sadly back to its original size (five).

"But nonetheless," continued Mr. Souperman, "we like to use the first day of each new school year to show you what it's possible to achieve. And so, without further ado, I would like to welcome you to Veterans Day: the day when we invite former Heroes' Alliance operatives to The School to spend time in your lessons. Last year, as most of you will remember, we were lucky enough to have a visit from Countess Fireball and her faithful sidekick, Dominic Sledgehammer."

Murph turned to Mary and jacked his eyebrows up a few notches in surprise until they met his hair coming the other way. This was brand-spanking-new news to him. He had joined The School two weeks late last year and hadn't heard one peep out of the others about Veterans Day or getting to meet actual Heroes.

"Oh yeah, Countess Fireball was pretty cool, actually," Mary acknowledged in a whisper. "The sidekick guy was a bit weird, though. He kept on breaking stuff and shouting, 'Hammer Time!'"

Murph calmed one eyebrow but kept the other at high alert. By now, the left-hand side of his face was beginning to ache, and he was actually quite looking forward to ditching this expression completely.

But he was forced to keep it, because just then Mr. Souperman spread both arms wide and announced grandly, "So please welcome our special guests for Veterans Day this year. **The Ex-Cape Committee!"**

There was a dramatic pause, followed by an even more dramatic c|ang from the hallway, and finally a loud whirring noise.

Everyone craned their necks to try to see what was happening—even Mr. Souperman, who by this time seemed anxious to be getting on with his assembly.

Just as the tension was becoming unbearable, a sleek silver wheelchair glided through the doorway. Sitting in it was a white-haired man with a keen, intelligent face and a neat beard. He was dressed in a natty gray jacket and had a red silk scarf knotted at his throat. The man moved smoothly through the hall, stopping only when he reached the foot of the stairs leading up to the stage.

Everyone in the hall now looked across at Mr. Souperman, who was standing up on the stage expectantly. Then they looked back at the man in the wheelchair. Then they looked at Mr. Souperman again, then back at the wheelchair, like they were watching the oddest game of tennis ever.

For a while nobody dared say anything, until one new student finally squeaked out, "How's he gonna get up the stairs?" before the people sitting on either side of him shushed him embarrassedly.

"Excellent question from our vole-voiced young friend there!" The man in the wheelchair grinned. He spoke with a clipped, upper-crust accent. *"Never* be afraid to ask a question. And here's your answer." He moved the fingers of his right hand across a small control panel set into the arm of the chair.

There was a click, followed by a low hum, and without fuss, the wheelchair rose slowly into the air.

"Oooh," said almost everyone.

"Oooh indeed," said the man in the chair, chuckling as he flew delicately around the room like an amused cloud. In a flying wheelchair. With a scarf on.

The chair passed right over the Super Zeroes as it looped across the back of the hall. Murph could just make out what looked like a bright metal fan spinning underneath, but he couldn't feel any downdraft. This was so puzzling he was forced to keep his quizzical expression in place; the left-hand side of his face was now cramping up quite severely.

At that moment Murph heard a familiar chuckle, and he followed the sound to the back of the hall, where Carl, the school janitor, was leaning against the wall and gazing up at the flying chair with an affectionate expression.

The wheelchair glided toward the stage, turning in midair. The man touched more buttons on the control panel as he swooped in and landed beside Mr. Souperman, who raised his hands and began clapping. Gradually, the whole hall followed suit.

While this impressive display of wheelchair aeronautics had been taking place, three more people had entered the hall and reached the top of the steps to the stage in a less interesting fashion. Two of them were slim elderly ladies, obviously twins, with long, straight silver hair and shrewd, intelligent faces. The other was a large, grizzled old man who walked with the aid of a stick. He was bald, with a strong neck and a red face. In fact, he looked not unlike Mr. Flash would have if you shaved off his mustache and then waited around patiently for forty years.

As the applause died down, Mr. Souperman introduced his guests, starting with the man in the incredible wheelchair.

"We are very honored to have with us today Sir Jasper Rowntree," he announced, "formerly known as 'Tech-Knight.'"

"Ah, yes. Tech-Knight," said Sir Jasper, inclining his head politely to acknowledge the headmaster's welcome. "That's a name I haven't heard in a long while. But in times past, tele-tech was indeed my Capability: the power to control electronics with my mind."

"And please also welcome the Gemini Sisters," said Mr. Souperman, waving a hand in the direction of the twins.

"Marian and Vivian to you," said one of the pair. "That's Marian there."

"Vivian and I were shape-shifters," added the other.

"We could squeeze through even the tiniest of spaces," her sister went on. "Very useful on missions back in the day."

"It certainly was," broke in the final member of the team, clomping his stick on the wooden stage as he stepped forward. "I fought alongside these ladies many

times, as the super-strong Lead Head. Tommy Biggs, at your service." He waved his stick out at the assembled students in salute, many of whom were regarding the quartet on the stage openmouthed.

The initial hubbub of excitement that had greeted the entrance of the flying wheelchair was gradually curdling into confusion as the true meaning of the Ex-Cape Committee's name dawned on the students.

"Those guys aren't Heroes! They don't even have Capes any more!" Murph heard someone say scornfully. He looked across to see Timothy, a student from his class and one of Mr. Flash's favorites, leaning back in his chair and folding his arms in a gesture of disdain.

"The people on this stage," continued Mr. Souperman loudly, waving a hand as if to try to dispel the air of disappointment that was spreading through the room like a suspect egg sandwich, "are founding members of the Heroes' Alliance, and we are privileged to have them here. They may no longer have Capes, but they were once operational and will have plenty of advice and tips . . . um, memories . . . that I am sure they will be glad to share as they visit your classes during the day. Ladies and gentlemen, the Ex-Cape Committee." He led The School in a final, noticeably less enthusiastic smattering of applause.

Under cover of the clapping, Hilda turned to the other Super Zeroes with her brow furrowed. She spoke in a tense, hushed tone, as if voicing her greatest fear . . .

"How can you lose your Cape?"

A LONG, LONG WAY AWAY, the man in black sat on the cold stone floor and listened.

He listened to the world far above, to the hum and buzz of a thousand conversations. And he singled out one voice in particular. A voice that whispered only to him. It said: "Master . . . can you hear me? I have returned."

"Welcome back, my friend," whispered the man in black. His voice croaked with lack of use. "Did you find everything as I had expected?"

"The laboratory is perfectly intact, master, just as you predicted," whispered the voice from the world above. "There has been no interference, and the . . . the project is undisturbed."

The man in black grinned thinly into the darkness, a grin without a morsel of warmth or friendship.

"Excellent," he murmured. "Everything is going according to plan."

"Soon, master," whispered the voice, "soon you will be free."

The man in black looked around his prison. His smile curled and warped like burning paper into a grimace of malice and hatred.

"Yes," he breathed. "Soon."

4

The A Stream

"**N**ot exactly role models, were they?"

"What a bunch of weirdos!"

"I thought this was supposed to be a day when some proper Heroes visit?"

"What's the point in talking to them if they don't have Capes anymore?"

Murph and the rest of his class had made their way to their homeroom after assembly, where the topic of conversation was still firmly fixed on their visitors in the main hall. And most of the class seemed about as impressed as they'd been last year when Katie Johnson was sick in the middle of an English lesson—and it had smelled so bad that five other people had been sick too. **"It's not my fault my mom made asparagus soooooooooup!"** Katie had wailed. Their

54

special Veterans Day guests seemed to be going down equally badly.

"Maybe he just invited them to keep Kid Normal company," sneered Timothy. His friends giggled sycophantically.

Murph was just cooking up a real zinger of a comeback—which may or may not have included an unkind comment about Timothy's hair—when the room was silenced by Mr. Souperman marching in, followed by Mr. Flash.

"Do please sit down," the headmaster told them, waving a benevolent finger. This confused things briefly, as everyone was sitting down already, but the class forgot all about it as they stared in surprise at the person who had slipped into the room behind the two teachers.

It was a young woman with long, dark hair. She was wearing a fringed leather jacket, skinny jeans, and boots. Deborah Lamington had only graduated from The School last year, and her reputation among students was legendary. She was one half of the Posse, the only team of working Heroes in the local area until the arrival of the Super Zeroes. Deborah's amazing

Capability to control objects in midair made her a force to be reckoned with. If the coolness scale went from one to four, she was nudging a strong nine.

"She's awesome," Murph heard someone whisper, and he fervently hoped it hadn't been him.

"Before you get started on lessons, class, I just have a quick announcement about staffing," said Mr. Souperman, raising a hand to quell the hum of speculation. "As most of you know, Mr. Drench has disapp— that is to say, Mr. Drench will not be joining us at The School this year due to, ahm, due to his current state of . . . nobody knowing where he is."

Unfortunately for the headmaster, these words only served to increase the excited hum. Mr. Drench was a short, molelike man with a reedy voice. Back in the Golden Age, before Heroes had started working in secret, he had been Mr. Souperman's sidekick—the Weasel. More recently, his job at The School had been to teach the less able students how to hide and control their Capes in public. But it had always seemed to Murph that the little man was bitter about being considered second best, both as a Hero and a teacher. When Nektar had attacked

The School last year, Mr. Drench had been one of the first people to become a drone, and after the battle was over, he was nowhere to be found. The mystery of his disappearance was a matter of huge gossip among the students, fueled by the fact that Mr. Souperman seemed spectacularly reluctant to talk about it.

The headmaster battled on. "As a result, I am delighted to say that one of our former students has agreed to fill in for the time being. Miss Lamington is familiar to many of you, of course, and I'm sure you'll make her feel very welcome."

Deborah swooshed her hair like a glossy horse and raised a hand in greeting.

"Miss Lamington will be teaching you CT this year," clarified the headmaster. "Everyone except the lucky few who will be joining Mr. Flash in the A Stream, of course. And I'm sure you're all anxious to know who those students will be . . ."

At this, the excited hum rose to deafening levels. Murph could see one of Timothy's friends patting him reassuringly on the shoulder. The most ambitious students in The School were desperate to join Mr. Flash's special lessons and they had been waiting months to find out who was going to make it.

"After all, as you will remember, there was a *slight* hitch with the Practical Capability Aptitude Test last term," Mr. Souperman reminded them, in a truly world-class display of understatement.

"What, when the school was attacked by that hideous wasp-man hybrid and taken prisoner?" asked Elsa, a girl whose Cape was freezing things, from the front row.

"And you were knocked unconscious by one of your own students and had to be rescued by five of the school's newest students?" added someone else.

"One of who has no Capability?" finished Timothy, with a sly glance at Murph and his friends.

"One of *whom*, Timothy," corrected Mr. Souperman, hoping that he might have won back the respect of the room with this small grammatical triumph. "Yes," he continued airily, "well, after that *slight hitch*, we have decided that perhaps the P-CAT isn't the most effective way of gauging your Hero potential."

Behind him, Mr. Flash tried to do that thing where

you do a cough that is actually the word "rubbish," but sounds cough-like enough to get away with. Unfortunately, subtlety was not the CT teacher's Capability, and all he did was bark the word "rubbish" in a slightly hoarse voice.

"Did you have something to add, Mr. Flash?" asked the headmaster blandly.

"NO, NO, NO, NO, NO, NO, NO. NO, NO, NO," replied Mr. Flash innocently. "No, not at all. No. I just coughed."

"My mistake," said Mr. Souperman. "It sounded rather like you shouted the word 'rubbish' in a slightly hoarse voice. Anyway,"—he turned back to the class— "this year, in collaboration with Mr. Flash, I have *hand-picked* the students who will be joining him for his special lessons from today onward. Mr. Flash?" He waved the CT teacher forward.

Everyone sat up a little straighter.

"RIGHT," Mr. Flash bawled, taking up position at the front of the class, legs braced, hands on hips, and, rudely, directly in front of Mr. Souperman. "It's time to sort the wheat from the goats!"

"I think it's 'sheep,' actually, Mr. Flash," ventured the headmaster, stepping out from behind him with a wounded air.

"Sort the wheat from the sheep?" scoffed Mr. Flash. "Don't talk pebble-dash."

Mr. Souperman let this slide with an almost imperceptible eye roll.

"All right, then," continued Mr. Flash, clasping his hands behind his back, "who has the potential to be a Hero? If I call your name, please come and join me at the front of the class."

He paused dramatically.

"TIMOTHY!"

Timothy punched the air like a mediocre tennis player. Scraping his chair back, he leaped to his feet and went to stand proudly at the front of the room.

"ELSA!" continued Mr. Flash.

Elsa, who had once frozen a very tasty muffin of Murph's, joined him.

"NATALIE!"

A girl with straight, dark hair marched proudly to the front.

"And . . . **CHARLIE!**" concluded Mr. Flash, and a boy with curly blond hair and thick glasses headed to the front of the room with a triumphant "Yessss!"

"These four have the potential to become the kind of Hero that the Alliance is looking for," said Mr. Flash loudly, pretending not to notice Mr. Souperman coughing loudly somewhere off to his left. "I will train them to the highest level in the hope that one day they will get the call."

The coughing had now reached an extremely high volume, and the headmaster was poking him hard in one arm.

"As for the rest of you, the remnants—stop poking me!—I wish you well. Goodbye and . . . **OW!**"

Mr. Flash had begun to usher his favorites out of the room, but Mr. Souperman had grabbed him by the upper arm. And when a Hero with the power of super-strength grabs you by the arm, you stay grabbed.

"Didn't you forget some people, Mr. Flash?" hissed the headmaster through a rather strained smile.

Mr. Flash looked very much as if he wanted to say

no, but the hand gripping his arm showed no sign of letting go. He sighed.

"Fine. And the, um, Super Zeroes as well," he mumbled.

There was total silence.

"I don't think the students quite heard you, Mr. Flash," said Mr. Souperman threateningly.

"All right, all right," burst out the CT teacher angrily. "The *Super*"—he stretched the word out like sarcastic chewing gum before spitting out the next in contempt—"Zeroes. You are also in the A Stream. Report for training immediately at the ACDC."

And with that, he wrenched his arm out of the headmaster's grasp, kicked the door open, and bundled his favorites out of the room as fast as he could. Which, considering he had super-speed, was really quite fast.

Murph, Mary, Billy, Nellie, and Hilda were still sitting at the back of the room, looking rather dazed. Even though they were actual members of the Heroes' Alliance, somehow they had never expected to be selected for Mr. Flash's elite class.

"Come on, then," mumbled Murph, pulling himself together and grabbing his bag.

As Mr. Souperman smiled benignly down at them, the five Super Zeroes walked out of the classroom, letting the door thud shut behind them.

The hallway outside was deserted. Mr. Flash had rushed the other four students off so fast that they had already rounded a corner and vanished. There was a distant sound of echoing voices coming from somewhere away to the right, and the Super Zeroes headed off hopefully in that direction.

"What did he call the place we should report to?" asked Murph as they trotted along. "The ACDC?"

"I have literally no idea," said Mary grimly. "I can't believe this! He obviously doesn't want us in his class. Did you see his face?"

"He's going to make our lives **utter, utter, utter, absolute hell,**" said Billy matter-of-factly, trailing along behind them. He was moving slowly, partly through sheer misery and partly because his left thigh had ballooned with anxiety, which was making it rather difficult to move.

At the end of the hallway they reached a T-junction. There was no sign of Mr. Flash, but two figures were approaching from the left—this was the source of the voices they'd heard. And one of them, with her comforting pink cardigan and friendly white cotton-candy hair, was exactly the person you'd want to see at such a moment.

It was their friend Flora.

As well as being Mr. Souperman's secretary, Flora had a secret. One of the most exciting secrets in the entire world of Heroes, in fact. For she was actually the Blue Phantom, a mysterious and legendary superhero whose specialty was swooping in and saving the day when all hope seemed lost.

Gliding along beside her, deep in conversation, was Sir Jasper Rowntree in his incredible wheelchair.

"Hello, hello, whatever do we have here? Young roustabouts, charging about the deserted halls like errant wildebeest! Surely there must be something amiss here, eh, Flora?" Sir Jasper's eyes glittered kindly as he spoke.

"You might be right," Flora said, spotting the

miserable expression on Murph's face. "I think perhaps the year's off to a sticky start. Jasper—this is Murph Cooper and his friends. The—"

"Super Zeroes!" finished Sir Jasper for her, widening his eyes and inclining his head respectfully. "To say I've heard a lot about you would be an understatement the size of a medium-to-large rhinoceros." He rolled forward and held out a hand. "It is my very great pleasure to meet each and every one of you," he told them solemnly, as they shook his hand in turn. "Now—unless my eyes completely deceive me, in which case I shall send them both to bed without supper, something is wrong here. How can we assist you?"

"Mr. Flash told us we're in the A Stream," Murph began, "but then ran off before we could find out where to go for the lessons."

"He said it was the, um, ADDC?" added Hilda hopefully. "Or was it the DCAD?"

Flora rolled her eyes. "Iain does love initials, doesn't he?" she said. "The ACDC, you mean—Advanced Capability Development Center. It's the gray door next to the geography classroom."

"I know it!" cried Mary. "But I just thought it was a cupboard. There's no sign or anything."

"Ha!" burst out Sir Jasper dramatically. **"Mysteries!** Unmarked doors that lead to adventure! The day can only get more interesting from here. Godspeed, my friends!"

"Um, thanks," said Murph as they hurried off. "Nice to meet you!"

"Jasper's staying for a few days, helping Carl out

with a project," Flora called after them before they rounded the corner. "Come and have a cup of tea one day soon and we'll show you. Well, one of you knows all about it already, of course."

This sounded intriguing, but there was no time to dwell on it now, so Murph filed Flora's comment in the "to be puzzled out later" department of his brain. Since he had started attending The School, this was by far the most overworked of all the different brain departments. If it had been a real-life office, the staff would probably have gone on strike, or gone mad and started smashing up their work computers with baseball bats.

5

The ACDC

Even in a normal school, there are a few places you never get to go into except on really special occasions. You never get to see the inside of the stationery closet unless you're given an important mission to locate some new highlighters. You never get to see inside the kitchens, which, believe us, is probably for the best. And you never, but never ever, get to set so much as the end of your nose inside the staffroom. Not even if you're on actual fire.

At The School, the Advanced Capability Development Center was all of these places rolled into one and then multiplied by ten. It was a mystery wrapped in an enigma, and then deep-fried and served with a creamy riddle sauce.

Mary eventually came to a stop beside a door that Murph must have walked past countless times but had never noticed. It was gray and unmarked, and appeared too narrow to have anything significant behind it. But when Mary pushed it gingerly, the door opened to reveal an imposing concrete staircase, much wider than the doorframe itself, which led down toward a set of double swing doors.

"Oh! A basement! Of course! It had to be in a basement," squealed Hilda. She was the only one of them who seemed even slightly pleased at the prospect of joining the A Stream. "All the coolest things are underground."

"Are they?" asked Murph.

"Yeah! Like rabbits!" Billy said. "And badgers."

"No, Billy, I mean all the coolest Hero things. Rabbits have nothing to do with it," said Hilda primly, leading them off down the staircase with a little skip.

"Moles too," mused Murph, following her.

"Good one!" said Billy. "Mary? Got any more?"

"Um . . . puffins?"

Even Nellie smiled slightly at Mary's idea. It's impossible not to be cheered by the thought of a puffin. But Hilda rounded on them and stamped her foot. "Will you all stop just naming subterranean animals! Animals are not Heroes."

"What about . . . Winky the Magic Worm?" asked Murph brightly as Hilda pushed through the double doors at the bottom.

"Gah! There is no such Hero as Winky the Magic Worm!" she bellowed, before realizing she'd just walked into a large, well-lit room full of people, all of whom were now staring at her. You know when everyone stops talking at exactly the same moment, just as you say something really embarrassing? Yeah, that. Hilda had just barged straight into a massive, great pool of silence, shouting about a nonexistent superhero called Winky the Magic Worm.

Murph clapped his hand over his mouth to trap the laugh that was trying to escape. The move was partly successful, and only a small stifled trumpet noise was heard.

Meanwhile, though, Hilda's face had turned the same color as the cushions on her grandma's sofa. Which, since you've probably never been to Hilda's grandma's house, we can assure you are a very deep shade of red.

The ACDC looked a bit like an enormous version of a traditional school gym. There were climbing bars attached to the walls, ropes dangling from the ceiling, and blue foam mats stacked everywhere. It had that gym smell as well—a mixture of wood polish, sweaty socks, and fear. Mr. Flash and the others from their class were nowhere to be found, but assembled at the near end of this gargantuan torture palace was the most terrifying crowd of people Murph had ever seen.

It's a well-known fact that all students in the years above you at school always seem bigger and more impressive than you. But this group really was bigger and more impressive than the Super Zeroes—even if the five of them had stood on one another's shoulders and dressed in a long coat pretending to be one giant person.

Closest to Murph, arms folded, were a pair of enormous final-year students with biceps bigger than his head. Behind them was a group of slightly younger teenagers who were all dressed in ripped jeans and

T-shirts, as if they were in a band. And worst of all, Murph could make out the mismatched gang of bullies who had targeted the Super Zeroes last year leaning against the wall at the back of the room.

Murph still didn't know their actual names—but he checked them all off in his head using the nicknames he'd assigned them: Gangly Fuzz Face, Frankenstein's Nephew, Corned Beef Boy, Crazy Eyes Jemima, and, of course, who could forget Pork Belly Pig Breath?

The five of them were glaring at the Super Zeroes as if they were tiny, tiny ants who had invaded their barbecue.

The atmosphere was as uncomfortable as an itchy neck after a haircut.

"OH, GOOD, YOU MADE IT," boomed Mr. Flash's voice suddenly, sounding about as sincere as a vegetarian waiter reading out the specials at a steak restaurant. He was approaching from the far end of the gym with the other four members of their own class trailing after him. "I've just been running Elsa, Charlie, Timothy, and Natalie through some of the main rules of the ACDC."

"And what are the main rules, Mr. Flash?" asked Murph brightly, trying not to be intimidated by the fact that just about every person in the room was staring at him and his friends as if they were suspicious stains on an expensive rug.

"THE FIRST RULE OF THE ACDC,' began Mr. Flash, fixing them with a fierce gaze, "is that you don't ever, never, not tell no one about the ACDC."

Murph's brain turned somersaults as he tried to work out whether this labyrinth of double negatives meant that he could, in fact, tell people about the ACDC and get away with it through the magic of grammar. But Mr. Flash cleared things up for him.

"THE SECOND RULE,' he bellowed like a bull with bronchitis, "is that if you tell anyone about the ACDC, I'll grind you into flour and use you to make scones!"

"So, quite similar to the first rule . . . ," began Mary, but she was silenced.

"RULE THREE,' screamed Mr. Flash, "is that no student outside of this room must ever find out about the ACDC. And rule four—"

"Is that the ACDC is a secret?" guessed Hilda.

Mr. Flash glared at her suspiciously. "How do you know rule four?" he growled, advancing on her with his mustache quivering.

"Lucky guess?" quailed Hilda, shrinking back toward the wall.

"AND, FINALLY, THE FIFTH RULE OF THE ACDC . . . ," concluded Mr. Flash, still looking at Hilda with hostility, "is that you do not talk about the ACDC."

"What you could do," suggested Mary conscientiously, "is say, 'The first rule of the ACDC is that you don't talk about the ACDC.' And then add, 'There is no second rule.' That'd be cool . . ."

"SHUUUUUUUUUT UUUPPPPPPPP!!"

Mr. Flash cataclysmed directly into her face. Mary felt as if a larger-than-average motorcycle had pointed its exhaust pipe at her. "Rule one around here—I make the rules!"

"I thought rule one was, 'You don't ever, never, not—'" ventured Billy.

"GRAAAAAAAAAAAGSCH!"

exploded the teacher. **"SHUT! YOUR! CHEESE! HOLES!** I knew it was a flippin' mistake to let you bunch of wimbling wet wipes in! The rest of us are supposed to be getting on with Hero training and you flounce in late like a load of blinkin' divas and start telling me what the rules should be!"

"That's a bit unfair," began Murph, but Mr. Flash was coming to the boil like a furious kettle and was about to make them a nice steaming-hot mug of humiliation.

"You"—he shook a frankfurter-esque finger at the Super Zeroes—"are not Heroes. Not in my book."

Murph thought grimly to himself that if Mr. Flash were ever to write a book, its title would probably be **HOW MUCH I HATE MURPH COOPER: A TEACHER'S TALE.** But Mr. Flash wasn't finished. "Sure, you snuck into the Alliance on a technicality . . ."

"Technicality? We rescued—" Mary tried to say, but Mr. Flash was on a roll.

". . . but you don't fool the rest of us. I mean—what have you actually done since you became . . . *Heroes*?"

He spat this last word out sarcastically. "I bet you haven't even been sent on a mission. They wouldn't trust you with one."

"We can't tell you about Alliance missions, you know that," Murph retorted, feeling stung.

"OHHH, VERY CONVENIENT!" roared Mr. Flash. "VERY handy, that! They haven't done anything at all!" he jeered to the rest of the class, who sniggered obediently.

"We have done missions!" squeaked Hilda angrily, her eyes shining with frustrated tears. "We have!"

Nellie stamped a foot, and Murph was sure he felt a ripple of electric fury radiating from her.

"Yeah!" added Billy, growing so incensed that he forgot about their vow of secrecy. "Like the Mysterious Case of Cat Woman!"

A couple of the other students looked quite impressed at this. "You battled Catwoman?" asked one of the muscly older kids. "Cool!"

"Well, no, not Catwoman. Cat Woman, two words," clarified Billy. "A woman who'd—"

"Lost her cat?" hooted Mr. Flash incredulously.

"Well, yes," confessed Billy, "but . . ." But it was too late. The whole class had erupted into mocking howls of derision.

It was like being slapped in the face with laughter. All five Super Zeroes stood, heads bowed, as the ACDC echoed with it.

"AH HA HA HA HA," bellowed Mr. Flash, looking like all his Christmases had been amalgamated into one Ultimate Super Christmas, delivered by glitter-covered magic robins with extra holly on top. "That's the best thing I ever heard, ever! A lost cat! Oh dear, dear, dear." He wiped his eyes theatrically.

"Catwoman's fictional anyway, you muppet," added the second muscle-bound student to his friend dismissively.

"Go on, get out of here!" Mr. Flash told the Super Zeroes, gesturing toward a door in the corner. "Go and clear out the storeroom! It could do with a good tidy-up. The rest of us have got Hero training to be getting on with."

Faces burning, the five of them shuffled awkwardly away across the ACDC.

"It wasn't just a lost cat . . . ," huffed Hilda. "They don't know about the nuclear accident, and the laser . . ." But Murph hushed her.

"Hilda, we can't talk about Alliance missions!" he reminded her. "Let them laugh."

"But what about the Giant Rat of Sumatra?" whispered Hilda as he pushed her through the storeroom door. "If they only knew about that . . ."

"The world's not prepared for that story yet," said Billy seriously.

As the door hissed closed behind them they could just hear Mr. Flash roaring, "Right. BURPEES! Let's go! On the floor! **MOVE, MOVE, MOOOVE!"**

The room they found themselves in was large and cluttered. In fact, "cluttered" doesn't really do it justice—it's like describing the Atlantic Ocean as "moist." There were overflowing filing cabinets with papers jammed haphazardly into the drawers. There were shelves upon shelves of cardboard boxes packed with random junk. There were piles of yellowing exercise books on the floor, reams of old-fashioned printer paper on the desks, an ancient, fat TV set on a stand, typewriters, broken lamps, and pieces of antiquated school equipment that none of them recognized. (If you are now wondering, "Was there an overhead projector?" then [a] yes, there was, and [b] you're a grown-up. Busted! But welcome.)

"So, that went well," said Mary sarcastically, wandering over to the shelves and poking around inside a crate full of black, book-size plastic boxes. "What is all this stuff?"

"What does it matter?" Murph retorted. "He doesn't even really care if we tidy up in here. He just wanted to get rid of us."

And with that, Murph swept a pile of books off a dusty old office chair and slumped into it. He was feeling less heroic by the second.

When Murph arrived home that evening, his mom was heading out to visit friends. They passed each other in the front yard.

She was looking happy and relaxed, carrying a bunch of flowers. Murph, on the other hand, looked like there should be a small, dark cloud hovering over his head, raining tiny drops of purest angst.

At the end of CT, Mr. Flash hadn't even bothered telling Murph and his friends that the lesson had finished. Sitting glumly in the storeroom, they had gradually become aware that the puffing, running feet, and shouting from next door had stopped—and when Mary looked at her watch she realized that it was halfway through break time.

By the end of the day, the confidence and happiness that had filled Murph Cooper on his way to school that morning had leaked out of him like sawdust from a very old and unloved teddy bear with a missing leg.

"Whoa, what's the matter?" his mom asked him, looking concerned. "You were full of beans this morning. Bad day?"

"Bad day" doesn't even begin to cover it, thought Murph, and he decided to express this in the time-honored talking-to-a-parent-after-an-awful-day-at-school manner.

"Mer . . . s'pose. Dunno."

Murph kicked moodily at a small stone, which

chipped up satisfyingly and disappeared down the well that stood in the middle of the garden. Normally this would have been a cue to put his T-shirt over his head and run around making the noise of a cheering crowd, but not today.

"Well, I'm here if you need to talk." His mom ruffled his hair, which is one of the more baffling things that parents like to do. Why on earth do they think making your hair slightly more messy will solve all your problems?

Murph was desperate for some advice—but that's the difficulty with going to a secret school. It's pretty hard to ask for guidance when your mom isn't allowed to know that you're a superhero. Where do you begin? But Murph was feeling down enough to give it a try.

"Well . . . ," he started.

His mom perched herself on the edge of the well, patting the bricks next to her for him to do the same. They sat together in a patch of late-afternoon sunlight and she wrapped a comforting arm around his shoulders.

"You know when you think everything's going well, and you're actually getting good at something?" Murph said. "And then you realize that, well, not everyone's giving you the credit they should?"

"I know exactly what you mean." His mom nodded. "But you've got to remember—there's only one person who can tell you if you're doing well at something or not."

"You're going to say it's me, aren't you?" said Murph with a reluctant smile.

"Of course!" she replied. "There's always someone ready to put you down—and they've always got their reasons for doing it. But it's their problem. Try not to make it yours. Plus, I'm out tonight—so you get to do the one thing that makes every problem feel a bit easier to deal with."

"Order pizza?" said Murph, feeling approximately 7 percent better already.

"Order pizza," confirmed his mom, smiling as she got up and walked away. "Andy's got my card. And try not to worry about whatever it is." She stopped at the end of the drive and turned back, a fake-innocent expression on her face. "Unless . . . it's not girl trouble, is it?"

Murph's internal mombarrassment gauge shot upward. "Gah! No! Shut up!" he snapped, getting up himself and making for the front door.

"Only . . . Mary seems to have been visiting a lot this summer . . ." His mom grinned widely.

"La la la la la la! Can't hear you!" yelled Murph, sticking out his tongue at her and slamming the door closed. "Now go away! And have a good night," he added through the mail slot before bolting up the stairs to his room.

He lay down on his bed, his internal movie theater screening an unwanted film entitled **THE VERY WORST OF MR. FLASH**, despite his mom's advice. He could still hear the laughter of the other students— and, worst of all, he could picture the wounded faces of the other Super Zeroes.

Are they embarrassed to be part of my gang now? Murph wondered. *Do they secretly want to hone their real-life Capes with the others, rather than being stuck in a junk room with me?*

The weather outside seemed to be mirroring his mood. A gusting wind was blowing the treetops about, and a shadow passed across the window. Then, all of a sudden, the HALO unit in Murph's pocket let out a small, piercing **brrring** noise that he'd never heard before.

He pulled it out and looked at it. The tiny green light on the top was blinking, and the screen was displaying a message in bright letters.

KID NORMAL . . . RESPOND.

"Um." Murph coughed and collected himself. That wasn't how Heroes responded. "Hello?" he continued uncertainly. The message changed:

GO TO THE BALCONY.

"Sorry, what?" Murph blurted in shock. "Why?"

NEVER MIND WHY . . . JUST DO IT.

Murph paused.

NOW.

"Okay, okay, fine," he said, jamming the HALO unit back into his jeans pocket, jumping up from the bed, and striding over to the double doors that led out onto his balcony.

As he pulled them open he realized just how windy it was. Filthy wet leaves from the gutters were swirling everywhere—one of them flew directly into his open mouth. He spat out this unwanted autumnal snack disgustedly, and it was only when he peeled another leaf off his right eye that he noticed what was different about the balcony.

Hanging in midair, right in front of him, was a rope ladder. *That isn't usually there*, thought Murph perceptively.

The ladder had a small, neat plastic sign attached to it.

HANG ON, it read.

Without stopping to think, Murph did exactly that. He grabbed one rung firmly with both hands and placed his feet on another.

The instant he did, he was jerked sharply skyward. Squinting up, Murph realized where the wind was coming from and what had caused the shadow that had blotted out the sun.

Hovering just above his house, but making almost no sound, was an enormous black helicopter, its rotor blades churning the air. The ladder that he was now clinging to for dear life swung crazily as it was gradually winched into a hatch on the bottom of the huge machine. Within seconds he had been grabbed by strong hands and pulled inside.

"Extraction successful," he heard a clipped, serious voice say.

The hatch slammed closed, and Murph felt himself pushed downward by the g-force as the helicopter shot silently up into the sky and away.

6

Shivering Sands

Once his brain had stopped feeling like a pinball machine full of weasels, Murph picked himself up into a sitting position and looked about him.

The interior of the helicopter was bare and functional, with black benches along either side underneath a row of round windows. An interior decorator might have described it as "miminalist," if there'd been one handy, but this isn't one of those stories where interior decorators pop up willy-nilly.

Looming over Murph and regarding him coolly with her arms folded was a person with almost zero interest in interior design of any kind. Her job as head of the Heroes' Alliance didn't leave much time for wallpapering. Miss Flint was a tall, stern lady with the sort of hair you don't argue with. Beside her was a broad-shouldered, unsmiling man in a black military-style uniform. Murph realized that he was one of the mysterious people known as Cleaners, who made sure that Hero activity was expertly covered up and kept secret. Once the Cleaner had satisfied himself that Murph was intact and unharmed, he turned on his heel and walked toward the cockpit at the front of the helicopter.

Murph struggled to his feet. Glancing out of the window, he could see that they were high above the clouds and moving fast—but there was still hardly any noise. Helicopters on the TV always made a huge clattering sound like a . . . well, you know. Like a helicopter. This one was smooth and quiet.

"Wow," he said to Miss Flint, "nice helicopter." This is just good manners. If someone has a really cool helicopter, it's always polite to point it out.

"It's electric," said Miss Flint simply.

"There's no such thing as an electric helicopter," said Murph, before he could stop himself.

"Luckily for you, Kid Normal, that's incorrect. Otherwise you'd currently be approximately ten thousand feet above"—Miss Flint glanced out the window—"the sea—with nothing to support you."

Murph peered closely at the fast-moving view and confirmed that they were, in fact, crossing the coastline. He caught a glimpse of a sandy beach and a small pier through the clouds.

He realized they must be traveling at incredible speed—his town was nowhere near the sea. The one time Mom had driven him to the coast over the summer it had taken absolutely hours. She'd reached the state of maximum anger and annoyance that he and Andy called DEFCON Mom when they were still more than twenty miles away from the nearest periwinkle. Sitting in a line of traffic in the boiling heat, they'd seen other people actually run out of patience and turn their cars around.

"I'm sorry, Jonty, but I simply cannot tolerate this any longer!" they'd heard a red-faced man shout, as he angrily reversed his expensive-looking car out of the line and away. All three of them had burst out laughing, and Mom's bad mood had evaporated. Murph smiled at the memory.

"Apologies for the rather . . . sudden summons," continued Miss Flint, sitting down on a bench and gesturing for him to do the same. "I hope you didn't have plans this evening, did you?"

"Well, I was going to order pizza . . . ," began Murph, but quickly realized that Miss Flint didn't actually care whether he had plans. It was a question that didn't really require an answer, asked only to be polite—or to give it its correct name, a slightly smug, irritating question.

"You see," she continued, pretending not to hear him, "I have a bit of a problem."

Murph raised his eyebrows, suddenly feeling rather important. Mr. Flash might think he and his friends were a complete waste of space, but when the head of the Heroes' Alliance has a problem, who's she gonna call?

He chanted the answer to himself silently:

Murph Cooper!

Miss Flint held on to her bench as the helicopter banked smoothly into a turn. Murph slid along it slightly but managed to stop himself with some nimble footwork, and silently congratulated himself. *Falling over when the most important Hero of all has just brought you on a secret mission would not be a good look*, he thought.

"So," he asked out loud, "how can I be of assistance?"

Miss Flint regarded him seriously for a moment before answering. "Do you remember the vow you took some months ago, Mr. Cooper? In particular, the part that refers to secrets?"

I promise to keep our secrets, thought Murph to himself, and nodded solemnly.

"Because," she continued, "you are now being taken to the most secret and secure facility operated by the Heroes' Alliance."

Cool bananas with awesome sauce, thought Murph, but he didn't say it out loud. He was doing his best to be all serious and Hero-y. "What sort of facility?" he asked instead.

"To answer that, you must first understand that the Heroes' Alliance is dedicated to fighting crime wherever we find it," said Miss Flint. "We operate in total secrecy to keep the general population unaware of the existence of Capabilities. Most cases that our operatives deal with are everyday stuff, perpetrated by ordinary people with no Capes. That's largely what you and your friends have been involved with over the summer. Good job with that awful Travers woman, by the way. And that work is, of course, carried out without anyone else finding out. We allow others to take the credit."

I promise to save without glory, remembered Murph, *to help without thanks . . .*

"But when a crime is carried out by someone with Capabilities, well—that's much more of a threat to our secrecy."

The cabin tilted slightly as the helicopter began to descend.

"People like Nektar?" Murph asked.

"Yes, would-be supervillains or people who use their Capes for evil: Rogues, as we call them in the Alliance. And, even more dangerous still, former Heroes who for one reason or another have turned against us." Miss Flint looked grave. "These people threaten to reveal our existence to the wider world. That must not be allowed to happen."

Murph's brain was whirring. He'd assumed that by promising to "keep our secrets" he'd just been vowing to tell nobody about the hidden world of Capabilities. But now he realized it also meant actively fighting against people who threatened that secrecy. "Are there really Alliance members who . . . who've gone bad?" he asked.

Miss Flint nodded solemnly. "Rogue Heroes, yes," she confirmed. "It's not common but it does happen. And with inside knowledge of Alliance operations, just think of the chaos they could cause."

"So, what happens once you've brought a Rogue to justice?" Murph whispered, feeling like he was on the edge of something huge. "Or a Rogue Hero?"

Miss Flint stood up without speaking and walked to the cockpit, where three black-clad Cleaners were busy at the controls. She pointed through the large windscreen.

"We bring them here," she told him grimly. **"We bring them to Shivering Sands."**

"Sands Control, HALO Five on final approach. Deactivate security systems. Landing on Tower Two," said a Cleaner into her headset.

Murph squinted through the glass, trying to make out what was ahead. The helicopter shook slightly as it passed through a layer of thin cloud.

"Roger, HALO Five, clear to land," crackled a voice over the radio.

Below them in the sea was an enormous bank of wind turbines—line upon line of them, turning lazily in the breeze. Then the helicopter banked to one side and, with a start, Murph saw their destination clearly. Rising out of the waves on huge, stout metal legs was a series of large, circular metal forts. They were old and dilapidated, discolored with patches of brown rust. Their tiny windows were grimy and rimed with sea salt.

Shivering Sands looked for all the world like a deserted, forgotten ruin left out at sea to gradually fall apart.

But as they flew directly over the towers and banked sharply once again, Murph realized this was far from the case.

At the heart of the complex was one central tower, with bridges leading out like the threads of a spider's web to the other towers arranged around it. Several more of the huge black helicopters were parked on top of the towers. And while the sides of the buildings still appeared rusted and rotting, their tops looked brand-new. They were black and shiny, with red and green landing lights arranged in careful rows across them. Murph could even make out black-clad figures scuttling here and there. More Cleaners.

One of the Cleaners guided the electric helicopter in as it made a smooth landing right in the center of an outside tower.

Murph watched as the pilots flicked switches in a businesslike manner, swiping at a large touchscreen control panel that bore a close resemblance to his own smaller HALO unit. He would have liked to linger, but at that moment Miss Flint tapped him on the shoulder and led him to the back of the cabin. There was a dazzling light and a smack of salty breeze as a ramp extended, and Murph was led down onto the metal platform. The air was chilly, full of the sound of gulls and the mashing of waves far below. He could make out the banks of wind turbines in the distance but could see no sign of any coastline off in the haze.

"Welcome to Shivering Sands," said Miss Flint, holding out a hand to indicate the structures all around them.

"It . . . it's a prison," Murph realized.

"Probably the most secure prison on the planet," she confirmed. "Let's get inside, shall we?"

She led the way down a sleek staircase to a fortified door, which slid open automatically as they approached. Once the door closed behind them, the noise of the sea and the gulls was silenced.

They were in a spotless, brightly lit, air-conditioned hallway. As Murph had suspected, the aging, rusting exteriors of the towers were a disguise. Inside,

Shivering Sands was state-of-the-art. He looked around at the gleaming metal fittings and found himself unable to stop wondering what the hand dryers in the bathrooms would be like.

A woman with a clipboard was approaching.

"Status report, please," Miss Flint commanded.

"Normal operating conditions," the woman replied efficiently, and her commander gave a satisfied nod.

"Very good. Is everything ready at Tower One?"

"They're prepared for your arrival."

Miss Flint turned to Murph. "This way, then, Kid Normal. I hope you don't have a problem with heights."

And without further explanation, she led the way to a large set of double doors set into the curved metal of the tower wall.

7

Rogues' Gallery

The sign beside the doors wasn't the sort that inspired confidence.

SECURE FACILITY was stenciled on it in bright red letters. NO ACCESS TO UNAUTHORIZED PERSONNEL UNDER ANY CIRCUMSTANCES. EXTREME DANGER OF DEATH OR SERIOUS INJURY. This was followed by a forest of smaller writing, which Murph didn't stop to read. He caught a glimpse of the words "mutilation" and "violence" and thought he got the gist of it.

"So, ah, why . . . why have you brought me to prison, please?" Murph felt this was a good time for an explanation. To his relief, Miss Flint seemed to agree, because she stopped beside the doors and turned to face him.

"Shivering Sands, as I told you, is probably the

most secure prison on the planet," she began. "And right in the middle of it is the most secure cell of all. It was built to hold the most dangerous enemy we have ever faced."

Murph's legs sparkled with apprehension, and his relief ebbed away as quickly as it had arrived. He emitted a tiny, nervous neigh. "The most . . . most dangerous?" he asked in a voice the size of an underdeveloped molecule.

"Indeed. The worst nightmare of everyone in the Heroes' Alliance . . . ," continued Miss Flint, ". . . apart from you."

Murph felt as if a phone had started ringing in a dusty room somewhere in the back of his brain. This all sounded strangely familiar.

"His name," said Miss Flint quietly, "is Magpie."

And suddenly Murph remembered. It had been in a CT lesson with Mr. Drench last year. The weedy, drably dressed little man had spoken bitterly about being sent into battle as bait many years ago—a battle in which he'd had some of his super-hearing Capability taken away from him.

My hearing has never been quite as exceptional since that day . . . he had said. *That's what happened to anyone who came up against . . . him.*

"Yeah, Magpie," repeated Murph, in awe, "I've heard about him."

Miss Flint looked surprised. "Really?" she asked sharply. "That's highly irregular. Most Heroes don't talk about him—they prefer to pretend he never existed. The battle to bring him to justice was . . . extremely painful. A dark day." Her face clouded over.

"And he can steal Capabilities?" Murph asked. The head of the Alliance answered him with a curt nod. "So none of you can get close to him without risking losing your powers," Murph continued, finally understanding where he fit into all this.

"No member of the Alliance has entered his cell for thirty years," Miss Flint answered. "And even if they had risked doing so, it would have been of no use to anyone. He has refused to say a word since he was imprisoned. But now, for the first time in decades, he has indicated that he is ready to talk."

"And he wants to talk to . . ." Murph trailed off.

"He wants to talk to you, Kid Normal," Miss Flint concluded, placing her hand on the control panel beside the double doors. They hissed open to the salt-spray smell of the sea and the cry of the gulls.

Stretching away ahead of them was a slim metal bridge. It led to the central tower at the heart of the complex.

Miss Flint stepped out smartly into the wind and began marching away from him. Murph followed a little uncertainly. The drop to the waves far below was dizzying. And to make it worse, the bridge was swinging gently.

Murph fixed his eyes on Miss Flint's back and kept going. After all, the alternative was to stay out there on the crazy-high swingy bridge. But he couldn't help thinking that this wasn't how he'd been expecting his evening to go at all. It was supposed to contain a great deal more pepperoni and much less blind terror. Murph swallowed thickly. Only an hour or so ago, he'd been weighing up whether to get cheesy garlic bread or doughballs to go with his pizza. He looked back on that moment now with a warm, sentimental glow. Life had been so much simpler then.

Murph wished he were a nice, warm doughball, about to plunge his bready face into a refreshing tub of butter. Doughballs wouldn't be forced to go to a prison in the sea to visit supervillains.

"Doughballs have it easy," Murph muttered to himself.

"What was that?" Miss Flint asked him.

"Nothing," said Murph quickly.

A couple of rather breathless minutes later, Miss Flint was activating yet another control panel, and yet another smooth-sliding door was admitting them to the middle tower. They were faced with five very burly guards, who snapped to attention as they entered.

"As you were," Miss Flint told them. "I'm just passing through. All quiet?"

"All quiet," confirmed the nearest guard, glancing down the long, wide corridor that led to the heart of the tower.

Miss Flint nodded in a satisfied fashion and proceeded to lead the way, but not before giving Murph a final warning. "Keep toward the center. We have to pass through the rest of the facility before we get to the cell where Magpie is held."

The passageway was lined with large, strong-looking doors. Each had a grilled panel set in the middle. It was a cell block, Murph realized with a cold spill of excitement and fright that wound its way down his back.

"This is the lower-security area," Miss Flint was saying over her shoulder. "The nearer you get to the center, the more high-risk the inmates become."

Murph looked from side to side as they walked. Occasionally, he caught a glimpse of a curious face peering out from behind bars. Once he was startled by a loud howling. A thin, fierce face was gazing out at him from behind strands of matted hair.

"Yellow Dog," said Miss Flint dismissively. "Don't be alarmed."

"Is his bark worse than his bite?" joked Murph in a rather strained voice.

"Not particularly," she replied, deadpan. "Right, this is the higher-security zone."

They had come to another curved wall. The

passageway was
leading them toward
the center of the prison
like a spoke on a bicycle
wheel, Murph realized.
Miss Flint opened the doors and
they stepped through.

Here, the cells were even more closely guarded.
Black-clad figures were stationed at intervals along
the way, their keen eyes checking for any hint of
trouble.

There was a sudden banging from away to one
side.

"Hey!" called a high, guttural voice. "Hey hey hey!"

With a slight sigh, Miss Flint stopped. Murph looked for the source of the noise, and was a little disturbed to see an enormous white face pressed up against the bars of a cell that seemed much larger than the others.

"Did you bring someone to party with me?" The face moved slightly, bringing a huge red nose into view, along with a patch of massive, red-lined mouth. "I like to party, you know."

Murph realized that he was looking at a clown— but not your normal-size clown. This was a bumper clown. A jumbo-size, economy-pack, mega clown. A really, really big clown, is what we're trying to get across here. And although Murph was okay with heights, clowns really did freak him out.

"Party Animal," explained Miss Flint in an undertone. "He ran his own circus for people with Capes, but they traveled from town to town creating chaos. Robberies, attacks, disappearances . . . He gave us quite a lot of trouble for a few years."

Murph thought back to the first time he'd been called to Mr. Souperman's office. There had been a picture on the wall of the headmaster in his days as a Hero, standing next to a gigantic unconscious clown. "Until Captain Alpha finished him off," he said.

Miss Flint cocked an approving eyebrow. "Yes, Souperman was the one to bring him in. You don't miss much, do you?"

But sadly, neither did Party Animal.

"Captain Alpha!" he hooted at enormous volume. "Captain Alpha! Oh, just you wait. One day I'll be out of here, and then he'd better watch out. He may have stopped my little carnival for a while, but I'll be back. And when I am . . . well, let's just say I'll invite the captain to a little party. Party party party," he muttered, turning his back on the door and wandering away from them.

"Let's move on, shall we?" suggested Miss Flint, spinning on her heel.

More faces peered out at Murph as they kept on toward the center of the tower, and at one point he heard one of the prisoners making an odd series of beeping and booping noises. He looked to one side, intrigued, and as he did so a thin, toneless voice cried out, **"Oooooh, look, an expected item in the bagging area."**

"That's Consumo," Miss Flint told him. "Tried to hold the whole country for ransom a few years back by releasing a virus into all supermarket self-service checkouts. He was demanding billions of dollars, threatening to stop anyone shopping for food. He has very advanced tele-tech and his virus was incredibly sophisticated. It turned many of the checkouts evil. They actually became self-aware and took delight in annoying shoppers. We still haven't managed to completely eradicate his software, to be honest."

"In there is Goldfish," she went on, waving her hand toward another cell and apparently starting to enjoy her role as super-prison tour guide. "He has one of the most brilliant criminal minds in all the world, but with one huge drawback: he has a memory that's only three seconds long. So he's capable of concocting spectacularly evil plans but then forgets them moments later."

Murph was straining to see through the bars and catch a glimpse of Goldfish, but he could see nothing except a bath full of water. It was like that frustrating moment at the zoo when all the pandas are in bed.

"The last time he was caught," explained Miss Flint, "he had made his way to the main vault underneath the biggest bank in the country. He'd written all the security codes to get inside on a bit of paper, but then put it somewhere for safekeeping and promptly forgot where it was. If he wasn't so evil, you might just feel sorry for him."

"So, how many—what did you call them—Rogues? How many Rogues are in this place?" Murph wanted to know.

"Dozens and dozens," she replied. "Anyone who is too dangerous to be out in the world. The Gremlin, Monsieur Trois, Colonel Vegetables . . ." She turned to Murph and looked even more serious than usual, if that were possible. If there was a Beaufort scale of serious expressions, she had just ramped up from "stiff breeze" to "hurricane." "And, of course, Magpie . . ."

And with that, she gestured toward a final set

110

of doors. Murph had seen a *lot* of doors that day—which tends to happen when you visit a prison. But this pair were, not to put too fine a point on it, the door daddies. They were curved and incredibly heavily fortified, reinforced with bands of grayish metal—the sort of doors that make other doors lie awake at night feeling inadequate. Stenciled across them in scarlet lettering were the words: MAXIMUM-SECURITY AREA. NO ADMITTANCE UNDER ANY CIRCUMSTANCES TO ANYBODY.

Underneath that was a warning sign like the ones you see near power stations, which show a cartoon man being struck by lightning. But in this case, the little stick figure was crouched down, clutching its head in agony while bolts of spiked, purplish energy swarmed around it. Beside it was written in stark black lettering: CAPABILITY LOSS ZONE AHEAD.

Miss Flint touched a final control panel.

The enormous doors clanked into life.

8

One for Sorrow

"This is where I must leave you," explained Miss Flint. "But before I do, listen to these instructions very carefully. They could save your life."

Murph decided, for the only time in his life so far, to pay attention to some instructions.

"First, I must ask you to hand over your HALO unit. As you'll see, Magpie's cell is designed so that he won't be able to get close to you, but he still has all of the Capes he has stolen over the years at his disposal, and there are a great many of them, believe me. We can't risk Alliance equipment getting into his hands."

Murph reluctantly pulled the HALO unit out of his pocket and handed it over.

"Now, here is my most important instruction to you," continued Miss Flint. "Whatever Magpie says to you, whatever he promises—*do not get too close to him*. I'll be watching, ready to extract you if anything goes wrong. But stay on the top level at all times. You'll understand when you get down there."

Murph nodded silently. He had no intention of getting any nearer to the planet's most dangerous supervillain than he absolutely had to.

"And finally," said Miss Flint, "here's something you'll need." She reached into her pocket.

At last, thought Murph. *This is where she gives me a really cool weapon that I can use to protect myself if this all goes bad.*

But all Miss Flint produced was some paper and a very blunt, stubby pencil. "Magpie says he wants to talk. So, find out what he wants to say to us. Note down anything significant," she told him. "No electronics can be risked down there, obviously, or anything pointy."

Hence the blunt pencil, Murph realized as he pocketed it.

With that, Miss Flint went back through the doors, leaving him alone at the very center of the prison tower.

So, armed only with his blunt pencil and paper, Murph stepped forward into the smallish, circular room ahead of him. It was lit by dim reddish lights. In the middle was a tall, round cage made of glass and strong metal mesh.

"Please enter the elevator," said the remote, metallic voice of Miss Flint, apparently now coming from a hidden speaker somewhere. "It will convey you to the maximum-security area of our facility."

With no other options available to him, Murph Cooper shrugged and stepped into the tube. It snapped closed and dropped sharply down into darkness.

Murph was able to take most things in his stride. Giant clowns were one exception, as we've recently discovered. But he'd also never been the biggest fan of elevators. Not since he was seven years old, anyway, and had gotten trapped in one during a vacation in Spain.

It had been very old and very clunky, and it had suddenly clanked to a halt somewhere between levels on the way up to their apartment. He'd sat on the floor staring at an old, faded poster for a bullfight that had been tacked to one wall while his mom had tried to use her basic grasp of Spanish to call for help.

"Assistance, thank you!" she had actually

been shouting. *"We is on the escalator!"* Eventually someone had heard them and fetched help, but ever since then, Murph had preferred to take the stairs when possible.

It's not possible today, he thought to himself, as his ears popped and the image of that old bullfight poster swam in his memory.

The elevator filled with greenish light as it continued to sink—and Murph realized with a start that he must be dropping deep underneath the sea, falling like a stone down through one of the wide metal legs that supported the huge central tower of Shivering Sands. His ears began to ache with the pressure, and he swallowed nervously to try to clear them.

This had just started to work when the elevator slowed to a halt. The door swung open and Murph stepped out into the most secure prison in existence. The area that, for thirty years now, had been the home of the single most dangerous individual who had ever lived. It smelled surprisingly nice, considering.

"You have reached Sublevel One," Miss Flint's disembodied voice crackled out of another speaker.

"I thought it would smell worse," said Murph, who had a habit of saying the first thing that came into his head when he was nervous.

"The air is filtered and we add a mild lemon scent," replied Miss Flint, who usually had an answer for everything.

Kid Normal took in his surroundings. Sublevel One was a single huge, round room built onto the seabed. Its walls were made of thick glass, which gave the whole place a weird, otherworldly greenish glow. The elevator came down at the outer edge of the circle—he could dimly make out the metal elevator shaft stretching above him into the watery gloom. The floor was carved from

116

cold, damp stone, and it fell away from him in row upon row of huge steps. Murph edged forward cautiously to take a better look: it was a gigantic stone amphitheater.

In the middle, on the very lowest level, Murph could make out a lone figure moving across the stone floor. There was a large white circle drawn in the center of this lowest level, and the prisoner was walking slowly, around and around, just inside the line.

Gradually, Murph became aware of a constant whirring and whining noise coming from above. He looked up. Arranged at intervals on the glass ceiling were countless cameras. The sound he could hear was their constant tracking and refocusing as they watched Magpie, following his every move as he paced his circular domain like a restless zoo animal.

The Heroes' Alliance had imprisoned its most deadly foe where he could be watched from every angle. He had nowhere to hide.

Murph was at the very top of the stone steps, and remembered Miss Flint's instruction to him to go no further. He could see the prisoner clearly now: an old man, bent forward with his hands clasped behind his back underneath a long, tattered black coat. With his large, beaky nose and stalking gait, he actually did resemble a bird of some kind. His face, hands, and bare feet were incredibly pale—perhaps bleached from decades without sight of the sun. His hair was long and raggedy, mainly black but shot through with streaks of white. Finally he stopped and cocked his head to look directly up at his first visitor in thirty years.

As Magpie turned his gaze upon him, Murph felt a curious and uncomfortable sensation. It was as if wings of thin metal were beating the air all around him, just barely brushing his skin. It was creepy—and oddly embarrassing somehow. He felt exposed, as if his every secret was being laid bare.

"It's true, then," rasped Magpie. Even though he was some distance away, his voice carried perfectly clearly through the unnerving undersea silence. "A Capeless child who rubs shoulders with Heroes."

"Kid Normal," said Murph uncertainly, nodding, squaring his shoulders, and trying to shake off the feeling that Magpie was able to see inside him. His hairline prickled as the man in black moved to one side to reveal the ominous words he'd scratched onto the stone floor. Bring Kid Normal to ME, the uneven writing read.

"Welcome, Kid Normal. Sit. Take a look around. Can you work out how my very special prison cell has succeeded in keeping me locked up for so long?" asked Magpie curiously.

Murph stared down into the amphitheater, at the thick white line that ran in a circle around the entire lowest level. And gazing back up at the glass walls, he now noticed red boxes at intervals with **DANGER: HIGH EXPLOSIVE** written on them. Finally, he looked up at the cameras once again, piecing it all together.

"If you move out of the circle . . . the whole place will explode," Murph said, unable to stop his mind imagining the glass walls blowing up and the sea rushing in. He shuddered.

"Very good," agreed Magpie, smiling placidly. "If the cameras see me step so much as a toe over that white line, those explosives will blow, and the whole cell will be flooded within moments. I can't even get too close to it . . . watch."

The old man took two large paces toward the outside of the circle. Before he could take a third, a mechanized voice broke out: **"BOUNDARY ENCROACHMENT WARNING. STEP BACK. STEP BACK. STEP BACK."**

"I've tried every power at my disposal—and, as you may have heard, I have a great many. But nothing works. This prison is not without irony, I must admit. The cameras are impervious to my tele-tech. And I can't slip past them. The system is so sensitive it can pick me out even if I'm a different shape."

Murph started as Magpie abruptly lay down on the floor and one of his arms elongated like a pale snake, slithering toward the white line. The mechanized voice intoned once again:

"BOUNDARY ENCROACHMENT. STEP BACK."

As quickly as it had grown, Magpie's arm shrank back to its usual size and the villain leaped to his feet. He was much more agile than his frail appearance suggested he would be. Murph was on high alert now. He fervently hoped that Miss Flint had been telling the truth about how quickly she could extract him if needed.

Magpie broke into his thoughts. "And it's not just me," he went on. "No living thing can cross the line without setting off the system automatically. So I can't get out, and nobody can come in. No one could free me even if they wanted to. It's ingenious, really. Foolproof, some might say. I'll admit that your friends in the Heroes' Alliance were quite clever in setting it up. A kind of underwater game."

Some game, thought Murph, imagining the thirty long years Magpie had spent down here and almost beginning to pity him.

Magpie started to pace once again, round and round the middle of the stone circle at the base of the steps. The cameras up above whirred constantly as they tracked him.

"You're probably telling yourself that I deserve this treatment." Magpie interrupted Murph's thoughts from far below. "I'm sure the Alliance has fed you a lovely story about how evil I am."

"Well, you did steal people's Capes," Murph retorted.

"Pah! I'm a . . . collector, that's all.

A lover of, ah, shiny things, if you like. These . . . powers. They interest me. And some are rather beautiful."

He held out a hand, palm upward, and suddenly a stream of tiny, bright-purple butterflies flew upward toward Murph's astonished face. They breezed past him and gathered in the ceiling space, fluttering around one of the cameras like jewels.

Murph shook his head, as if to clear his thoughts. For someone who had been described to him as a hugely dangerous enemy, Magpie was coming across more like a slightly sad old man, resigned to his fate.

"Why did you want to see me?" Murph asked, eager to get on with his mission.

"Well . . ." Magpie considered this for a moment. "I suppose I was . . . a little lonely, I must confess. I thought they might consent to send you down to visit me, talk a little, you know. Only active members of the Heroes' Alliance are allowed at Shivering Sands, and since you are the first and only member of the organization without a Capability, there's been nobody they would consider sending, until now. I was rather fascinated to hear talk about you . . . ."

Murph mulled these words over. *Hear talk . . .* he mused to himself, remembering once more what Mr. Drench had told him about having his superhearing Capability partially taken away. Could Magpie be using this somehow, to hear things? He thought uneasily about Magpie sitting down here, on the seabed, listening to conversations in the world above. Was it possible?

"Well, I'm here," Murph told him. "So what do you want to talk about?"

"So much to choose from; where to start?" said Magpie idly, stopping to look up at Murph once again. "After so much time spent down here with only my own thoughts for company. Oh, I know," he said, almost casually. "I have written a poem. Would you like to hear it?"

"A poem?" asked Murph blankly. Perhaps he should have been surprised at this turn in the conversation, but by this point it was just a weird little cherry on top of the Super Strange Sundae of a day he was having.

"Yes," said Magpie—and if Murph had only been closer, he might have seen a tiny spark of hatred flare somewhere deep within Magpie's dark eyes, like a supernova in a distant galaxy. "A poem."

Murph rummaged in his pocket for the paper and pencil. He had to take *something* back to Miss Flint.

So, as Magpie recited his poem in a sing-song voice, Murph dutifully jotted down every word:

One for a stranger,
Two, an old thief.
Three for anger,
And four for grief.

Five for a follower,
Four for a friend.
One to seek,
Three for a sad end.

Four, she falls,
And three, she flies.
Six, she can live again.
Three, she dies.

* * *

"All this effort for a . . . poem?" raged Miss Flint incredulously.

The head of the Heroes' Alliance didn't have much time for poetry (an attitude that's almost always a mistake).

Murph was holding out the piece of paper upon which he'd jotted down Magpie's poem as best he could.

"It's just an old nursery rhyme," she went on in disgust. "I can't believe he didn't say anything useful. Nothing about why he wanted to see you. Nothing about why he'd written your name on the floor."

Murph shrugged. "Well, perhaps he meant it when he said he was lonely and I was the only one you'd send down there."

Miss Flint made a disgusted pt'chah! noise and led him back down the corridor through the prison, ranting as she went. "Nothing but incomprehensible whispering under his breath for thirty years, and now when he chooses to speak out he's decided to become a poet. I should have known this would be a waste of time." She said this last bit almost to herself, as they crossed the bridge back to the helicopter that was waiting to take Murph home.

Murph felt his stomach swoop in disappointment: Miss Flint had been counting on him, and he couldn't help feel as if the failure was his fault somehow.

"Right." Miss Flint turned to Murph on the landing platform and fixed him with the most serious of her wide selection of serious expressions. "Before you leave, I must ask for your complete discretion, Kid Normal. You must not, under any circumstances, tell anyone about your visit to Shivering Sands today. Is that understood?"

Murph nodded.

"This facility is top secret. Especially Sublevel One. I had to take a chance and send you in there, in case Magpie had some real information to give us." She looked slightly embarrassed. "It appears he was simply . . . toying with us, I'm sorry to say. But that's all the more reason for you to keep this close to your chest. I don't want to go alarming the rest of the Alliance for no reason. Do I make myself clear?"

"Crystalutely," Murph confirmed.

"Utter secrecy, remember?"

"Understood."

"Tell absolutely no one."

"Roger and wilco."

Far below, Magpie sat back down cross-legged on the floor and listened to them, smiling a dangerous crocodile smile.

He rubbed his pale hands together in delight.

He heard the rotor blades beat the salty air as the Alliance helicopter carrying Murph took off from the top of Shivering Sands and flew away across the waves.

He heard the footsteps of Miss Flint as she returned to the control room.

And he also heard a noise that nobody else in the entire complex was aware of. It was the rasping breath of a small figure who was scratching around in a trash can behind the Shivering Sands kitchens.

Magpie's friend in the outside world. His only ally.

"Oh, Drench . . . ," cooed Magpie, knowing that with the remains of his superhearing Capability, the little man would be the only person who could hear him as he whispered the words from down in his cell.

"Yes, master?" replied Mr. Drench, poking his face out of the trash can. He had a banana peel on his head.

"I heard the helicopter departing. Is everything satisfactory up there?"

"All has gone according to plan."

Underneath the sea, Magpie grinned his cruel grin.

Let your plans be dark and impenetrable as night, he thought to himself. *And when you move, fall like a thunderbolt.*

9

Nellie's Secret

"**S**o . . . hang on," said Mary, holding up a hand. "Miss Flint sent you in . . . on your own . . . to talk to the most dangerous enemy the Heroes' Alliance has ever faced?"

It was morning break, and the Super Zeroes were sitting along the front porch of the wooden pavilion that stood at one edge of The School's large playing fields. Murph had spent a great deal of time here the previous year sweeping up, and it had become one of their favorite places to hang out.

"Um, yeah," said Murph simply. It was only hours since he had sworn a solemn promise of silence to the head of the Alliance:

"*Utter secrecy, remember?*"

"*Understood.*"

But that obviously didn't apply to his four best friends

and crime-fighting partners, right? That had to be in the small print somewhere.

"So—why just you?" asked Hilda, looking miffed. "Why not send all of us? We are a team, after all."

"They couldn't send any of you down to Magpie," Murph consoled her. "He could have stolen your Cape."

Hilda shivered at the very thought of someone taking her horses away. Nellie looked down at her hands and made a small noise of fright and determination that's very difficult to write down but would be something like **eep.**

"You're right, Murph," Mary piped up, trying to break the fearful mood that had taken hold of them. "You were the only safe bet. I mean, what was Magpie going to steal from you? Your incredible meatball-eating ability?"

Murph rolled his eyes and cuffed her on the shoulder affectionately.

"So . . . what's he like?" asked Hilda, wide-eyed. "Is he a . . . massive bird or something?"

Murph thought about his answer carefully. The truth was he didn't really know what to make of the most dangerous supervillain on the planet. "He's . . . really,

really creepy," he said. "He was trying to make out that he's this harmless old man—but there was something really unpleasant in the atmosphere down there. Almost like a gas coming from him, you know?"

"Yeah, you often get that with old men," began Billy sagely. "My grandad—"

"No," Murph cut in, "it was honestly really unnerving. There were loads of security systems and stuff—but you couldn't be in a room with him and feel safe."

They were all silent for a moment.

"Can I see the poem he read to you?" asked Mary finally, looking thoughtful.

"Yeah. It's like some kind of nursery rhyme, I think," Murph confirmed. He pulled the piece of paper out of his pocket.

"That is a secret message. Absolutely. Definitely. No doubt. One hundred percent," said Mary, after studying it for a while.

"Well, Miss Flint didn't seem to think so," said Murph doubtfully. "She thought the whole thing was a waste of time."

"No, nope, nuh-uh, no way," replied Mary. "This"—

she waved the paper at the rest of them—"this isn't a poem."

Everyone looked at her blankly.

"It's our next mission," she told them. "Not a Heroes' Alliance mission—our *own* investigation. Miss Flint doesn't even think this poem is worth bothering with. It's up to us to prove that it is. Think of how brilliant it would be if we foiled a secret plan devised by the Alliance's most dangerous enemy."

It was clear that Mary was as annoyed as Murph at how everyone seemed ready to dismiss the Super Zeroes' abilities—first their classmates, then Mr. Flash, and now even Miss Flint's belief in them felt like it was in doubt.

"But why would Magpie send *me* a secret message?" queried Murph. "I mean, I'm just . . ."

"He's just Kid Normal," chipped in Hilda.

"I don't know yet," admitted Mary. "But I refuse to believe that one of the most dastardly supervillains in history just fancied a bit of company and a quick chat. He must be planning something, and this poem is the key to it."

"Perhaps it's a secret code," said Murph. At Mary's words, his curiosity had sat up and begun sniffing the air like an inquisitive puppy. And if there was one thing Murph loved doing, it was taking the Puppy of Curiosity out for a walk. You never knew what it would stick its nose into.

"Let's all take a copy of the poem and start thinking about what it could mean," he told his team. "But in the meantime, we need to find out everything we can about Magpie. Where he came from, who he really is, why he's started speaking after all these years, how he ended up in that prison. How he got his name. Everything. We need to know how his mind works. It'll give us the best chance of understanding what this message might mean." He got up from the wooden porch and dusted himself off.

"I love a good mystery," said Billy excitedly. "When do we start?"

"Now. And I know just *where* to start too," said Murph decisively. "In Carl's workshop." He set off across the field, with the rest of them trailing behind him.

"Why there?" Billy piped up.

"I want to talk to Sir Jasper. Flora told us he'd be sticking around for a while, working on something with

Carl, remember? Well, when I was in Magpie's cell, he changed shape. And what did the Gemini Sisters say their Cape used to be?"

"Shape-shifting!" Mary cried triumphantly.

"Right," said Murph. "I think Magpie is responsible for taking the Ex-Cape Committee's powers."

"Ooh, our first lead! We're just like the Famous Five," said Hilda excitedly. "I can be Julian! Which one do you want to be, Murph?"

"I dunno," said Murph, "John?"

"There isn't a John," sniffed Hilda.

"Um, Michael?"

"Stop just saying names," said Hilda, marching off ahead of him. "You can be Timmy."

"Okay, whatever," said Murph, stifling a laugh. Then he paused. "Hang on, wasn't Timmy the dog?"

Hilda was striding ahead, smirking to herself.

"Wait!" shouted Murph, running after her. "I don't want to be the dog! Stop!"

"Here, boy!" Hilda teased him, clicking her fingers. "Walkies!" Even Nellie turned and gave a little whistle, smiling shyly at him from behind her green-tipped hair.

* * *

The Super Zeroes could tell Carl was in his workshop not only by the trickle of smoke coming from the chimney but also the persistent banging sound that was audible from across the playing field.

Murph marched up to the front door, glancing with affection at the handwritten sign that read *Fortress of Solitude,* and knocked.

The banging stopped, and a second later the door was opened, not by Carl but by his wife, the Blue Phantom herself, bearing a mug and a beaming smile.

"Oh, hi, kids!" exclaimed Flora delightedly. "Come for that cup of tea, have you? Lovely."

"That's right, yep, the cup of tea," said Murph brightly. "Love a cup of tea." Flora was sharp, and they'd need to be subtle if they were going to keep the fact that they were investigating Magpie from her. "But we were hoping to grab a chat with Sir Jasper as well. Is he here? We didn't get a chance to talk to him on Veterans Day—we were stuck tidying the ACDC for Mr. Flash."

Flora laughed kindly and ushered them inside Carl's workshop—a long room lined with wooden workbenches and filled with gadgets. Carl was a brilliant engineer who supplied working Heroes with equipment when he wasn't busy keeping The School spick-and-span.

"Jasper will be delighted to chat with you," Flora said as she went. "Between you and me, he didn't really get many takers the other day, and he's a bit sore about it. Seems most students weren't very interested in the stories of ex-Heroes with no Capes, I'm sorry to say. Very shortsighted of them, if you ask me."

The door leading to Carl's main garage was usually kept securely locked, but today it was standing open. They all headed through.

Bright lights had been strung from the wooden ceiling. They were shining on the polished fuselage of a sleek, bullet-shaped car with a single wing set across its back. This *ooh*-inspiring vehicle was the *Banshee*, the Blue Phantom's pride and joy. Built and piloted by Carl, it had been severely damaged in the fight against Nektar last year when Carl and Flora were forced to make an emergency crash landing.

But it seemed that the janitor had been busy since then—a few metal panels were still missing from the wing, and one of the jet engines had been removed and placed in pieces along a wooden workbench, but otherwise the silvery-blue machine looked very nearly as good as new. Carl and Sir Jasper were bent over the bench, chattering contentedly like two old hens trying to fit together the world's oiliest jigsaw puzzle.

"Ah, you've lost part of the subsonic inlet, that's the trouble here, old chap," Sir Jasper was saying, guiding his wheelchair forward to prod the area with a wrench.

"Yeah, yeah, I know. I can sort that easily. It's the compressor that's the real problem: all the blades are bent out of shape. Look!" Carl held up something that looked like a twisted, blackened airplane propeller. "And it's still got bits of robot wasp stuck in it as well! Now, I wonder where I put my stiff-bristled brush? It's a right old mess in here. I can never find anything."

Before he could wonder much longer, the brush in question had been placed in his hand.

"Ah, here it is," said Carl gratefully. "Thanks, Little Nell."

The other four Zeroes stared in amazement at Nellie, who had located the brush behind some paint pots within seconds.

"Now grab me the Allen wrenches and we'll see if we can get this fixed and fitted, shall we?"

Nellie trotted to the other side of the garage and started rummaging in a large metal toolbox.

"Hang on . . . who, wha—how does Nellie know where everything is?" Murph wanted to know.

"Hasn't she told you?" replied Carl.

"Told us what?" replied Mary. "She doesn't really tell us anything much, so . . . no."

"Well then, Super Zeroes: meet my new apprentice." Carl gestured toward Nellie, who was now marching back over, dangling a set of Allen wrenches from an oily finger. "Nellie's been helping me out with the repairs to the *Banshee* all summer."

Nellie squeaked slightly with pride as her four friends gazed at her enviously.

"Wow. How cool! You're full of surprises!" said Murph to Nellie. "Carl only ever trusted me with the sweeping," he added, feeling a little jealous but also proud of his friend. "You haven't flown it without us, have you?" he added urgently, turning back to Carl.

"Nah, she's not quite ready for that yet," the janitor replied, "but we're not far off now, are we?"

"Indeed no," replied Sir Jasper, spinning his chair around and motoring over to inspect the miraculous flying car. "Do you remember when we first worked on her together, eh, old sausage? Sixty-five, it must have been. Miraculous, shiny lady that she is," he added, tapping a hand affectionately on the hood.

Mary prodded Murph gently in the ribs. He knew that she was eager to question Sir Jasper about

how he'd lost his Cape, but now Murph was dying to know all about Jasper and Carl working together back in 1965. Between Magpie, the *Banshee*, and Nellie's secret summer, Murph's brain was swimming with so many questions it felt like an overcrowded fish tank, and he didn't know which to ask first.

"Have questions!" he blurted out finally. Everyone stopped and looked at him.

"Well, let's hear them, then, young sir," coaxed Sir Jasper. "An inquiring mind is a wonderful thing. Almost as wonderful as a delicious pork pie with a suggestion of fine tangy mustard." He smacked his lips.

"Question one: Did you . . . help *build* the *Banshee*?"

The old man seemed surprised, stroking his neat beard before saying, "Yes, in part. Carl and I have worked together for many years. He's a brilliant engineer, and when I still had my Cape—tele-tech, you know—we were a great team. He did the mechanics, I sorted the electrics. The Alliance still uses a lot of our inventions."

Murph thought of the electric helicopter that had flown him to Shivering Sands. He was sure that Jasper must have had something to do with it.

"In fact, Jasper here is one of the very few people who knew my secret identity while I was still operational," Flora said quietly. "He's been a loyal friend for years." At this the Super Zeroes gasped—very few people knew Flora's secret identity even now. If she and Carl had trusted Jasper with it for so long, he must be very special.

"They were good days," Sir Jasper went on. "I inherited the old family pile, of course. Witchberry Hall. A large country house," he explained further, seeing Murph adopting his notorious "confused owl" expression. "Gave us all a place to work—and a little cash to start out with as well."

"Uh-oh," Flora broke in. "I can see this is ramping up into a full-on reminiscence session. I had best put that kettle on. We're all going to need a cup of tea for this."

"In that case," said Murph, "question two: Can I have a hot chocolate instead?" Before anyone could answer, Hilda burst in:

"And question three: Can I have a coffee, please?"

Drinks requests took them all the way up to question six, but a few minutes later, while Flora was away in the kitchen preparing the most complicated tea round ever, Murph was ready to ask question seven, the most pressing of the day.

"Right, next question. Why did you say in assembly that tele-tech *used to be* your Cape? What happened to it? Was it . . . Magpie?"

At the mention of Magpie, Carl peered anxiously around the corner of the workshop, as if to see if Flora could overhear what was being said. **"Where in blazes did you hear that name?"** he asked, unusually sharply.

"Oh, it was just something Mr. Drench said in a lesson last year, that's all," Mary broke in, hoping to cover their tracks.

"Now listen, my young friends," said Sir Jasper, exchanging a significant glance with Carl before gliding over toward them with a serious expression. "There are some things that are best left in the past, you know. Some . . . events that we don't really talk about. I won't talk about how *I* lost my Cape, but perhaps I can tell you about the first time Magpie appeared."

At this Carl seemed to relax a little, before coughing

and standing up. "I think I'll see how Flora's getting on with those drinks."

Once he had left, Jasper brightened. The twinkle in his eye returned. "Very well, then, you curious little cauliflowers," he said. "I'll tell you about the first hero to have their Capability taken away from them. It's not something you need to fear these days, so I don't see that telling you about it can do too much harm. What I am about to relate happened, **oooooh . . . at least thirty years ago . . ."**

10

The Dashing Escapades of the Dandy Man

It's flashback time. Everybody ready?

We are now going to travel back in time more than thirty years. It's a complicated process, and you must follow our instructions very carefully. First, you must put your socks on your hands. Then go to the nearest window and shout "I AM LORD BANANA HEAD!" as loudly as you can.

Now run around in circles going "Wee-oo-wee-oo-wee-oo" until you are dizzy. Then do the same thing backward until you feel better. Pop off and do all that, and we'll see you in the next paragraph.

All finished? Great. Welcome to the past. Don't we all look young?

1985

It was a Friday evening in the 1980s, and multimillionaire Wayne Blaze was making a snack in the kitchen of his mansion. He sang to himself as he buttered two slices of bread, dressed in nothing but a black silk dressing gown embroidered with a huge dragon, satin pajama bottoms, and a pair of unacceptable slippers with straw soles.

"Jitterbug . . ."

Blaze slipped one of the slices of bread into his very latest high-tech gadget, a brand-new sandwich toaster. He added a few pieces of cheese, followed by the second slice of bread, and closed the lid. He started to sing louder.

"JITTERBUG . . ."

"Is everything okay, Master Blaze?" came a voice through the doorway. It was his butler, Butler.

"Ah, Butler! Come in here and take a look at this!" marveled Blaze as smoke began to stream from the sides of the toaster. Butler slid into the room, dressed as usual in an impeccable black suit. He looked at his employer's dressing gown with mild alarm.

A **ping** sounded. Blaze flipped up the lid of the toaster.

"Incredible," he said enthusiastically. "It's toasted both sides of the sandwich . . . at the same time! And look at the delicate seashell-like pattern that it's branded onto the bread. Modern technology is incredible!"

"Most impressive, sir," agreed Butler insincerely, thinking how difficult it was going to be to clean.

Wayne Blaze was now trying to extract his grilled cheese from the hot metal plate to which it had become fused. He managed to get a knife underneath, but then half the sandwich came away with it, spilling molten orange 1980s cheese all over the marble worktop.

Just then the phone rang.

"Blaze Mansion, one Friday evening in the mid-1980s," began Butler. "A hostage situation, you say? He'll come right away. Goodbye."

He turned back to his employer, who had burned his tongue trying to bite into his hot sandwich too soon.

"Wha' wa' tha'?" Wayne Blaze asked, flopping his tongue out to try and cool it off in the air-conditioned atmosphere of the kitchen.

"Apparently there's an emergency at Nakamura Tower," replied Butler.

"Tha' sows li' a 'ob for 'andy wan," mumbled Wayne Blaze dramatically, with his tongue still out.

"That sounds like a job for the Dandy Man?" clarified Butler helpfully. "I couldn't agree more, Master Blaze."

Together they raced through to the oak-paneled room next door, delayed only slightly when the pocket of the black silk dressing gown got caught on a door handle.

Butler strode over to a huge bookcase and pressed the spine of a large leather-bound volume entitled ***THE WIT AND WISDOM OF GARFIELD.***

All at once, one of the wall panels slid smoothly to one side to reveal a gleaming fireman's pole and, arranged on a chair beside it, the costume that would transform Wayne Blaze into his alter ego. Butler politely turned away as the dressing gown slid to the floor like an unfashionable snake and the slippers were kicked away into a corner, where they belonged. Within moments, they had been replaced by gleaming black riding boots, tight pants, a white shirt with huge frills down the front, a black eye mask, and a massive highwayman's hat.

"Time to save the eighties once again,"

yelled the hero as he shrugged himself into a military-style coat with epaulets on the shoulders and adjusted his black eye mask. **"The Dandy Man is coming!"**

With a final incomprehensible shout that sounded something like "Da diddly qua qua!," he leaped onto the fireman's pole and dropped out of sight.

Butler rolled his eyes and went to try and scrape congealed cheese off the kitchen counter.

Several floors below, the Dandy Man was struggling to open the complicated doors of his sports car. Instead of opening sideways like normal doors, they flapped upward like beetles' wings. Finally he located the handle and managed to step back just in time to avoid being hit on the chin as the door sprang up.

It knocked his hat off as he sat down, though, and he had to lean uncomfortably out of the low driver's seat to pick it up. Then he realized he couldn't reach the handle to close the door and had to get halfway out of the car again to grab it.

Eventually though, the Dandy Man was ready to roar into action. He pulled out a small lever marked Choke and turned the key in the engine. After mere minutes of making an odd coughing noise, the powerful car burst into life and sped out of the secret garage into the city night.

The guests at the party to celebrate the opening of the city's tallest skyscraper, Nakamura Tower, were all dressed in the very latest fashions. Fingerless lacy gloves and neon leg warmers mingled underneath an array of frankly alarming hairstyles.

But halfway through the evening, things had gone very wrong. With a shout of "Everybody freeze!," several men had burst in carrying guns and proceeded to shatter the huge windows that looked out from the top floor. As broken glass flew everywhere, the guests huddled in the center of the room, feeling increasingly chilled by the night breeze that was now whistling through the building.

"So sorry to break up the party," a measured voice had said finally.

Some of the braver guests raised their heads to see a nondescript-looking man wearing a long black coat over a black suit coming through the door, surveying the scene calmly.

"I shouldn't have to inconvenience you for much longer, but do please stay exactly where you are for now or my colleagues here will . . . deal with you."

The man in black selected a comfortable chair, brushed the broken glass from it, and sat down to wait, lacing his fingers together and carefully crossing one leg over the other.

The Dandy Man's car squealed to a halt beside Nakamura Tower. "Vogue!" he exclaimed to himself, squinting up to the top floor, where he could see light streaming through the missing windows.

After only a minute or two struggling with his car door, the hero was striding toward the entrance lobby, his feet crunching on the broken glass that littered the road.

The Dandy Man took a flying leap at the doors and aimed a kick at them with his high black riding boots, his frilly shirt and tricorn hat flowing in the breeze as he went. As he burst through, he was surprised to find just the one guard inside, armed with a single small knife. This was something of a disappointment, as he felt that his dramatic entrance had been wasted, but he didn't let it faze him. Striding up to the guard, the Dandy Man pointed at his weapon and chuckled.

"That's not a knife," he taunted the guard. "This is a knife." And with that, the Dandy Man's hands began to elongate and transform into shimmering metal blades, until finally his arms were tipped with two gleaming swords. He brought them together in front of his face in an X shape with a resounding clang.

Then he paused. "Well, in fact it's a sword. A pair of swords," he said.

"Well, this also isn't a knife," replied a guard who had been hidden at the other end of the room. "This is a high-powered assault rifle, and I'm about to shoot you with it." Which was a fairly persuasive point.

With a huge roar and a flash of flame, the guard opened fire—and the Dandy Man leaped into action. It didn't actually happen in slow motion, but it's far more fun to imagine it that way.

"I don't think so!" cried the Dandy Man, although since we're imagining it in slow motion it sounded more like **"Ooooooooooh doooooooooooooooooooon't thoooooooooooooooooonk suuuuuuuuuuuuue."** He sprang up, chopping at the air with his hand-swords at a speed that defied belief, even in slo-mo.

Bullets pinged to the floor as he sliced them away, somersaulting down the long lobby toward the new guard. He landed in front of him with a thump of his black riding boots. The guard looked at him in amazement, and not just because of the tight pants.

"Stand and deliver." The Dandy Man grinned, swishing his swords.

Neither guard seemed eager to stick around—they bolted down the hall and out the doors. Their vanquisher looked after them with a satisfied sigh, then turned to the row of elevators beside him.

"Well, that was suspiciously easy. But now for the main event. **I am SUCH a righteous dude.**"

Even at the time this sounded a bit embarrassing, so it was lucky that nobody heard him.

Some of the hostages screamed when they heard the clatter of a machine gun several floors below, but the man in black continued to recline calmly in his chair.

"What is it that you want?" a man in a suit with huge shoulder pads shouted at him. "Money? Gold? We'll give you anything. Just please, let us go!"

The man in black silenced him with a wave of his hand. "Money? How quaint. That's not what I'm interested in. There's only one thing worth having in this world. Power. That's what I'm here for. And unless I'm much mistaken, my delivery is arriving . . . now."

Ping!

The elevator doors at the end of the room slid open, revealing the impressive silhouette of the Dandy Man, his shirt fluttering in the breeze and his swords gleaming. "Release the hostages and I may spare your life!" cried the hero in his most dramatic tone of voice.

The man in black stared silently at him. After a moment he flicked a hand at his two remaining guards, who were stationed by the window. "Let's see what this frilly man's made of. Attack!" he told them calmly.

Someone uttered a high-pitched scream—it was the man with the huge shoulder pads. The guards started toward the elevator and began taking what looked like rather lazy potshots at the Dandy Man.

Before the guards could hit their stride, the hero immediately leaped into a perfect scissor kick with his shiny boots and slammed the bullets out of the air with his swords. He somersaulted toward the guards—knocking one unconscious with a flying roundhouse kick and booting the other into the now-empty elevator.

The doors closed.

"Looks like you're going down, creep," quipped the Dandy Man, and he turned to face his main enemy once more, hoping for a ripple of applause from the hostages at the very least.

One person did clap. It was the man in black, and if the Dandy Man hadn't known better he would have thought that it sounded more than a little sarcastic.

The villain got to his feet and walked away from the hero toward the large windows that looked out over the city. "Well, it appears I have been beaten," he said, sounding anything but.

"Does that mean . . . we can go?" squeaked the man with the big shoulder pads.

The man in black shrugged.

It was all the crowd needed. They surged toward the exits in a tide of neon, leaving espadrilles and scrunchies discarded in their wake. Within seconds there were only two people left on the top floor of the skyscraper.

"Swords for hands," mused the man in black. "An unusual power. Yes, I suppose that could be useful to have." He turned to face the Dandy Man, his face twisting into an expression of angry concentration.

"Useful?" laughed the hero. "It was more than enough to defeat—**aaagh!**"

Flashes of purple lightning had started to appear in the air. Like snakes, they wound around the Dandy Man's arms, until the two men were linked by a bolt of dancing purplish fire. The Dandy Man's eyes widened in horror as his twin swords shriveled, shrank away, disappeared—and then popped back into existence on the ends of the arms of the man in black. These new swords were curved like scimitars: deadly-looking, and somehow even brighter and more impressive than his own had been.

At last the purple lightning flashes subsided. The Dandy Man staggered backward and fell to his knees, his vision swimming. Desperately he tried to produce his swords—but nothing happened. He flapped his hands in front of him frantically, tears springing to his eyes.

"In the name of Salt-N-Pepa! My swords! You've taken them!" he gasped.

"Oh, don't worry. They're in good hands," replied the other man drily. And without further conversation, he ran to the edge of the building and jumped out into the night, reaching inside his coat to pull a rip cord as he did so.

The Dandy Man dragged himself over to the window and gazed out across the city. He could make out far below, but moving away rather than downward, a hurrying black-and-white shape, its coat fluttering in the wind as it sped through the air underneath a narrow black parachute. He could just see the twin swords glinting as they caught the moonlight.

"He stole them . . . ," breathed the Dandy Man to himself, the enormity of what had just happened catching up with him. "A thief—a flying thief . . ."

His head slumped to the floor.

"A thieving magpie!"

11

The Perils of Annabel

For the rest of the morning, Murph's brain circled around and around—first to Magpie in his prison, and then back to everything Sir Jasper had told them about Magpie's first Capability theft. It seemed as though every answer Jasper had given the Super Zeroes had just thrown up more questions.

By the time lunchtime arrived, Murph was brooding harder than a hen flicking through an egg catalog. As he entered the main hall, he glanced up at the Heroes' Vow, and that single line popped out at him once again:

I promise to keep our secrets.

How far is the Alliance prepared to go in order to keep their secrets? he wondered to himself.

Murph's reverie was interrupted by a loud cry of **"Mind yer backs!"** as the school's head chef,

Bill Burton, whizzed by dangerously close to him with a huge piping-hot tray of meatballs on a little trolley. Bill was a frantic little chap, who zipped around the lunchroom attending to each station like a clown spinning plates at the circus.

Incidentally, Bill was also very good at spinning actual plates. It was his Cape—and it made him an excellent catering manager—but he had been banned from using it at The School, as it encouraged the children to try spinning plates too.

In fact, at one point, plate spinning had been so popular that the school lost 35 percent of its crockery, causing Mr. Souperman to send a stern letter home. The letter was widely mocked by parents and students alike, and in some instances, spoof versions began appearing mysteriously, posted on the walls of various classrooms. Here's an example of one of them:

Dear Parents,

It has cucumber to my attention that several students are causing absolute haddock in the dining room through the mindless act of trying and failing to spin plates. What's more, despite serious prawnings that action would be taken, these students have continued to fishobey me. As the breadmaster of this school, I shouldn't have to waste my thyme writing letters about such nonsense, butter the situation has gotten serious. Peas tell your children that they mustard stop doing this immediately, otherwise they will have their lunch privileges bacon away from them.

Best fishes,

Mr. SouperTheDayMan

"Roll up, roll up!" said Mr. Burton in his chipper voice as Murph reached the front of the lunch line. "Fresh batch of meatballs over here!"

Meatballs were Murph's favorite, and he loved it when he got the first spoonful of the unspoiled servings.

"Ah, Mr. Cooper!" said Bill Burton loudly. "Will you be having your usual, sir?!"

"Yes, please, chef!" Murph laughed as he playfully saluted the smiley meatball provider. He liked Bill a lot. It was hard not to, really: he was a very happy, excited fellow who seemed to absolutely love his job.

Bill nodded, saluted back, and proceeded to flamboyantly scoop up the delicacies and present them atop the spaghetti on Murph's plate.

"*Et voilà!*" he exclaimed. "Do enjoy!"

"Thanks, Bill," said Murph, forgetting his Magpie-based woes for a moment, and he wandered off to scan the tables for the rest of the Super Zeroes, hot tomatoey steam wafting into his face as he did.

Finally he caught a flash of yellow—Mary had saved him a seat next to her. The rest of the Zeroes were already there too, busy shoveling in meatballs.

"It's your lucky day, Meatball Murph!" she told him as he approached.

Murph squeezed in between her and Hilda and started scooping his lunch into his mouth as fast as he could.

"Wobbler fink abba fur emission?" Murph mumbled, his mouth full of spaghetti.

"Wobbly . . . *what now*?" asked Mary, puzzled and slightly grossed out by Tomato Mouth next to her.

Murph swallowed and wiped his face with a hand.

"What did you think of the first part of our mission?" he clarified. "We've already found out how Magpie got his name—and a bit about how his Cape-stealing power works. Not a bad start, huh?"

"Ah, right. Thanks for translating that from gross mouth-full-of-pork language," said Mary. "Yes, very helpful. That purple lightning stuff sounds weird, but at

least it gives people some kind of warning sign that he's trying to take a Capability. It sounds like he just used to set up crimes to lure Heroes to him, then steal their powers and escape. No wonder he was such a danger to the Capable community."

"I know," said Murph. "And now, after years of everyone thinking he's safely locked away, he's planning something new."

"He might not be planning anything at all," Billy argued. "He just messed around with that Dandy Man person, didn't he? Wasted his time with those guards just to test him out. Maybe that's all he was doing with you. He heard about you and was curious, like he said."

Murph could see Nellie shaking her head. She didn't think that sounded likely, and neither did he. "No, I think there's more to it," he said seriously. "I've got a bad feeling about this." He slightly spoiled this dramatic and quite heroic declaration by doing an accidental but rather large meatball burp.

Mary cowered away. "I've got a bad feeling about your guts," she joked.

"Sorry," Murph replied bashfully.

It was Mary who realized that the answers the Super Zeroes needed could be right under their noses. Meatballs managed, they were preparing to spend another CT lesson hanging around in the ACDC storeroom while the rest of the class trained to be Heroes.

"Look at all this!" Mary said, leafing through a folder full of papers. "Old Alliance records—details of missions. This place is a gold mine! I bet there's something here that will tell us a bit more about Magpie! Let's split up and see if we can get some of this stuff in order and find something useful."

"Hang on," said Billy, "are you saying that we're *actually* going to clean up the storeroom? The next part of our mission is, in fact, a bit of tidying?"

" 'Tidying' isn't a dirty word, Billy," sniffed Mary. "Quite the opposite, in fact."

But before they could start investigating properly, the storeroom door suddenly opened, admitting Mr. Flash's head and shoulders.

"HEY!" he shouted. "What are you doing malingerin' in here, you bunch of muscleless cockles?"

"We're, you know, tidying the storeroom?" said Mary tentatively.

"Like you told us to?" added Billy.

"WELL, STOP IT!" he snarled at them like an unreasonable tiger. **"COME AND JOIN THE LESSON."**

The Zeroes exchanged bemused looks, then filed back out into the ACDC. The rest of the class looked at them as if they were unwelcome worms in the apple of Wednesday.

"We're staging a mock rescue mission today," said Mr. Flash, four decibels louder than necessary. "And we need an even number of people on each team."

"Ah, now I get it," whispered Murph to Mary. "He just wants us to make up the numbers."

"SHUUUUT UUUUUPPPPP!" yelled Mr. Flash at him predictably. "NOW, this is going to be a realistic simulation of the kind of operation you might be sent on if you ever do actually join the Heroes' Alliance. Annabel there is in terrible danger." He pointed a maroon finger toward the other end of the ACDC, where a life-size stuffed rag doll was dangling limply at the top of a very tall wooden ladder. She was dressed in an old-fashioned frock and had a smiling, painted face with long eyelashes.

Between the class and the doll, Mr. Flash had placed piles of mats, vaulting horses, hurdles, and other gym equipment to form a makeshift assault course.

"Half of you are going to play the villains today," he continued. "Although, of course, the Heroes' Alliance doesn't refer to them as villains. The official term is—"

"Rogues!" Murph interrupted, earning himself a filthy look and a grudging nod.

"Yeeeeees," said Mr. Flash, extremely reluctantly. "Kid Normal is correct. Rogues. So some of you will be playing the part of Rogues who are holding the lovely Annabel prisoner. And the rest of you will be trying to climb that ladder and get her out. Alive."

"Looks a bit late for that," fluted a voice from the back.

Murph thought it sounded like Corned Beef Boy, and shot him a little glance. Corned Beef Boy glared right back, and then did that slightly embarrassing thing that people think looks cool but doesn't, where you point at your own eyes with your fingers and then point at the person you're trying to intimidate, as if to say "I'm watching you."

Mr. Flash noticed Corned Beef Boy's little show and decided to volunteer him. "Right, Roland, since you seem so eager, get yourself up here. You can lead our Rogue team today."

Corned Beef Boy trudged to the front of the class.

"And who's going to be head Hero . . . ," mused the teacher. "How about you, Elsa?"

"Okay," replied Elsa brusquely, and she shouldered her way to the front.

"Right then, you two, hurry up and pick your teams," Mr. Flash encouraged them.

Even before they started, Murph knew that he and his friends would be chosen last. It was as inevitable as that moment when you call your primary schoolteacher "Mommy" by mistake, and just as humiliating.

The kids with combat skills were chosen first. Then those with superspeed or the ability to fly without an umbrella. Then those with advanced tele-tech or X-ray vision.

After a couple of minutes, the whole class was staring at the five Super Zeroes, who remained standing at the edge of the Development Center, feeling as out of place as five carrots who have accidentally wandered into a tangerine convention.

There was a silence as awkward as the one that follows the moment when you call the teacher "Mommy."

"Go on, then," coaxed Mr. Flash, nudging Corned Beef Boy, whose turn it was. "Get it over with: pick one of the remnants."

"Don't want any of them," he grumped. "They're useless. We stick." He led his team off to the other end of the hall, where they ranged themselves threateningly across the width of the room.

"Looks like we're with you, then, Elsa," said Hilda brightly, cantering across to join the rest of the team and standing next to Gangly Fuzz Face, who looked at her furiously. The other Super Zeroes shambled nervously into position too.

"Right!" shouted Mr. Flash, throwing his hands into the air. "Heroes, to count this as a successful mission, Annabel must be delivered back to me unharmed. And remember that this is a drill—so go easy on each other, all right? Strike to disable only. Three . . . two . . . one. GO!"

Elsa beckoned her team together for a pep talk.

"Okay, we've got the best Capes, so this will be easy," she told them. "You"—she jerked her head at Gangly Fuzz Face—"your force fields are cool. Use them as soon as you can." She gestured to Frankenstein's Nephew. "Use your fire to keep them at bay. Basically, let's just get in there and kick some serious shin."

"Um . . . what should we do?" Hilda wanted to know.

Elsa did a sort of scornful snort. "You stay behind us and try not to get in the way."

"Yeah, but what's your actual rescue plan?" Hilda persisted.

"I just told you! Steam over there and use our Hero powers to save the day! Weren't you listening?" demanded Elsa arrogantly.

"Not strictly a plan . . . ," began Murph, but it was too late. With a shout of **"CHARGE!"** Elsa had led the rest of their group off across the hall, firing blasts of ice from her hands. As she ran, Murph could have sworn he heard her singing to herself, but for legal reasons we should point out that the song was not about letting it go, being one with the wind and sky, or the cold never bothering her anyway.

The opposing team seemed to have been caught slightly off guard by this sudden onslaught. Elsa's Cape was already coating much of the center of the ACDC in ice and frost and, faced with the other team barreling toward them, Corned Beef Boy decided to tackle the attack head-on.

"GET THEM!" he roared, lumbering toward the increasingly snow-covered middle of the room.

Watching the scene unfold, Murph thought it looked a bit like opening time at a Christmas Village—if someone had announced that the first person on Santa's lap would be given a private jet. The two sides reached the icy area at around the same time, their feet slipping all over the place as they desperately tried to engage the other team.

Gangly Fuzz Face used one of his force fields to stop Corned Beef Boy in his tracks. Corned Beef Boy fell over backward in a shower of sparkling ice crystals. Two enormous older students had been placed on opposing teams, and they squared up to each other. One raised her hands like a conductor, creating a tornado in the air that whirled particles of ice upward into a blizzard that spread across the room, stinging eyes and faces. Her friend opened his mouth like he was about to be sick, but instead a powerful stream of water shot out of him like a fire hose. He raked his head from side to side, knocking several people off balance before Elsa froze the jet of water, blocking his mouth with a huge ice cube. Enraged, he flew at her and grabbed her by the hair, all Capes forgotten as they grappled with each other.

Before long, the center of the ACDC was a mass of brawling, struggling figures only dimly visible through the snow. Grunts, slaps, and the occasional word that isn't suitable for this book filled the air.

"Narnia's really gone downhill recently, hasn't it?" said Mary drily, sheltering with the other Super Zeroes behind a frozen vaulting horse.

"What on earth are you all doing?" screamed Mr. Flash from the other end of the room. "I've never seen such a bunch of bumbling beavers! **SOMEBODY DO SOMETHING, FOR THE LOVE OF JOHN!**"

Elsa's ice blasts had by now covered a large part of the ACDC, including Annabel's ladder, which was hidden behind a sheet of frozen water.

"How are we going to rescue the hostage now?" grunted Frankenstein's Nephew from the crook of someone's elbow. "Shall I melt it?" He ignited one of his hands hopefully, but before he could do anything, a member of the opposing team, who'd transformed her entire body into stone, knocked into him and sent him flying headfirst into a snowdrift.

Nellie—a small icicle hanging from her nose— grabbed Murph by the sleeve. She widened her eyes and pointed urgently toward the far end of the room, where Annabel was dangling sadly above the blizzard. Murph realized what his friend was telling him. The coast was clear; the entire defending team was caught up in a ridiculous snow battle. This was their chance.

"She's right," he told the rest of the Super Zeroes, earning himself a quarter-of-a-second smile from Nellie in the process. "While they're all busy holding the Annual Snowman Smackdown, we could just get in there, have Mary fly up, grab Annabel, and win the battle! Billy, can you help us get a bit closer? We could use some cover."

"That I can do," said Billy, ballooning himself and beginning to roll toward the other end of the hall like an out-of-control wobbly tire. The other Super Zeroes followed behind, dashing toward the foot of the ladder while explosions and ice jets crackled and snapped around them.

Murph glanced over his shoulder, satisfied that the rest of the class was busy brawling with one another and showing off.

He tapped Mary on the back: "Now, go!"

Mary popped out her umbrella, rising smoothly

out from behind Billy and scooping Annabel from the top of the ladder in seconds flat. She made landfall again without any of the rest of the class even noticing what had happened.

"Nice to meet you, Annabel," said Murph seriously to the doll's smiling face, shaking her by one limp cloth hand. "We're here to rescue you."

"We've just got to get you back to Mr. Flash," said Hilda tensely, as Billy unballooned to his more customary size beside her.

The center of the room was still almost completely blocked by the battle that was raging in the snow— Murph could just make out the figure of Mr. Flash right at the other end of the ACDC, hopping around and shouting something about "uselessness" and "most ridiculous load of tangling terrapins I've ever seen."

"Back down the side," Murph decided, pointing to the edge of the room that still seemed relatively clear.

They made a break for it, trying to crouch and run at the same time, with Mary dragging Annabel by the foot. But just as they began to feel like they might make it through, a shout brought them up short.

"Hey! Losers!" It was the hoarse voice of Frankenstein's Nephew.

The Zeroes stopped in their tracks.

"What do you think you're doing?" he continued, as more of the class stopped fighting one another and turned to look. The clouds of ice crystals filling the air gradually began to settle.

"They've done it . . . ," said Gangly Fuzz Face in surprise, letting go of Crazy Eyes Jemima's hair. "They've rescued the hostage."

"Nah, I don't think so," snarled Frankenstein's Nephew, jabbing his hands toward the Zeroes. "I don't think Annabel's gonna make it out of this alive." He laughed a grunting laugh and shot two fat jets of fire directly toward the cloth dummy.

"HEYYY! They're on our team!" cried Fuzz Face. But nobody heard him, because right at that moment Murph shouted, "Oh no you don't!" and dived straight in front of Annabel.

There was a blur of noise and movement.

The next thing Murph knew, he was back at the end of the hall, tucked under Mr. Flash's highly muscled left arm. The teacher had raced in and saved him from the jets of flame. Annabel, on the other hand, was now a small pile of smoking ash.

"What in the name of Heck, Hades, Hull, and all points north do you think you're doing, you ridiculous cabbage?" bawled Mr. Flash, putting Murph down and striding over to inspect the damage.

"Um . . . rescuing the hostage?" replied Murph, trotting after him.

"Fighting without fear," added Mary, looking at him proudly, which made Murph's insides go strange. "Saving without glory." There was a flick of green as Nellie violently nodded her head in agreement.

"Learning what it means to be a true Hero," finished Hilda, hands on hips.

Mr. Flash grunted dismissively before rounding on Frankenstein's Nephew. "And what about YOU? Were you trying to burn down the flamin' Capability Development Center? What's the matter with you?"

Frankenstein's Nephew shuffled his large feet and looked sideways at Gangly Fuzz Face for support.

But the leader of their gang just grimaced slightly and said, "Yeah, not cool, pal" in an undertone.

"WELL," screamed Mr. Flash to the class. **"WHAT DO WE THINK WENT WRONG WITH TODAY'S MISSION?"**

"The hostage got burned to death?" suggested someone meekly.

"The hostage got burned to death," confirmed Mr. Flash grimly. "I sewed that doll myself as well. It'll take me ages to make another one." He collected himself. "RIGHT! Well, consider yourselves a bunch of complete, half-baked, soggy-bottomed failures. Why didn't any of you help these kids out once they'd rescued Annabel, eh?" He gestured toward the Super Zeroes, who had gathered together sheepishly.

"Because they're lame!" said Corned Beef Boy, or Roland, as we now know he is called. "What superheroes do you know who prance around with umbrellas and stupid little horses?"

There were a few giggles at this, but Murph noticed that Gangly Fuzz Face didn't join in. Instead he met Murph's eye before looking away awkwardly.

"WELL, THEY BEAT THE LOT OF YOU!' said Mr. Flash, looking as if the words had to be dragged out of his mouth with pliers. "Go on, get out of here; it's nearly break time."

The class straggled off, with the Zeroes following last of all.

Mr. Flash watched them go with a slightly strange expression. Murph caught a glimpse of it as he left the ACDC. If he didn't know better, he might have thought it looked a teeny, tiny bit like respect.

12

Magpie and the Weasel

Now, those of you with Olympic-standard memories will remember that something very intriguing happened earlier. You know—when we found out that Mr. Drench is now living in a trash can and helping Magpie. This is what is known in the authoring world as a cliff-hanger. We chuck in a bit of information like that, then throw our authorial scarves over our shoulders and swan off to talk about something completely different for a few chapters. It's extremely irritating, so please accept our apologies. This is the chapter when we explain everything and we can all be friends again.

To rescue you from the literary cliff from which you are now dangling, we must go back to the day that Mr. Drench first disappeared. The day of Nektar's defeat.

Being captured and mind-controlled by an evil man-wasp had a rather unexpected effect on Mr. Drench.

All the time he was doing Nektar's bidding, a tiny part of his brain was realizing that, for the first time in many, many years, he was actually enjoying himself. He really rather liked being evil. He might have been able to recover from this with a good nap and a cup of tea, and possibly some pictures of cute kittens to remind him about being nice. But unfortunately, that's not quite how things turned out.

Instead, Mr. Drench was hit very hard on the back of the head with a large frying pan and knocked unconscious, which did his already scrambled brain no good at all. Then, when he came around, it was to the sound of several Cleaners in the corridor outside shouting things like **"Room clear!"** and **"Locate possible hostiles and neutralize!"** as they swept through the building.

They're looking for the bad guys, thought Mr. Drench to himself woozily. *I'm one of them. Hide!* He stood up sharply, which delivered another blow to his head, as he was underneath a table. Then, as the clomping of boots got even closer, he dashed across the room in sheer panic and dived through a large, shattered windowpane.

His fall was broken by a Dumpster on the ground below. Well, we *say* his fall was broken, but in fact he hit his head again on the way in, which made a surprisingly pleasing noise, not unlike a large bell. Mr. Drench sank to the bottom of the Dumpster, which was full of waste from the kitchens, and lay there in a daze as the Cleaners carried out their search around him.

As he trembled in the trash, something very strange happened to Mr. Drench. The series of blows to the head, the aftermath of being mind-controlled, the fact that being evil had come quite naturally to him . . . they all merged inside his addled brain as he lay among the food scraps and discarded packaging. Then and there, he decided that he was finished with being a mild-mannered teacher. He had had a taste of sweet villain-honey, and he liked it.

A very slightly mad-sounding chuckle escaped from his lips, soon growing into a cackle of crazed laughter.

Mr. Drench felt a powerful affection for the trash that had protected him and kept him hidden. This would be his habitat from now on, he decided, chewing meditatively on an old, moist teabag. He would live among the cast-offs as he plotted revenge on the Heroes who had underestimated him and taken him for granted. No longer would he be the meek and mild sidekick known as the Weasel.

And he would never wash, or be nice to people, ever again.

The story of Mr. Drench's first few weeks as a sneaky, trash can–dwelling villain is a very bizarre one, but we haven't got time to tell you about it now because as we're writing this our dinner's nearly ready and we're having fries. Let's just skip to the part where he arrived at Shivering Sands. Because after a while he decided that to become a true supervillain he had to learn from the best—and surely the best was Magpie, the most feared Rogue of them all.

Stowing away on one of the ships that brought supplies out to the rusting towers in the sea, Mr. Drench slipped unnoticed into the waste-disposal systems of the prison. He slid into pipes and burrowed through bins. He existed on a diet of food slops and rainwater. With his superhearing he listened to the conversations of the guards and prisoners, gradually building up a mental map of the whole prison and its security systems.

Before long, he worked out that there was no way he could get in to see Magpie in person. The elaborate security system for Magpie's cell operated on a different electrical circuit from the rest of the prison. The Heroes' Alliance was taking no chances—there was no way for anyone to override the auto-destruct mechanism on Sublevel One. So instead, Mr. Drench decided to bide his time.

During this time-biding period, he also befriended a small rat, which made a nest in the pocket of his tattered, garbage soaked tweed jacket. He had decided it could be his sidekick, when he had learned enough to commence his reign of evil, and he named it Ratsputin. It became his constant companion—he would feed it leftovers from the leftovers that he ate himself—and he would sit and talk to it for hours, telling it his plans.

"It won't be long before I find a way to contact Magpie," Mr. Drench was telling Ratsputin one day, a few weeks after he'd arrived at Shivering Sands. He was crouched in the bottom of his favorite hideout—a large wheelie trash can that stood on a platform outside the kitchen block. Privately he'd nicknamed it the Weasel-y trash can. "Then I shall learn how to be truly evil. The Alliance will regret taking me for granted for so long."

"Yes, my friend," answered a smooth, whispering voice, "soon they will learn to fear you." Mr. Drench was rather taken aback by this. Cute as he was, Ratsputin had never shown any particular talent for speaking before.

"Um, yes, that's right," he answered uncertainly. "I didn't know you could talk, actually."

"It's not the rat speaking," answered the soft voice—perhaps a little sharply. "It is I, the one you seek."

Mr. Drench narrowed his eyes. "Magpie?"

"Yes, my friend. I can hear you. I know of your plans. And I can help!"

"You will help me to be truly evil?"

"Of course! I will help you achieve your true destiny."

"And I shall no longer be a sidekick?"

"Do as I tell you, and you will never be a servant again."

A voice at the back of Mr. Drench's mind told him that the phrase *"Do as I tell you"* was generally something that people said to sidekicks, but he silenced it. This could be his big chance.

"When a part of your power was transferred to me," Magpie went on, "it gave us a very special connection. I am the only one who can hear you whispering in the trash cans up there. And you . . . you are even more special. You are the only person in the world who can hear me. So, shall we begin to lay our plans?"

Over the following days, Mr. Drench told Magpie all he knew about the Heroes' Alliance, the Super Zeroes, and The School. And Magpie—supremely clever and wicked beyond imagination—realized that he had all he needed to hatch the plot that he'd been pondering for many long years. The final piece of the jigsaw had clicked into place. Kid Normal . . . he could ask to see

Kid Normal. And perhaps, because Kid Normal didn't have a Cape, the Alliance would consent to send the boy to him.

"We are almost ready to begin," he had told Mr. Drench one day (about a week before this book began, if you're really obsessed with the timeline). "I just need you to make a journey for me, my friend, to make sure that my . . . *work* . . . has been undisturbed all this time."

"Certainly, master," said Mr. Drench. The little voice at the back of his mind complained that it felt more than a little sidekick-like to be calling someone "master," but old habits die hard.

And so Magpie had sent his new servant off on a special mission to make sure that the secret lair he had left behind thirty years ago was still intact. Then, once he knew that everything was as he had left it, he had summoned Kid Normal to him.

Now, with the boy back at The School with his very special poem, all Magpie had to do was wait.

As Murph and his friends were battling to save Annabel in the ACDC far away, the supervillain and his loyal servant were speaking once again.

"How do you know that the boy will deliver your

message?" asked Drench, nervously gnawing at a moldy chicken bone.

"I know how these Heroes operate," rasped Magpie scathingly. "His curiosity will do most of our work for us, and his friends' pathetic obsession with working as a team will do the rest. It is nearly time to mount our attack."

Mr. Drench reached a finger up and flicked a blob of cold porridge off his left ear before popping it into his mouth. "It is nearly time . . . ," he whispered excitedly to Ratsputin, who squeaked and washed his ears in a not-particularly-evil fashion. "Time for the attack. And then will come the moment to reveal my new identity."

"Your . . . new identity?" asked Magpie from his underwater cell.

"Yes! I shall be meek and mild Mr. Drench no more! I am no longer the pathetic sidekick known as the Weasel. **From now on . . . I am . . . DoomWeasel!**"

"Seriously?" asked Magpie before he could stop himself. But he soon rallied. "Yes, yes, um, DoomWeasel. Excellent," he soothed.

In the trash can, Mr. Drench chuckled delightedly to himself, spitting out a bit of eggshell halfway through. **"DoooooooomWeasel . . . ,"** he murmured to himself madly. **"Once I was but the sidekick . . . Now I am the main . . . kick."**

13

The Scarsdale Incident

Thanks to the Annabel episode, it wasn't until the following day that the Zeroes managed to put Mary's plan of searching the storeroom into action.

When they arrived, Mr. Flash actually tried to get them to join his CT session again, albeit in a very grudging fashion.

"S'pose you can come and do some jumping jacks with the others this morning. You know, if you want to," he told them in an unnaturally quiet voice.

"No thanks, Mr. Flash," replied Mary brightly. "We'll get on with tidying the storeroom for you. Must get it all nice and shiny!" and before the teacher could recover from the total shock he was experiencing at this response, she dragged the rest of them through the door to the cluttered side room.

"Right!" she said, quietly turning the key in the

lock to prevent any more interruptions. "We're looking for anything that mentions Magpie, or Sir Jasper, or the Dandy Man, or losing Capabilities. Anything!" She pulled open a drawer and extracted an armful of dusty folders, sat down cross-legged on the floor, and started thumbing through.

Hilda decided to enlist some help and called for her horses to trot off underneath the tables and sift through the dense piles of clutter. Meanwhile Nellie and Murph started on the boxes of junk on the shelves.

Billy grabbed a broom and started sweeping.

"Not really what I had in mind, Billy," Mary sighed. "We should probably be focusing on the paperwork."

"Oh right, yeah, sorry," he said, solemnly returning the broom to its corner by the door. He joined her by the filing cabinet and started to investigate.

As they rummaged, they could just make out the sound of running footsteps from the other side of the wall, accompanied by the foghorn-like voice of Mr. Flash shouting, "Drop and roll! Immediately! If this was a real-life mission, you'd be mincemeat!" Clearly the teacher was coping without them after all.

Presently, there was a tiny neigh and a scuffling from one of the lower shelves in the far corner. Hilda's horses had pushed over a cardboard box, spilling its contents all over the floor. It was full of plastic book-size objects—all plain black apart from the white labels on their spines.

"Naughty horses!" scolded Hilda. "We're supposed to be cleaning up, not making more mess!"

But Mary had raced over to the scene of the spillage and was appraising the debris quizzically.

She bent down and dusted off one of the black objects.

"What even is that?" asked Murph.

"No idea," said Mary, turning the object over in her hands. It had a transparent window on the front and two round white holes in the back. She looked at what was written on the label.

"*Carol Concert '92—exploding shepherd/laser Jesus*," she read out loud.

"It's an old videotape," piped up Billy, walking over to join her. "My dad has loads of them."

"How do we watch it?" asked Murph, wandering over and picking up more tapes. Surely the world's oldest tapes must require the world's oldest tape player.

"With that," replied Billy excitedly, pointing to a large, old-fashioned black machine underneath the brown TV set. "I'll see if I can find the leads and get it connected up."

"Right away, Billy. Quick!" said Murph suddenly.

"Why are you so desperate?" said Mary. "Why do you want to watch a Christmas play so urgently?"

"I don't," said Murph. "I want to watch this."

He was holding up another tape. Its label read:

CLASSIFIED. SCARSDALE INCIDENT.

Next to that, someone had written in pen: **MAGPIE.**

"Holy guacamole!" said Billy, sorting through tangled wires like a frantic bomb-disposal expert. After a few anxious minutes, he stepped back and turned the video player on.

It clunked and whirred into action.

"Right. Give me the tape, then," he ordered.

Murph handed it over and Billy inserted it into the mouth of the ancient machine. The TV screen flickered; the picture fizzed, wobbled, and eventually came into focus. Two words appeared:

THE END

"Oh, nuts. We need to rewind it," said Billy as he rushed forward and mashed some of the buttons on the front of the device. It began to make a high-pitched whirring sound.

The Super Zeroes waited impatiently.

"Is this really how people used to watch movies?" asked Hilda incredulously. "It must have been absolutely terrible!"

After what seemed like an hour, the video machine clunked some more and finally burped into action. The Super Zeroes grabbed chairs and clustered around the TV.

They didn't know it, but they were about to witness the darkest hour of the Heroes' Alliance . . .

The TV screen faded to black, and after a moment a deep voice spoke in dramatic tones.

(You might want to read this bit out in a British accent. Unless you already are British, in which case just read it out in your normal voice. But deeper. And more dramatically.)

The year was 1988, intoned the deep, dramatic voice, deeply and dramatically, ***and the world of Heroes was facing the greatest threat to its existence ever encountered. In response, a great number of Heroes agreed to band together to combat their most dangerous enemy. Until that day, Heroes had worked alone, or in small groups—individual fighters for justice.***

But the peril they now faced was so extreme, they came together for the first time in history. And a mighty battle was fought . . .

"This is SO EXCITING!"

squeaked Hilda, tipping backward on her chair.

The TV began showing grainy images. They seemed to have been shot on a handheld video camera. A series of figures in outlandish costumes were running through a patch of woodland.

This, explained the voice-over, *is the first footage of what is now known as the Heroes' Alliance. Nobody who fought that day came home unchanged. And some . . . did not come home at all.*

Suddenly, there was a flash of light, and the camera tilted sharply to one side before righting itself, as if the person holding it had fallen over.

Mud and sparks rained down, and some of the brightly clothed figures could be seen racing for cover behind trees.

"We're under attack!" someone shouted. **"Advance! Capes at the ready!"**

"I've got a bad feeling about this . . . ," another voice warned.

"Any news from the scouting party? They should be back by now!"

"Here they come!"

Two hunched figures were hurrying toward them through the woods. One, dressed in a tight-fitting red costume, was supporting the other—a smaller man in drab brown overalls, who was moaning and clutching his head.

"He's been hit!" panted the man in red.

"That voice . . . yes! It's Mr. Souperman!" exclaimed Murph.

And indeed, they could now clearly see

that the Hero in red was a younger version of their headmaster.

"And that's Drench!" added Mary.

Here, we can see Captain Alpha and his faithful sidekick, the Weasel— two of the founding members of our organization. They were in the vanguard as the Alliance closed in on its first and greatest enemy at his hidden base: the abandoned tunnels of Scarsdale Quarry.

"He was ready for us!" Captain Alpha told the rest of the group. "We crept into the quarry so Weasel could listen out for clues, but as we got close, he was hit by that horrible purple lightning. It came out of the tunnels with no warning. I managed to drag him clear, but . . . part of his Cape's gone."

"My hearing!" wailed the smaller man. "Why weren't any of you there to back us up?"

"No time for that kind of thinking, my friend," Captain Alpha said. "We've lost the element of surprise. We all have to get in there before he has a chance to flee. Let's roll!"

As one, the Heroes sprinted back through the woods, retracing Captain Alpha's steps. The film was old and the camera kept shaking, but Murph thought he could see a pair of tall, slender women who looked very much like the Gemini Sisters among them.

They all gathered at the tree line, looking down at a large, bare hill. In the middle of the slope, like a bite out of a big green apple, sat a white quarry with steep stone sides.

"There's no cover!" someone quailed. "We'll be sitting ducks!"

It was on this day that the Heroes' Vow was first taken. In order to save the world of Heroes from its greatest threat, these exceptional men and women had made a solemn promise.

"We vowed to fight without fear, remember?" Captain Alpha told them. "Fear is his greatest weapon."

Voices rose in agreement.

"We're with you all the way."

"We stick together."

"For the Alliance! Come on, CHARGE!"

The Heroes raced out of the woods and began streaming down the rocky slope toward dark openings at the bottom of the quarry. But as they approached, several things happened at once: they were met by a volley of explosions, then a strange forked lightning arced out toward them, sending sharp stone shards flying in all directions. Some of the Heroes were blown off their feet by a huge energy force. Others suddenly slumped to the ground, as if they had run into an invisible wall. And strangest of all, several large boulders rolled terrifyingly *up* the slope toward them, bouncing and crashing, obliterating anything in their path.

"It's Magpie, using all his Capes!" marveled Hilda.

The Heroes might have promised to fight without fear, continued the voice-over, **but the Rogue they were up against was determined to attack without mercy. His name was Magpie.**

The Super Zeroes looked at one another, wide-eyed.

Magpie's power was unique—and terrifying. He had the ability to steal another person's Capability.

By sheer force of will, some of the Heroes had finally succeeded in reaching the base of the quarry. The camera zoomed in, revealing that the dark circles in the rock face were tunnel entrances. The largest of these was sealed with thick metal doors.

All at once, there was a flash of purplish light and a huge crash, and the doors caved in. Brightly clothed figures disappeared inside with a confusion of shouts and explosions.

"Watch out for that lightning!" Murph heard someone cry.

"Keep your eyes peeled! Don't leave any escape routes open!" yelled someone else.

The camera panned around to show Captain Alpha crouched at the top of the slope, one comforting hand on the shoulder of the Weasel, who sat morosely beside him. Other Heroes were taking up positions around them, eyes fixed on the tunnel entrances below.

Occasionally the footage would jerk about as more explosions resounded through the quarry. The air was filled with flying debris and flashes of lightning. For a brief moment, the camera pointed upward into the gray sky as a rainbow of different shades of blue streaked across it. Murph and Mary exchanged a significant glance. They knew of only one vehicle that produced that effect: the *Banshee*. Clearly the Blue Phantom had been involved in this battle somehow, but they looked in vain for her trademark silvery-blue armor.

There was another massive explosion.

"He's coming!" a woman's voice shouted, followed by a terrified scream.

The footage went static and grainy for a few seconds.

By the time the camera refocused, smoke could be seen pouring from the tunnels—and several figures were lying on the ground outside. A dark silhouette was racing unnaturally fast up the rocky slope, surrounded by crackling bolts of electricity: Magpie himself. Those Heroes who were still on their feet were dashing frantically around the top of the quarry to head him off.

Magpie was ruthless, said the voice-over. **Determined to evade the newly formed Alliance at all costs, he carried out a shockingly evil act. Using all the Capabilities at his command, he had rigged the entire area to explode, and while brave Heroes were still inside searching for him, he brought Scarsdale crashing down on top of them.**

The Super Zeroes were all silent and open-mouthed now, bathed in the blue light of the TV screen. Hilda reached out a hand and squeezed Murph's shoulder.

If the footage hadn't been so old and primitive, the Super Zeroes would have been convinced that what happened next was nothing more than a special effect. As they gazed on in horror, the whole quarry began collapsing in on itself. A huge cloud of dust spread from the center outward.

Before the cloud closed in, Murph caught a glimpse of what was taking place on the other side of the quarry. The small, dark silhouette of Magpie had reached the top, but by now several other figures were converging on the same spot. One figure got close, only to be surrounded with purple fire and dropped to the ground. Then, still wrapped in that unearthly light, the figure was picked up, as if by a giant invisible hand, and flung over the quarry edge.

"Sir Jasper!" gasped Murph. "Magpie took his Cape! Then dropped him!"

"That's what happened to his legs!" Mary exclaimed.

Rising dust was cutting off their view of the scene, but they could make out more purple lightning bolts striking yet more Heroes.

Just before they lost sight of Magpie

completely, a large figure leaped
on him from behind and knocked
him to the ground.

*Heroes refer to that fateful day
as the Scarsdale Incident. Many
brave men and women were lost;
many more had their Capabilities taken.
But thanks to their sacrifice, Magpie was
captured and brought to justice. This
film is intended to serve as a reminder
that it is only by working together that
the world of Heroes can survive and
flourish. That is the founding principle
of the Heroes' Alliance.*

And finally, the words they'd seen
earlier:

THE END

There was total silence in the room. The Super Zeroes
looked at one another, stunned and unable to find
words to describe what they'd just seen. At last the
tape began to rewind itself with a click and a hum.

"Magpie . . . he killed so many Heroes!" said Hilda
in a tiny, horrified whisper.

"No wonder nobody likes talking about it . . . ," said Murph. "Sir Jasper, Mr. Souperman, Mr. Drench—they all must have lost friends that day."

"And Flora was there," added Mary. "Carl too. Remember in his workshop yesterday? He didn't even want her to hear the name Magpie. I wonder what *they* lost?"

Murph pondered this question, thinking back to the stooped old man he'd visited in prison the previous week and finally realizing exactly what this man was capable of. He shivered.

Miss Flint gazed out of her office window at Shivering Sands, across the gray sea. One hand toyed idly with her HALO unit. She was brooding on Kid Normal's visit to Magpie.

She'd brushed it off at the time as a bust, pure and simple. Nothing had been gained, but as long as the boy didn't tell anyone, she had lost nothing either. Since then, though, as she'd been busy with the day-to-day running of the Heroes' Alliance, that stupid poem wouldn't leave her alone. The words nagged at her, like an irritating song you can't get out of your head.

Three for anger . . . four for grief.

There was a tentative knock at the door, and a weedy voice fluted out the words, "Trash collection!"

"In!" Miss Flint called sharply, being one of those people who are far too managerial to use the full phrase "Come in."

A shabby-looking little man shuffled in, dragging a large metal trash can behind him.

"It's over there in the corner," Miss Flint told him dismissively, in a tone of voice that implied "Be quick, please, I'm busy." She indicated the small wastepaper basket, and turned her attention back to the view across the waves.

"Lovely . . . ," said the little man, sidling toward the corner.

As he did so, a truly hideous stench met Miss Flint's nose. It smelled like someone had taken garbage juice, distilled it into a pungent perfume, and then decided to wear the whole bottle. She gagged slightly, hoping the trash collector would finish his job quickly and leave.

"We'll just put this one over here," said the man to himself in a sing-song voice. "And this one . . . **on your HEAD!"**

That was an odd thing to say, thought Miss Flint, but before she could turn around, the large metal trash can had been clanged down over her head.

"What on earth!" she managed to exclaim, before there was a huge crash as Mr. Drench jumped up onto the desk, pirouetted like an extremely smelly ballet dancer, and kicked the side of the trash can as hard as he could. Miss Flint was knocked out cold.

"Yes! Yes! Hahaha haaaa! Victory! DoomWeasel strikes again!" cackled Mr. Drench maniacally—even though, strictly speaking, he'd never actually struck before. But somehow "DoomWeasel strikes again" sounded more dastardly and impressive than "DoomWeasel strikes for the first time!"

He capered on top of the trash can like a crazed, stinky little monkey, banging the metal with his fists and chanting, **"Doom, doom, doom, doom, weasely, weasely, weasel!"**

In a momentary break from his banging, DoomWeasel heard the croaky voice of Magpie rise from deep under the sea. "Excellent work, Dre— I mean . . . DoomWeasel. Now, my friend—bring her to me. Quickly! We must act fast to bring my plan to fruition!"

"I will not fail!" spluttered Mr. Drench, jumping off the trash can and beginning to roll it toward the door.

"For I am DoomWeasel! And I have strucked! Strucken! Strickened!"

Below the ocean, Magpie rolled his eyes slightly, but there was nobody there to see.

Miss Flint awoke some time later with a headache and a ringing in her ears, as if she'd been to a loud concert and stood too close to the speakers. Or, more accurately, like she'd had a trash can shoved over her head and a mad weasel-like person had kicked it before proceeding to hit it repeatedly with his fists.

She wondered groggily where she was. The light was dim and greenish-tinted, and the floor beneath her was damp, cold stone.

"Welcome," said an unfamiliar voice from below her.

Miss Flint shivered involuntarily. There was something about the tone of the voice that chilled her to the marrow. Desperately trying to shake the fog from her head, she peered into the gloom and saw a ragged, pale figure dressed in black far below her.

She sat up in total panic.

"Magpie!" she shrieked in alarm. "What . . . how on earth did I get down here?"

"The what and the how are very much the least of your worries," croaked Magpie, stalking toward her. "It's the why that you should be terrified about."

Miss Flint heard the cameras up above moving as they tracked Magpie. She sighed a tiny sigh of relief. At least the security system that kept him imprisoned was still working. Plus, she could see that he was still safely contained within the white circle on the floor. But as she plunged a hand into a pocket to grab her HALO unit and call for backup, her eyes widened in horror. There was *something* in there, but it certainly wasn't the cold metallic casing of the communications device. She pulled her hand back out to reveal an ancient blackened potato, covered in hairy green sprouts and oozing with slime.

"Looking for this?" hooted a second voice.

A pungent but horribly familiar waft floated past Miss Flint's nostrils. She turned to see another, much smaller man standing above her at the top of the stone stairs. He was hopping from foot to foot, waving the

HALO unit triumphantly over his head and cackling. "It worked! It worked! I have defeated the Heroes in one fell swoop! For I am DoomWeasel! Most evil and most powerful of them all."

"Did you put this revolting potato in my pocket instead?" asked Miss Flint in disgust.

"A little souvenir from my home," slobbered DoomWeasel as he continued to brandish the HALO unit boastfully. But his hands were slippy with trash-can slime, and he almost dropped it.

"Careful, you idiot!" snapped Magpie with biting sharpness. He swiftly recovered himself. He still needed this creepy little spud-concealer if his plan was going to work. "Just . . . make sure nothing derails our plans at this late stage, my little friend. Now, throw the unit to me, and we shall show these . . . pah! . . . these so-called Heroes who is really in charge."

DoomWeasel had looked a little crestfallen at being called an idiot, but he perked up at the mention of the Heroes' imminent downfall. "With pleasure," he said, and he threw the HALO unit to Magpie, who caught it deftly and laughed in delight.

Miss Flint tried to struggle to her feet, but she was still sick and dizzy from her recent imprisonment in the garbage bin—or bin-prisonment, if you will.

"I'll deal with you in a moment," said Magpie casually. "First, we need to . . . even the playing field. You've been in charge a little too long. Things have gotten stale. I think it's about time we gave your Heroes' Alliance the leader it really deserves. Someone who truly understands the purpose of power."

DoomWeasel clapped his hands delightedly and capered around. "He's talking about himself!" he cackled.

"She knows that," snapped Magpie irritably, before once again regaining his temper. He needed to concentrate for this. It was a moment he had planned for years.

Holding the HALO unit in one hand, he gestured toward it with the spindly fingers of the other. Purple lightning crackled around the handset as it rose into the air of its own accord, spinning around faster and faster, trapped in a web of dancing purple light. Magpie's expression was fixed, his eyes glazed over as he concentrated.

After a few moments the lights subsided, and the HALO unit sank back into his outstretched palm. Only now, instead of green, its screen glowed an eerie purple.

"The HALO system is ours!" squeaked DoomWeasel with glee. "We can contact Heroes! Summon them! Or find out where they are! We control the entire Heroes' Alliance!"

"You are absolutely correct, my friend," Magpie mused. "And that being the case, I am sorry to say that you"—he fixed his eyes on Miss Flint—"are now surplus to requirements."

He stabbed his hands toward her viciously. Miss Flint screamed as she was enveloped in a web of purple lightning.

14

The Heroes' Memorial

"How . . . how many Heroes do you think were in his base when it exploded?" asked Hilda in a small voice.

"Well, we saw loads of them running down into the quarry, didn't we?" answered Murph solemnly. Hilda shook her head in dismay.

It was the end of the school day, and the five Super Zeroes were trailing down the passageway toward the front gates. Deborah Lamington was on duty at the main doors, keeping a watchful eye on the constant stream of students heading out into the afternoon sunlight. Mary gave her a little wave.

"Scarsdale is puzzling me," Mary said to the rest of the Zeroes. "Does Magpie's poem have anything to do with the Heroes who died that day? There's got to be something we're missing . . . ."

"What are you guys up to?" asked Deborah. "You've got plotting faces on."

Murph noticed that she had swapped her usual fringed leather jacket for something quite different.

"Nice cardigan," he said, with a slight smile.

"Hmmm, do you really think so?" replied Deborah. "I'm not sure about it. I'm trying to be a bit more teacherly. Or teacher-esque . . . But I think I sort of hate it. Anyway," she continued, "why are you all going on about Scarsdale?"

Mary reddened. She must have been speaking more loudly than she intended. "Oh, it's just a name we saw on an . . . old videotape," she said, earning herself a quizzical look. "Do you know anything about it?"

"A videotape? Old-school!" said Deborah. "I thought you must have seen it written on that old stone monument in the woods."

All five Super Zeroes tried desperately not to look like this was exciting new information that they wanted to investigate immediately. But Nellie couldn't help grabbing Billy's arm, giving him a small static shock, and Hilda did an involuntary tap dance of anticipation.

Deborah regarded Hilda curiously. "You guys are in a weird mood today," she said slowly.

"Worms," said Murph, pointing a thumb at Hilda, who smiled innocently. "Um . . . so, this monument? It sounds intriguing. I love, you know, monumental architecture and stuff. Bit of a hobby of mine. Must go and have a look when I have a spare half hour. Where did you say it was again?" He raised his eyebrows, attempting to look casual, when in fact he looked about as relaxed as a balloon in a pin factory.

"Dirk and I found it when we needed somewhere private to train," replied Deborah. "It's right at the back, in the bit that's fenced off. The part you're not supposed to go in." She pointed toward the playing field at the back of The School. "Oh, that's probably not a very teacherly thing for me to admit, is it?"

"No, no, it's very interesting," said Murph in his most laid-back tone of voice. "We must ask permission from the proper authorities to have a look one day. No hurry. Well, good to see you. We'll be off now. Oh, hang on, I seem to have left my bag in the classroom."

He gestured urgently to the others. "Let's all just pop back for it, shall we?"

"You're holding your bag," Deborah pointed out.

"Oh, I meant my other bag," said Murph, backing away. "My . . . knitting bag. Another hobby of mine. I *love* it. Bye!"

"Knitting bag?" demanded Mary, when they were out of earshot.

"I panicked!" said Murph. "I couldn't think of another kind of bag."

"Sports bag?" suggested Mary. "Lunch bag? Sleeping bag?"

"Well, yes, with hindsight, those would all have been better things to say," huffed Murph. "But can we not get sidetracked here? This could be a massive clue! There's a monument on the school grounds with 'Scarsdale' written on it. It must be a memorial to the fallen Heroes! Come on!"

The patch of woods at the back of the school was red and golden with autumn colors. Fallen leaves and horse chestnuts crunched under their feet as they picked their way down the slope. Soon Murph caught a flash of silver away to the left—a reflection from the tranquil pond that stood in back of Carl's huts. Murph could just make out a wisp of smoke through the leaves. *Carl's pipe*, he guessed, imagining the old janitor sitting in his favorite deck chair and gazing contentedly out across the water, as he often did at this time of day.

But they weren't heading for Carl's huts. The Super Zeroes knew that part of the woods well, and they had never seen a monument of any kind there.

Instead, Mary led them diagonally down the slope into the thickest and most inaccessible part of the woods. After working their way through the trees for a while, they came to a wooden fence with signs placed at intervals reading **KEEP OUT.**

"Nobody ever got to be a Hero by taking notice of signs," said Murph quietly as he climbed over. Even though there was no one around, it felt appropriate to whisper. It was quiet and eerie among the tall trees.

His friends followed him over the fence, and they carried on through the undergrowth. Presently they came upon a narrow, well-kept path, and followed it until it came out into a small clearing. It was lined with bushes that were coated with dark purple flowers. Several butterflies were fluttering around them.

And in the very center of the glade was a tall monument made of pale gray stone. Standing on top were four statues of Heroes adopting combat postures. The grass around it was neatly tended. Even from a distance it was easy to read the large engraved letters at the very top: **SCARSDALE.**

As they edged closer, Murph could see that every face of the stone had a list of names carved into it, and around the base was a large inscription. He walked around the stone column, reading as he went:

In memory of friends
Who fought without fear.
Their names live forever,
Heroes to the end.

"We were right! It's a memorial!" he told the others. "A list of the Heroes who . . . who didn't come home from the battle with Magpie."

Solemnly, Mary began to read the names in turn, starting at the top. "Adams, John, aka Spitewinter; Anderson, Victoria, aka Badger Girl . . ."

But before she could read further, the sound of a voice made them jump.

"What on earth are you kids doing here?"

They spun around in shock. Carl had walked into the clearing behind them. He was carrying a bunch of flowers, and the expression on his face made Murph's insides curl uncomfortably. He had never seen the janitor look so miserable.

"You shouldn't have been there. Plain and simple. It's not a place to go messing around in," said Carl a few minutes later, leading them into his workshop and shutting the door.

His misery had turned into anger. "It needs to be treated with respect. It's out of bounds for a reason."

Murph looked up at him sheepishly. "Sorry, Carl, we were just—"

Carl cut him off. "What happened at Scarsdale was devastating. You won't find many Heroes who will talk about it. The battle cost us a lot."

"But why *is* the memorial out of bounds?" asked Mary tentatively.

Carl looked at her with a "don't push it" expression. "Because it just *is*. All right?" he said sharply. "Quite frankly, it's not any of your business. The past needs to be left in the past." He paused. Then he sighed. "What has gotten into you lately, eh? You've been acting very strangely. First you're asking about losing Capes and Magpie; now you're sneaking around the Scarsdale memorial."

"Scarsdale?" came Flora's horrified voice from the *Banshee*'s garage next door. "Why on earth are you talking about that?" She came through into the main workshop carrying a wrench.

"The kids were at the Heroes' Memorial. Heaven

knows why, dear," answered Carl. "Been asking me a load of questions on the way back about . . . about *him*."

"Magpie?" said Flora quietly. "What do you want to know about him for? He's safely locked up—has been for years. He's nobody you need to worry about."

"Well—I kind of can't *help* worrying about him," said Murph, embarrassed.

"What on earth for?" replied Flora. "He's gone, a memory. History."

A million thoughts were sprinting around Murph's head. He had wanted so much for the Super Zeroes to solve this mystery for themselves and prove their worth. Miss Flint had sworn him to secrecy. And the more he found out about the damage Magpie had wrought, the more he felt that it wasn't right to worry any of the older generation of Heroes by telling the truth about what was going on. But this was Carl and Flora, their friends, and lying to them now would be too painful.

He took a deep breath and let it out, making that flappy-lipped noise more commonly associated with horses. He looked at Mary for confirmation and she nodded.

"I went to see him," said Murph softly.

"What?" roared Carl.

"I went to see Magpie. At Shivering Sands."

Flora came toward them with a serious, sad expression. "Okay. We need the whole story, Murph," she said, glancing Carl's way. "Tell us everything."

Murph looked to his closest advisor for another nod. Mary obliged.

So he did. He told his friends about his visit to Shivering Sands, his time in Magpie's underwater cell, and the Super Zeroes' investigation into Magpie's history.

Flora looked at Murph intently as he finished his tale. She took a breath, as if to consider her response, and then broke into a slightly forced smile.

"Well, you certainly are a lot of worriers, aren't you?" she told them. "Scurrying around, trying to save the world from Magpie. Listen." She swallowed. "The world doesn't need saving from him. We did that years ago."

Murph was surprised at her reaction. He couldn't help but think that her mouth was saying one thing and her increasingly pale face was saying another.

"Okay. Well, I'm glad I told you, Flora," he said quietly. "Sorry for keeping things secret from you both."

"At least I've been able to set your minds at rest. That's how teams work, isn't it? Now," she went on, with another glance at Carl, "where's this silly poem you mentioned?"

Murph fished in his pocket for the piece of paper. "Miss Flint thought it was just some weird nursery rhyme," he told her, handing it over. "Maybe she was right."

Flora squinted down at the poem, mouthing the words to herself. "It certainly seems like gibberish," she told him. "And we know one thing for sure: nothing that Magpie has got to say is going to be good news, for you or anyone else. Just you forget all about him. That's the best place for him: out of sight—out of mind—out of memory." And, crumpling the paper in her hand, she marched abruptly back into the garage.

"Bye, then," Murph told Carl awkwardly as the Super Zeroes turned to leave. But the old janitor seemed lost in thought and only vaguely waved a hand in their direction as they filed out.

15

Breaking the Code

That night, Murph couldn't sleep. He stayed awake into the early hours, stewing like a slow cooker, and by morning his brain had prepared a rich casserole of self-loathing dotted with fluffy dumplings of guilt. He felt terrible that he had upset Carl and Flora so much with his investigations and forced them to think about a time that obviously held such painful memories. He felt stupid too—he'd gotten so carried away with trying to prove that he could live up to the Alliance name that he didn't think about who he was hurting.

It seemed that most of the Zeroes had been feeling the same way. Mary, Billy, and Hilda were waiting for Murph at the front gates of The School the next day, and they all had identical bags under their eyes. Together they headed straight for the janitor's huts before classes started. They wanted to apologize properly, smooth things over, and promise to stop asking any more difficult questions.

"That's weird. There's no smoke," said Mary as they got close, peering up at the tin chimney.

"Carl!" shouted Murph, banging on the front door. There was no sound from inside. "I'll go and check around back," he told the others, setting off along the path that ran down the hill and into the woods. It circled around behind the huts to the wooden porch.

But there was no Carl sitting there in his usual spot, only his wooden deck chair neatly folded away and propped against the wall. Murph climbed the steps and listened at the back door.

As he pressed his ear to it, the door slammed open, catapulting him forward to land on his face with a mouth full of dirty sneaker. The shoe in question belonged to Hilda, who had opened the door from the inside. Billy and Mary were behind her.

"How did you get in?" asked Murph, spitting out the end of a shoelace and scrambling to his feet.

"The door was just . . . open."

"So there's no one here, then?" said Murph, puzzled.

"Not unless they're playing hide-and-seek," suggested Billy brightly. "But they're probably a bit old for that, and in any case they'd be doing it wrong. They shouldn't both be hiding."

"Not really helping, Billy," Mary informed him.

"Have you checked the garage?" Murph asked. "Perhaps they're working on the *Banshee* again." He dashed over to the large doors in the center of the workshop.

But when he flung them open, they revealed bare, oil-stained floorboards.

The *Banshee* had gone— and in its place was Nellie, sitting in the middle of the floor with her hair covering her face. She held a small scrap of paper in her hand.

As Murph entered, she slowly stood up and silently handed him the note.

Murph read aloud:

One for a stranger,
Two, an old thief.
Three for anger,
And four for grief.

Five for a follower,
Four for a friend.
One to seek,
Three for a sad end.

Four, she falls,
And three, she flies.
Six, she can live again.
Three, she dies.

"It's Magpie's message!" Murph said. "Flora didn't throw it away."

"And now," continued Mary, "she's vanished!"

"I don't understand," Hilda said. "Flora told us it was nothing."

"Well, maybe she was telling the truth," said Billy, "and she and Carl have just taken the *Banshee* for a spin. You know, to test the repairs?"

Murph breathed a sigh of relief. "That's possible," he said. "Maybe we're worrying for nothing."

"No," said a small voice from behind him. It belonged to Nellie.

Murph stared at her in astonishment.

"NO!" she said again, and there was real worry in her voice. Murph was shocked to see tears pooling in her eyes. "No, it's not that. Carl promised me that the first time he took the *Banshee* out after the repairs, I'd be with him. I was going to be his co-pilot. He wouldn't break a promise." Nellie was becoming more and more upset, her speech faster and more frantic. "Well, I hope he wouldn't? Maybe he would. No! He wouldn't! I think Magpie's message was meant for

Flora and Carl, and now they've gone off, goodness knows where, without telling anyone or wanting anybody to know and I hope they're okay and, and . . ."

Murph could see how upset Nellie was—and not just because of the tears she was busily trying to wipe away. She had just uttered more words in that single sitting than in the previous year of their friendship.

The realization hit him like a ton of bricks in a giant lead bucket. Nellie was right. Wherever Flora and Carl had gone, they'd left in a hurry, and in secret. It must be important.

"So . . . what was the message Magpie left for them?" asked Hilda. "What does it mean?"

Mary looked at her seriously. "That's exactly what we're going to have to work out," she replied, looking at their worried faces. "As soon as we can. Who knows where Carl and Flora could be by now?"

Back in Carl's deserted main workshop, the Super Zeroes pulled up chairs and pored over the crumpled scrap of paper.

"Anger . . . grief . . . ," muttered Hilda to herself. "We know that Magpie has caused a lot of those. But who's he talking about in the last bit? Four, she falls, and three, she flies? Does he mean Flora?"

"But Flora doesn't fly," Billy cut in. "She goes invisible."

"I hope he doesn't mean Flora," said Murph fearfully. "Look at the end—six, she can live again, three, she dies."

They all glanced at one another silently, feeling as if Magpie had reached out from his undersea prison to snatch their friends away.

"What about the numbers? Is it the numbers?" Billy asked suddenly. "Look, it goes: one, two, three, four in the first verse. Then five, four, one, three. Then four, three, six, three. Maybe it's a combination or something?"

"Or the words at the end?" mused Hilda. "Stranger, thief, anger, grief. Follower, friend, seek, end. Falls, flies, again . . ."

"Dies," Murph finished for her grimly. "We've got to find out what's going on here."

"But what if it's something really dangerous? What if he's trying to lead them into a trap?" asked Billy.

"That's exactly why we've got to find out where they've gone," replied Kid Normal. "And then follow them."

235

* * *

The Super Zeroes were so desperate for answers they even tried asking Mr. Flash during CT that morning. They cheerily joined in with his physical training session, jogging around and around the ACDC until they were pouring with sweat.

"Sir," puffed Hilda after their fifth lap. "Was there ever a Hero called Follower, or one called Friend?"

"Or Stranger or Thief?" added Murph.

Mr. Flash looked at them suspiciously. "What do you bunch of recycled shrimp want to know that for?" he barked.

"Oh, we just found this weird poem . . . around the school," said Murph vaguely. "We're trying to work out who it belongs to—in case they . . . lost it and want it back." He handed Mr. Flash his own crumpled copy.

The teacher's crimson brow furrowed like an expensive velvet curtain as he read through the verse. **"LOOKS LIKE COMPLETE EGG-PLATED NONSENSE,'** he growled. "There was someone called the Stranger, I think. But not a Hero. One of the other group."

"A . . . a Rogue?" said Murph excitedly.

"Yup," confirmed Mr. Flash. "Long time ago, though. Don't see what it's got to do with this claptrap. Now come on, push-ups! **MOVE!**"

The Super Zeroes discussed this excitedly as they headed back up the stairs into the main part of The School for geography. They were still moist and steaming, like five soggy, undercooked brownies.

"So the Stranger was a Rogue," said Murph thoughtfully. "Do you think it's a list of Hero aliases, then? A list of people that Flora and Carl have got to try and find, perhaps?"

"But why? Why would they go off to track them down and not tell anyone?" said Mary, biting her lip. "It doesn't make sense."

For the rest of the day they showed the poem to every teacher they could corner, concocting more and more elaborate stories about what they were asking for as they went, but nobody could shed any light on Magpie's mysterious verses.

Murph headed home that afternoon feeling downhearted. His head was busy. In fact, it was thoroughly congested. Like downtown at rush hour, on the Friday before a long holiday weekend. He couldn't kick the feeling that it was all his fault Flora and Carl had headed off in the *Banshee* to goodness knows where. He wished he'd just left it alone, not let Magpie get into his head.

But it was too late for moping. Magpie *had* gotten into his head, and he'd used Murph to get to his friends.

After dinner, he headed up to his room and lay on his front on the bed, staring at the piece of paper intently as if he could work out the message just by sheer force of will.

But, of course, that's not how brains work. They are odd things, always clanking and beavering away in the background when you're doing other stuff. That's why you often come up with solutions to problems when you're thinking about something completely different. Or while you're asleep.

And that's exactly what happened to Mary, who sat bolt upright at five o'clock the following morning—suddenly bright-eyed and alert—and realized that she had figured it out.

Murph loved waking up early in the morning and realizing he didn't have to get up for another couple of hours.

It is indeed a wonderful moment. That first half opening of an eye, and then the realization that the beep of your alarm is still eons away. You can go back to sleep—delicious, extra, bonus sleep. A flip of the pillow to get the cool side, a stretch of a foot out from under the duvet to test the air, and you're ready to turn over for a really top-notch spell of snoozage.

Murph had just found a massively comfortable position and was about to drift back to sleep like a warm dormouse that has invested its savings from the Dormouse Bank in a really high-quality mattress, when there was the thump of rain boots landing on his wooden balcony outside. Then came the tap of a metal umbrella tip on his window.

For a while he tried to pretend it wasn't happening. He was too warm and comfortable to do adventuring right now.

But adventures don't wait for you to have a nice lie-in. They have notoriously inconvenient timetables. The tapping continued.

Murph sighed, sat up, and ruffled his hair with a sleepy hand. He knew without turning his head that

Mary was on his balcony, hopping about excitedly and mouthing something.

He turned his head.

Mary was out on the balcony, dressed in her yellow raincoat and her most "open the window RIGHT NOW" expression. She was hopping excitedly from boot to boot and mouthing something.

"I can't hear you," said Murph quietly. "Hang on."

He shuffled across the room in his pajamas and opened the large window that led out onto the wooden platform.

"I said—**open the window RIGHT NOW!**" hissed Mary as she stepped through. "We haven't got any time to lose. I've solved the poem."

"What? Really! Mary, you are the actual, literal best!" Murph was suddenly wide awake. Unfortunately his hair hadn't gotten the memo and was still sticking up in "too early in the morning" mode. "What's the message, then? What does it all mean? Was it in the words or the numbers?"

"It was both. Look."

Mary dug in her pocket and pulled out her copy of the poem. Murph could see that she'd circled certain letters.

"It's a code. So, in the first line we have 'One for . . . a stranger.' So 'one' means that we need to take the first letter of the words 'a stranger.' "

She had drawn a ring around the letter *A* in red pen.

"Okay, so then, second line," Murph tried. " 'Two,

an old thief.' Two means we take the second letter of 'an old thief.' That's . . . N."

"Right," confirmed Mary.

Murph worked his way down the circled letters in the first verse. "A, N, G, E . . . is it a name? Angela?"

"Keep going," Mary told him, looking serious and even, now that Murph glanced at her again, a little frightened.

He carried on: "Right, second verse. L . . . so it could be Angela. No, wait, it's I next. Angeli? Is that, like, more than one Angela?"

"Stop saying Angela," a frustrated Mary told him. "This is nothing to do with Angela, or the plural of Angela."

"Sorry," said Murph. "Right then, carrying on . . . S, A. Angelisa. Then it's L, I, V . . . E. Live. No, wait, alive."

Mary waited almost patiently for his brain to catch up.

"Someone is alive . . . Angel! Angel is alive?"

"ANGEL IS ALIVE. That's what the message says," Mary confirmed intently. "That's what made Flora and Carl disappear."

The paper with its circled code was trembling slightly in Mary's hand. Murph looked at his friend open-mouthed as a question formed in his mind.

"Who's Angel?"

"That, Kid Normal, is very much the question of the day." Mary nodded. "We need to find out the answer, and fast. It's the only way we'll know where Flora and Carl have gone."

16

Unrehearsed Bassoon Recital Emergency

Murph bounded down the stairs like a rhino late for a "who's got the gnarliest horn" competition.

"See you later," he shouted to his mom, and was halfway down the front path before the words had made it as far as her ears. He skidded around the corner in what would have been a hand-brake turn, if boys had hand brakes, and sprinted off down the street.

"You go and get Hilda, I'll grab Nellie and Billy," Mary had told him before taking off and flying away, backward and rather stylishly, over the roof of his house. "We'll get to school before anyone else and find out anything we can about who Angel might be. Even if it means breaking into Mr. Souperman's study."

Murph covered the distance to Hilda's house in about the time it took you to read that last paragraph, which is convenient, as we wouldn't want to have to pause the story and wait for you to catch up.

We say "Hilda's house," but it was more like a small mansion, really. It stood at the end of a long, curving gravel drive, where about a thousand windows reflected back a mirror image of the lush chestnut trees that lined the front lawn. Murph had walked home with Hilda a few times, and he always expected to see a butler or footman polishing the shiny Rolls-Royce that was usually parked outside.

Murph crunched his way toward the front door, tugged hard on the old-fashioned bell pull, and after a moment the door swung open to reveal a rather plump man wearing black pants and an extremely expensive-looking waistcoat.

"Hello." The man smiled. "Who do we have here?"

Murph hesitated. Was this Hilda's dad, or an actual real-life butler? Until he'd seen Hilda's house he'd always thought butlers only existed on the sort of TV shows his mom made him watch with her on Sunday nights, but anything was possible where Hilda was concerned.

"I'm Murph, Mr. . . . um . . . sir," he replied cautiously.

The man broke into an even wider smile. "Ah, the prodigy! The young maestro! Come in, come in."

He ushered Murph through into the hall, which was hung with paintings and a brass barometer.

"She's upstairs," continued Hilda's dad, or possibly Hilda's butler. "Why don't you head on up?" Then he trotted toward the back of the house and said, "It's a great pleasure to finally meet you," before vanishing behind an enormous potted palm.

Murph climbed the stairs. They were huge and made of dark wood, which meant they were exactly the sort of stairs a detective might clomp down when he was about to solve the murder of a young heiress in a Sunday night TV show. Murph wasn't exactly sure what an heiress was, but he did know that their life expectancy on Sunday TV wasn't great. He shook his head, suddenly remembering that he had bigger things to worry about, and stared down the large landing.

It was a fairly safe bet which room was Hilda's, because the door was decorated with glittery stickers of horses. Murph knocked softly and pushed the door open.

Hilda was sitting at a desk over near one of the large windows. She had her back to him, and was so busy writing or drawing something that she hadn't heard him come in. Murph headed toward her, stepping over a large stuffed toy horse, a riding helmet, and other equine-based items as he did. Now that he was closer he could see what Hilda was working on.

It was a comic strip, entitled **EQUANA: MISTRESS OF HORSE!** The title frame showed a muscled heroine with flaming red hair ordering two massive stallions into battle. It was, Murph admitted to himself, pretty awesome, and he was silently admiring the artwork when Hilda spotted his reflection in the window and turned around with a shriek.

"Gah! What are you creeping up on me for?" she scolded him, grabbing some blank pieces of paper and covering up her work.

"Sorry. I didn't mean to creep. But your . . . dad? . . . said I should come upstairs and find you."

"Oh, right," replied Hilda, mollified. Then she reddened. "Did you see what I was drawing?"

"Um, well, yeah. It's really good!" enthused Murph. "Like, amazing. Can I have a closer look?"

"Not until it's finished," said Hilda primly, although she looked like she was secretly rather pleased at Murph's praise. "Anyway, why are you here so early?"

Murph suddenly remembered that he was on an emergency Hero-type mission and not just popping in to admire Hilda's drawings.

"Mary solved the code," he told her seriously.

Hilda took one look at his solemn face and nodded. "Then what are we waiting for?" She carefully replaced the caps on her felt-tips and followed him to the door.

"By the way," said Murph casually as they went down the stairs, "your . . . dad? He called me maestro or something. What's all that about?"

"Um, I've been meaning to tell you abou—" began Hilda, before being interrupted by a cry of "Ah, here he comes now. The young woodwind genius!"

The plump, elegant, friendly man was at the foot of the stairs, and he had now been joined by an equally plump, elegant, friendly lady.

"Hi, Mom; hi, Dad," piped up Hilda, solving Murph's

whole butler conundrum in an instant. "Murph and I have to head to school early this morning; is that okay?"

"Yes, yes, of course." Her dad smiled. "But we can't meet the great Murph without him giving us a quick sample of his talent, now, can we? You must allow us five minutes, Master Cooper—and then we'll save you some time by driving you to school in the Rolls. You'll still get there nice and early. Come, come!" And he beckoned them to follow him into a nearby room.

"So . . . you know we've been out, um, Hero-ing quite a few evenings this summer?" whispered Hilda. "Well, I had to tell my parents something to explain why I was never in, and . . . ."

Murph had one of those impending doom sensations, where the back of your hair goes all cold. "What have you told them?" he muttered grimly.

"I said that I've been going around to your house, because . . ." She chewed her lip nervously.

"Yes?"

". . . because you've been helping me with my bassoon practice. Mom and Dad think you're, like, one of the country's best young bassoonists."

The realization of what was about to happen hit Murph like a medium-size whale. "So are you telling me," he hissed through clenched teeth, "that in about five seconds' time I will walk through that door and your parents are going to make me play the . . ."

The five seconds were up. Murph stepped through the door.

". . . bassoon," he finished weakly, seeing a large, polished-wood instrument propped up by the fireplace waiting for him.

"It really is so nice to meet you at last, Murph," said Hilda's mom delightedly. "Hilda's told us so much about your extraordinary talent! We are a family of bassoon lovers, you know, and it's so rare to find a fellow appreciator." Murph tried to smile but it just looked like he was choking on lemons.

"Now, we don't mean to pressure you," Hilda's dad said reassuringly as he sat down on the ornate sofa. "Any piece of music you want to play will be a delight. But don't hold back! Hilda tells me your Dvorák is world-class."

Murph had no idea what Hilda's dad was talking

about. This was even worse than the time in his first year when Mr. Flash had tried to get him to fly in front of the entire class. At least back then he'd been able to confront his fears and tell the uncomfortable truth. This time he had to keep his mouth shut or he'd risk exposing their whole secret life as Heroes.

There's nothing in the Heroes' Vow that covers this, thought Murph mournfully as he grasped the gleaming bassoon with both hands and held it uncertainly upright in front of him.

In case you're not familiar with the bassoon—and after all, why would you be?—it is a long, upright wooden tube with a lot of pipes and buttons around the outside. The one Murph had been presented with was a highly polished specimen that looked as if it cost a lot of money. Sticking out at around head height was a thin, gleaming metal tube that snaked toward his mouth. It was tipped with a thin brown reed that, Murph guessed, he was supposed to blow into.

He glanced over at Hilda, who had taken a seat in a chair to one side of her parents. She nodded to encourage him, then licked her lips exaggeratedly.

Murph tried to do the same, but nervousness had sucked every ounce of water from his mouth. He sandpapered his lips with a catlike tongue and gripped the reed between his teeth.

"This will be a real treat," Hilda's mom said with a smile.

Now, playing any woodwind instrument for the first time is tricky. You've got to know what you're doing to make any kind of noise at all. And this is doubly true of the bassoon, which is the wild stallion of the orchestra.

So let's give Murph his due. The fact that he managed to make a sound at all is really very impressive; it just happened to be very different than what his audience had been anticipating. They were expecting the sweet, mellow tones of an expertly blown bassoon. What they got was the noise of an angry donkey with a sore bottom backing into a huge clump of thistles.

The kind smiles froze on Hilda's parents' faces. (Both the apostrophes in that last sentence are in the correct position, we checked.)

"Sorry, I'm a bit nervous," said Murph through his mouthful of bassoon.

"Yes, of course," Hilda's dad said soothingly, settling himself back into the hugely expensive sofa in anticipation of some less donkey-like sounds.

Murph steeled himself to have another try at it. We have no idea why. The chances of him spontaneously working out how to play actual classical music with absolutely no training were embarrassingly slim. But luckily, he was about to be reminded of one of the great advantages of being part of a team of crime-fighting superheroes. Someone's always got your back.

The doorbell rang.

Hilda's dad hauled himself out of the sofa to

answer it, and after a moment Murph heard a familiar voice from the hall. "I'm terribly sorry to disturb you, but I think someone's blown up your Rolls-Royce," Mary was saying.

Hilda and Hilda's mom leaped out of their seats as if the starting gun had been fired for the annual Baker family one-hundred-yard dash. As Murph placed the bassoon gratefully back against the wall, he hoped heartily that he would never have to see it again.

Out on the driveway, Hilda's dad was inspecting his pristine green car, which was leaning dangerously to one side. One back tire was several times its normal size, the rubber bulging and creaking as if it were about to burst.

Billy and Nellie were standing nearby. Billy glanced at Murph and gestured anxiously with his thumb in the internationally recognized signal for "Let's get the cheese-and-pickle salad out of here!"

"Hope you get it sorted out, Dad! Looks like we'll need to walk to school after all," fluted Hilda as they all edged off down the driveway.

"Yes, yes," he mumbled distractedly, fiddling with

the valve on the side of the tire. A huge blast of air shot out and, startled, he fell over backward into a small, conveniently placed puddle.

"Nice to meet you," called Murph as they neared the gates.

"But we still haven't heard you play . . . ," Hilda's mom wailed after them.

"Another time, Mom, promise," called Hilda. Murph aimed a gentle kick her way. "See you later!"

"Right," said Mary, "that woodwind-related setback has cost us twenty minutes. Let's get to school, quick!" It was the only time in history a twelve-year-old girl had uttered those words. Mary didn't know that, of course. We just threw it in as an interesting extra.

And so the Super Zeroes rushed off down the road, accompanied by very dramatic music that you must supply in your own head. Whether it involves a bassoon or not is up to you.

17

A Secret Never to Be Told

As the five friends turned into the scruffy, nondescript road where The School was located, a memory kept tickling the back of Murph's brain.

Angel, he kept thinking . . . *Angel*. It was as if he'd seen the word written down somewhere significant, or heard someone mention it . . . but he couldn't bring it to mind properly.

He was so frustrated with his own brain that he actually let out a little growl of rage as they raced through the school gates and across the front yard. The unrehearsed bassoon recital had really held them up. By now they only had about half an hour until classes started and an entire school to search for references to one cryptic name.

"Flora's desk, that's the best place to start," decided Mary. "She keeps all sorts of things there."

As the school secretary, Flora had a desk that was located just outside Mr. Souperman's study. They found it covered in its usual jumble of papers, but as they turned them over, there didn't seem to be anything significant among them.

Murph scanned the pictures on the walls and the knickknacks spread all over the bookcases, looking for further clues. Flora kept her little waiting area like a junk shop: it was full of friendly clutter and intriguing artifacts. Murph studied the print of a snowy mountain, a shark's jawbone, an instrument dial from an old airplane . . . but nothing seemed to link to the word "angel." There wasn't even an angel-shaped ornament, he thought to himself desperately— and Flora had more ornaments than you could shake a stick at. In fact, as he searched, he realized that the answer to the eternal question of "Who on earth buys all that stuff in museum gift shops?" was "Flora and Carl." Or "Flora, Carl, and Murph's mom," actually. She couldn't go to a gallery without buying a thimble or two.

And then he got it.

"Wait!" he told the others. "I know where I've seen an angel. Lots of angels, in fact. **Carl has a whole shelf full of them!"**

The memory had finally burrowed its way right to the front of Murph's brain. While sweeping out Carl's workshop during his first year at The School, he'd been bemused to see Carl's collection of angel ornaments. He had so many, and all of different types and sizes.

"Come on!" urged Murph, as they arranged Flora's paperwork back into some sort of order and hurried down the stairs.

By now, the corridors were starting to fill up with teachers and early arrivals. The Super Zeroes hustled their way through the back doors and out across the playing fields, squinting against a light rain that had started to fall.

"Murph," said Mary as they raced toward the workshop, "I've been thinking. The message said Angel is alive. Well, that must mean that until now . . . everyone thought Angel wasn't."

Murph considered this. "Um, yeah—I guess so."

"Well," Mary went on, pointing into the patch of

woodland that was coming into view up ahead, "where might you find the name of someone who's . . . who's not alive anymore?"

Murph stopped in his tracks. "Of course! The Heroes' Memorial. Angel could be the name of a Hero who died at Scarsdale. We wondered what Flora and Carl might have lost that day. Right"—he gestured to Billy, Hilda, and Nellie—"you three, go and look at the things in Carl's huts. See if there's anything written on them, anything weird about them . . . just *anything*. You"—he grabbed Mary by the hand—"come with me."

Together the two of them ran along the edge of the woods and down the narrow, hidden path that led to the stone pillar. Once more, it was eerily quiet—there was only the slapping of their feet on the leaf-coated ground and the soft pittering of tiny raindrops among the branches overhead.

Finally, Mary and Murph burst into the forest grove where the Heroes' Memorial stood. The rain was dripping down across the carved names, as if the stone itself were weeping. They approached slowly, feeling a little somber, before Murph steeled himself.

"Look for a Hero with the code name Angel," he told his friend, releasing her hand. He'd forgotten he was still holding it. "Or maybe *the* Angel." They split up and began scanning the list.

In the workshop, Billy, Hilda, and Nellie were examining the angel statues. They were all gathered carefully together on one shelf, as though they were a special collection. They were made from all kinds of material—wood, pottery, glass. But there were no words written on any of them.

Hilda even counted them: "There are thirty. Might that mean something important?"

"Look at this," piped up Billy, who had begun to look elsewhere. He was pulling a large box out from among the jumble of tools underneath the bench. "It's full of photos!" He tipped the pictures out onto the workbench. Some of them had names written on the back in pencil, he realized.

"Look for Angel!" he told the others, beginning to thumb through.

* * *

It was Murph and his keen eyes who discovered her first: on the side of the Heroes' Memorial, carved at the very end of the list of the names of those lost. He had almost given up hope. None of the fallen Heroes had the code name Angel.

"Venn, Otto, aka the Steamroller. Waites, Polly, aka First Frost . . ."

And then, there she was:

Walden, Angel

"Mary!" he called urgently.

Mary came to stand behind him, and he heard her gasp as she read the name. "Angel isn't a code

name after all! It's a first name, a girl's name!"
she exclaimed. "And look at her surname. It's Walden!
Angel Walden! She must have been related to Flora
and Carl somehow . . ."

"Do you think she was a Hero?" Murph wondered.
"Her name's on the memorial, but she has no code name.
All we know is that she was Flora and Carl's relative."

They raced up through the woods, not bothering
to stay on the pathway in their frantic hurry to get
back to Carl's workshop and tell the others their
discovery. Brambles plucked at their clothes as they
skirted the pond and climbed the steps to the back
door.

Murph burst through: **"We found her!
Angel Walden! She must have been
Carl and Flora's—"**

"Daughter," Billy finished for him, quietly. "She was
their daughter."

Billy, Hilda, and Nellie were marveling over a small, square photograph. It showed a much younger Flora and Carl beaming into the camera, holding between them a rosy-cheeked, smiling baby girl. As Murph and Mary approached, Nellie turned it over and pointed to the writing on the back:

$$Angel, 1975$$

"She was their daughter," repeated Billy.

"Not 'was,' Billy, 'IS'!" Mary breathed. "Magpie's message said 'ANGEL IS ALIVE.' The memorial's wrong. She didn't die at Scarsdale. **She's still out there!"**

"Destination is three hundred feet ahead," intoned the calm voice of the *Banshee*'s GPS.

Carl craned his neck closer to the rain-splattered windshield in an effort to see through it better, which as we all know makes no difference whatsoever. But despite the poor visibility, he could just make out the gloomy towers of Shivering Sands.

"Be careful; they'll have radar," said Flora from

the copilot's chair. "We don't want them to see us come in."

"I'm doing my best, dearest," said Carl, with the merest hint of tension. "This isn't the first time I've stormed a prison. Remember Alcatraz in '79?"

"Oh yes," she replied, "that *was* fun."

It wasn't being *seen* that should have worried them, though: it was being overheard. Far below, nestled in the bottom of his trash can and sucking on an old fish head, DoomWeasel had heard their whole conversation.

"You were right, master," he said softly, knowing that on the seabed Magpie would be waiting for an update. "Just as you predicted, the Blue Phantom is approaching." He used the pointy bones of the fish head to comb Ratsputin's matted fur.

"Excellent," came the voice of Magpie from beneath the waves. "Let's make sure that her passage to my cell is as smooth as possible."

Magpie's pale fingers tapped at Miss Flint's hacked HALO unit. A message appeared on the screen, underneath pictures of Flora and Carl:

ROGUE HERO AND ACCOMPLICE:

APPREHEND AND DETAIN.

ALL COMBAT UNITS PROCEED IMMEDIATELY

TO LAST KNOWN LOCATION: THE SCHOOL.

Instantly, the message was beamed to the HALO unit of every single operative in the Heroes' Alliance.

As the *Banshee* descended, Flora and Carl were shocked to see several black helicopters lift off from the top of the rusty towers below and speed off into the storm.

"I wonder where they're all off to?" Carl mused.

"Don't look a gift horse in the mouth, dear," said Flora.

"Wouldn't dream of it," replied Carl. "Wouldn't want to look any kind of horse in the mouth, to be honest. It's a very strange thing to do, unless you're a horse dentist."

Rather like Murph, Carl had a habit of making jokes when he was nervous. And here, as they were about to try and break into the most secure prison on the planet to question the most dangerous Rogue who had ever existed about the daughter they thought they'd lost thirty years ago . . . well, that's about as nerve-racking as it gets.

"Anyway, shall we land?" said Flora anxiously.

"Imagine the size of the toothbrush," said Carl to himself as he piloted them toward an out-of-the-way landing platform.

Magpie heard the scream of the *Banshee*'s jets as it touched down on Shivering Sands.

"Aaaaah," he breathed to himself. "Visitors. I do love visitors. I wonder if they've brought me a gift . . ."

18

Lockdown

"It's just so sad," Hilda said. The Super Zeroes were looking through more pictures from Angel's life—here she was a toddler riding on Carl's shoulders, here they saw her at five or six in a homemade version of Flora's amazing Blue Phantom costume.

Murph was looking at a picture that he realized he'd caught a brief glimpse of the previous year. It was a head-and-shoulders portrait of Angel at about their own age. She had striking silvery-blond hair. "If Angel was born in 1975," he mused, "and Scarsdale happened in 1988, then she wasn't much older than us when Carl and Flora lost her."

"I wonder if she wanted to be a Hero too?" added Hilda, who had picked up a wooden angel and was turning it over in her hands thoughtfully.

"Maybe she already was one. If they thought she

was at Scarsdale when it exploded, perhaps she was part of the mission," Mary reasoned. Nellie nodded.

"She's Flora's daughter—so I bet she had an amazing Cape," said Billy.

Suddenly Murph stood up. "It's no use wondering. What we need to do is find Flora and Carl. They must have gone to Shivering Sands to see if Magpie is telling the truth. They've got a massive head start on us, which means they're probably already there. So we need to find someone to help us get a message to Miss Flint." Murph shivered. "I'm done with secrets. We're supposed to be an Alliance, a team. Teams don't keep secrets from one another. And Magpie is obviously planning something major."

"What, though?" said Mary, sounding frustrated and tense.

"I don't know," admitted Murph. "But he's managed to lure the Blue Phantom to him. That can't be good news. She needs backup."

Truthfully, he felt like an idiot. Magpie had used him to get to his friends, and now they were in peril. He'd carried a message without even realizing what it was, or how dangerous it could be. And his own investigations into Magpie suddenly seemed like a childish waste of time. There had been a much bigger game going on all the while.

"Murph's right," said Mary. "We need to get help. Who might be able to contact Miss Flint? Deborah? Mr. Souperman?"

"School's started," Murph said. "They'll all be in the main hall for assembly."

"Then what are we waiting for?" said Mary. "Like you said, the time for secrets is over."

Bursting out of the wooden workshop door, the Super Zeroes rushed back in the direction of the main school building as if their lives—or, at least, the lives of their dearest friends—depended on it.

As the five of them slammed dramatically through the doors into the main hall, Murph felt like he was in one of those hospital-based dramas where the heroic doctor runs into the operating theater in slow motion just in time to save the day.

Of course, he wasn't in a slow-motion scene in a

hospital-based drama. He was in a school, moving very much at normal speed and not in possession of a white coat or a stethoscope. But it felt exciting, and before he could stop himself he was imagining shouting, **"I need a scalpel, ten ccs of plasma, and a doughnut, stat!"** at some nurses. He wasn't exactly sure what "stat" meant, but TV doctors always seemed to say it.

In any case, Murph's mental drama was cut short at this point by the arrival of actual real-life drama.

Everyone in the room had stopped to stare at the Super Zeroes. Mr. Souperman was onstage, apparently in the middle of some classically unsuccessful public speaking. "We must pilot the, ah, train of knowledge," he had been saying, "toward the airport, if you like, of your own brains." But five students slamming through the door like drizzle-drenched doctors had put him off his stride.

"Sorry we're late," cried Murph.

He caught sight of Deborah at the side of the hall. She was standing next to Mr. Flash and a gaggle of A-Stream students.

"Don't mind us," Murph went on airily, as the Super Zeroes all sidled toward the two teachers, to a chorus of grumbles from the rest of the students. It was like walking through an amusement park based on the theme of glaring. "Do go on, Mr. Souperman. Something about airports, was it?"

"WHAT THE PEA AND HAM SOUP ARE YOU DIMWITS UP TO?" Mr. Flash whisper-roared at them as they got there, but Murph ignored him and turned to Deborah.

"We need your help!" he said. "Do you know how to get in touch with Miss Flint? It's really important; we need to tell her something!"

But Deborah wasn't looking at Murph: she was staring in disbelief at the screen of her HALO unit. At the same time, Murph's own handset started buzzing manically, and his hand went to his pocket.

"What's this, an Alliance call?" Mr. Flash's eyes lit up. For all his talk, Mr. Flash had never actually been an active member of the Heroes' Alliance, and his eyes gleamed at the prospect of being so close to a real mission. "Let's have a look, then! **MUST BE SOMETHING BIG IF YOU'VE BOTH GOT THE CALL.'**

Murph hesitated. The look on Deborah's face was scaring him, and somehow he knew that he wasn't going to like what was on the screen.

He dug it out anyway, but immediately stopped in astonishment. The green light was blinking urgently, and on the screen were pictures of Carl and Flora.

Deborah had recovered from her shock. "This is unbelievable!" she told Murph breathlessly. "Flora and Carl— they've been declared Rogue Heroes!"

The manic whispering from

their corner of the hall was attracting the attention of students nearby. Corned Beef Boy had overheard Deborah.

"What, the janitor?" he scoffed. "And the school secretary? That's crazy."

"It's an Alliance order—all Heroes!" said Deborah to the Super Zeroes. "We're duty-bound to capture them! Where are they?"

"They've gone," shouted Murph in a panic, silencing the whole room immediately. **"But they're not Rogue Heroes! You have to believe me!** There's so much going on here that you don't understand! That's what we came to tell you."

The tension in the hall was so thick you could have cut it with a knife. Not an ordinary knife either. You would have needed a special razor-edged, diamond-sharpened tension knife.

Deborah was looking at Murph intently. It was like that moment in a cowboy film where two gunslingers face each other in the middle of the road. Which, if you think about it, is an inconvenient place to stage a gunfight. What if they got run over by a stagecoach or something? But there's no time to ponder that now. Let's get back to the action.

Murph had just begun to think he could see a softening in Deborah's eyes when the lights on both HALO units began blinking once again. Like the moment in the cowboy film where the tension breaks and everyone goes for their gun, they both looked down to see a new message on the screen.

Murph's face paled, and he showed the message to Mary, who had come to stand beside him. **KNOWN ASSOCIATES OF ROGUE HEROES—APPREHEND AND DETAIN,** the message read. Above these words were photos of all five Super Zeroes.

As the squadrons of helicopters had begun taking off from Shivering Sands, a delightful little idea had occurred to Magpie.

"Since they're going to look for Rogue Heroes," he purred to himself like a spiteful cat, "why not give them a *really* exciting day out?" His spindly fingers toyed with the master HALO unit. "And I must thank

Kid Normal for delivering my message so efficiently. I'm sure a battle against the rest of the Heroes' Alliance will teach him and his friends a valuable lesson. Namely: you can't trust anyone."

Magpie gave a chilling chuckle as he put the HALO unit back into his coat pocket for a second time, dousing the purple light from its screen, and listened for the footsteps of his enemies growing closer.

Slowly, Murph and Deborah raised their heads and stared at each other.

Murph tried to contort his face into an expression that said: "I know this looks really bad, but I have information that the Alliance doesn't know, and would you please pretend you're not a superhero for a minute and let us go?"

It's a lot to squeeze into one expression—and in the end it just looked like he was trying to hide a bee in his mouth.

Deborah's face was much easier to read. It said: "I'm about to leap into action, and it's not going to be much fun for you."

Murph's expression changed subtly, until it said something far too rude to write down here.

"Stop them!" shouted Deborah to the A Stream students gathered nearby, at exactly the same time that Murph turned to the rest of the Super Zeroes and shouted, **"Run!"**

The Zeroes turned and pelted out of the hall at maximum speed, with the students of the A Stream stampeding after them like a stampede of stampeding stampeders.

Mr. Souperman, who fortunately for everyone hadn't brought his HALO unit with him to assembly, started to move down the stage steps to find out what was going on. He was left dumbfounded by the sudden burst of activity. **"What about the train of knowledge?"** he shouted after them, but he couldn't be heard above the chaos.

The Super Zeroes smashed back through the doors and into the corridor, but the A Stream were hot on their heels like a pair of insulated socks with innovative heel-warming pads built in.

Everyone spilled out into the hallway more or

less together, creating a huge, pulsating heap of small battles. Deborah was hopping about, spinning her lasso and crying desperately, **"Get out of the way!"** but nobody was listening. Billy was being wrestled by Corned Beef Boy, but had ballooned himself to such a large size that the bully's hands couldn't find any place to grab on.

Mary had initially adopted a combat stance with her umbrella like an elegant fencer, but she soon had to resort to bashing people with it like an angry old lady fending off purse snatchers. Hilda tried to help her by stamping hard on the toe of Crazy Eyes Jemima, who hopped about in agony before barreling into Bill Burton, who was wheeling a cart toward the hall laden with dishes to begin setting up for lunch. It went flying, sending plates and silverware spilling out across the floor, and Bill, enraged, started spinning plates through the air toward anyone who approached him. It turns out there was one thing that made the friendly guy lose his cool, and that was anything that came between him and his ability to deliver a prompt and efficient lunch service.

A rumble of thunder came from outside as Nellie prepared her Capability; she was edging down the hallway with her hands raised like a conductor about to begin a symphony.

While all this was going on, Murph was trying to restore order and get his team out of there. But before he could act, he found himself pinned to the ground with his hands behind his back. He struggled furiously but couldn't get free. The air was filled with the sounds of battle—umbrella thwacking, rumbling thunder, screeching, and stamping. But then a low voice spoke directly into his ear, cutting through the noise.

"Stop struggling. Tell me what's going on."

With a gargantuan effort, Murph managed to twist his head slightly to see the blotchy, patchily mustached visage of Gangly Fuzz Face. It was he who was holding Murph down.

"Get . . . off! You . . . oaf! You don't understand. None of you do! You're going to ruin everything."

"What do you mean?" asked Fuzz Face. "Listen. Is the secretary really a Rogue Hero?"

"NO! Of course not!" Murph grunted into the floor. "It's complicated, but . . . we've got to try and help her. She's in danger! So's Carl! It's a trap! Why doesn't anyone trust us?"

There was a pause. Then Murph felt the grip on his arms loosen.

"I trust you," grunted Fuzz Face.

Murph thought he must have taken a stray hit to the head from Mary's umbrella. "Sorry, what?"

"I trust you," repeated Fuzz Face. "You guys might be a bit lame . . . but you know what? You were right about that wasp guy last year. You saved us all and I believe I owe you a favor. So here it is. Go! Quick! I'll hold 'em up for as long as I can. Tell your friends to get on the floor!"

And with that, Fuzz Face leaped to his feet, raising his hands as he activated his own Capability.

"Zeroes, get low! Drop!"

Murph yelled wildly, and he watched open-mouthed as Fuzz Face's invisible force fields began pushing the whole battling, yelling mob of people down the corridor and back into the main hall until they were all trapped behind an invisible wall.

The Zeroes dusted themselves off. Murph and Fuzz Face regarded each other for a moment. At last Murph held out a hand.

"Thanks . . . Fuzz . . . Face . . . um, Furry . . . fur . . . gotten your name actually."

"Nathan," replied Gangly Fuzz Face, holding out

his own hand and shaking. He glanced over at the rest of the students, who were glaring at him from their transparent prison, then back to Murph. "Run, then!" he suggested.

There was a squeaking of sneakers on the polished floor as all five Super Zeroes leaped to their feet and hotfooted it out of there at maximum speed.

"Running again," said Billy, panting, as they made for the back doors, "always running, backward and forward, run, run, run." His right elbow puffed out slightly with the effort. But when they actually made it out onto the field, his entire head blew up in panic at what he saw landing on the grass ahead of them.

It was a huge black helicopter, and several figures in black were already jumping off the ramp at the back and running toward them in a way that said "when this running is finished you're not going to like what happens next."

But before the burly Cleaners could reach them, there was a blur in the air. Murph felt as if he'd been hit by a sudden tornado as he and his friends were gathered up, lifted off their feet, and whisked away in a fraction of a second. The Cleaners looked around in disbelief as their targets seemed to vanish before their eyes.

"Fan out! They can't have gone far!" instructed their leader, gesturing with her gloved hand.

The Super Zeroes found themselves at the side of The School, clutched in the burly, bulging arms of Mr. Flash. The CT teacher had scooped them up at lightning speed, the same way he'd stopped Murph being burned alive earlier in the week.

"KEEP QUIET," said Mr. Flash loudly. "They won't take long to find us. I couldn't carry you guys very far." He was wearing an odd expression, and it took Murph several moments to decipher it. Mr. Flash was . . . *smiling.*

"Go on, then," he prompted them. "Off you go and save the day. Flora would never betray the Alliance, I'm sure of it. Which means you must be right, and she's in trouble. I'll hold them off for as long as I can."

Murph's mouth opened and closed a few times

but no sound came out. He looked like a fish playing an invisible tuba. First Fuzz Face—aka Nathan—and now Mr. Flash. This day couldn't have gotten more surprising if the Easter bunny had suddenly appeared and smashed an egg in his face.

"Um . . . thanks?" he finally managed to blurt.

"There they are! All units engage!" came a shout at the same time. A large group of Cleaners had come around the corner and caught sight of them from afar.

"GO ON, YOU MANGY SATSUMAS. HOP IT!" bellowed Mr. Flash, sounding a little more like his old self. He turned toward the Cleaners, slapping one fist into the other palm and murmuring, "Come on, then, let's see what yer made of!"

"Let's get out of here," urged Murph. "Once we're clear of the Cleaners we can figure out another way to get to Shivering Sands."

"Hang on!" sang Mary, reaching for her umbrella. They all grabbed onto the handle, and just as the men and women in black reached Mr. Flash, the Super Zeroes rose elegantly up into the air. Shouts and slaps came from below them.

"Up there!" shouted a Cleaner, who had spotted them from the playing field. "On the umbrella!"

"Back to the chopper," ordered another. "Prepare for aerial combat. Move, move, move!"

"They won't get far," they heard a third Cleaner add. But he was wrong. The Super Zeroes were about to get very far indeed.

Before the Cleaners could reach their helicopter, the air was filled with a droning clatter, and Mary had to hold tight to her umbrella to stop it from bucking in the strong wind that had blown up out of nowhere.

Screwing up his eyes, Murph glanced behind them. Hovering nearby was a jet-black car. It flew with the aid of two silvery rotor blades that stuck up on either side, beating the air furiously. For some reason, it immediately reminded him of the *Banshee*. This car was smaller, and it was a matte black rather than the *Banshee*'s silvery blue, but it was just as sleek and effortlessly cool.

A door in the side popped open, and the Zeroes

were startled to see the grinning face of Sir Jasper Rowntree looking out at them.

"Need a lift somewhere, young chaps and chapesses?" he piped in his upper-crust accent.

The friends needed no more encouragement. Mary steered them toward the hovering car and they piled in through the door as fast as possible.

"All aboard?" asked Sir Jasper. He flicked a switch above his head and the door whisked shut behind them, blocking out the noise of the wind and the unfolding chaos below.

"Nice car," gasped Murph weakly, collapsing to the floor. Now that they were inside, he could see that Jasper's wheelchair slotted cleverly into the control panel at the front of the vehicle's cockpit.

"I call her Gertie," declared Jasper affectionately, as the miraculous car rose higher into the air, leaving the Cleaners—still scrambling back to their helicopter—far too late to give chase.

"Seriously?" blurted out Hilda.

"And what, pray tell, is wrong with Gertie?" retorted Jasper, sounding a bit stung.

"Oh, nothing," said Hilda airily. "It's just a really, really cool car. So I thought that it might have a really, really cool name to match. Like, oh, I don't know, the Sky Panther."

"Or Air Beast," suggested Murph.

"Black Vengeance!" added Mary.

"Or Blades of Fury," chimed in Billy.

Nellie stuck up a thumb. Clearly this was her preferred choice.

"Gertie just sounds like the name of a cartoon cow," Hilda complained.

"Well, excuse me, I'm sure," said Sir Jasper, widening his eyes and smiling. "But if you've quite finished, I'd like to get on with the business of rescuing our friends."

This sounded like an extremely high-quality idea to everyone.

"Whither shall I direct old Gertie, young Murph?" Sir Jasper asked.

"To Shivering Sands!" said Murph. "As fast as you can!"

Sir Jasper couldn't hide his look of astonishment as he piloted Gertie rapidly above the clouds, and they were lost to sight.

19

Party Time

Flora and Carl stepped slowly into the elevator that would take them to Magpie's underwater cell. They'd been expecting to have to use the full extent of their skills and experience—not to mention Flora's invisibility Capability—to get this far. But instead, their path had been left suspiciously clear of guards and Cleaners, and as they worked their way toward the center of the main tower, the doors they needed to pass through had their security systems disabled.

"I think we can safely say that he knows we're coming," said Carl, as yet another door slid open to let them through without the need for a command or an access code. Their footsteps echoed loudly on the metal floor.

"I don't like it one bit," Flora replied grimly. "It feels like a trap."

"Well, of course it's a trap," Carl told her, grabbing her hand and squeezing it reassuringly. "But you know what we do with traps, eh, Flo?"

"We spring them," responded Flora, with a slight smile. "Then we kick some serious bottom."

"That's the spirit," said Carl, trying to sound more confident than he felt. If there was the smallest chance that Angel might be alive, they had to grab it with both hands. Even if that meant playing the game by somebody else's rules.

Under the sea, Magpie waited. He could hear the elevator descending, and he licked his lips in anticipation. "Of course I know you're coming, you imbeciles. Now, let's make sure that nobody is able to follow you. One last security measure . . ."

He turned to his HALO unit once again and ran a finger across the screen. A plan of the prison tower appeared, and as Magpie concentrated, the message **SECURITY SYSTEM DISABLED** flashed across it.

Up in the main prison, every single cell door popped open with an almost imperceptible click.

That should keep the attention of any remaining guards firmly away from us. If only my own cell were as easy to override, Magpie thought ruefully. *I might have escaped years ago. But no matter. Soon I will have what I require.*

With a smile he imagined the many Rogues of Shivering Sands emerging from their cells and tasting the air of freedom. If all went according to plan, he would soon join them.

Magpie's eyes narrowed as the elevator finally hissed open, and Flora and Carl stepped out into the murky light of his lair.

Yes, very soon indeed.

Carl and Flora were on their guard as soon as they set foot in the cell. Magpie looked entirely too pleased to see them.

"Welcome!" Magpie's voice was jovial. "Come in, come in, make yourselves at home. I've been looking forward to seeing you again for quite a while now. A very, very, very long while, in fact."

As he spoke, his face twisted into an expression of

pure hatred. "I take it you received my message, then? I knew the boy would be efficient. I knew it wouldn't be long before he had to rely on the help of some more *Capable* friends. Nothing if not predictable."

"Yes, very clever, well done, you," blustered Carl, wanting to show no fear in front of this villain. "Murph showed us the message. Bravo. Now stop wasting our time and tell us what you know."

"I've been stuck down here alone for three decades, and it was your wife and her heroic colleagues who made sure of that, not you," Magpie hissed, slowly and quietly. "So it's the legendary Blue Phantom I want to speak with now, the greatest Hero of all time"—his voice was scornful—"not her Capability-free chauffeur. Hold your tongue, you bumbling fool, and let the grown-ups talk."

Carl started toward the top of the stone steps, red with anger, but Flora grasped his hand to hold him back. "No. You know how this cell works. If you cross that line down there we're all done for. Don't give him the satisfaction," she said tightly, before turning to address Magpie for the first time.

"You deserve never to see the light of day again," said Flora carefully, but her voice betrayed her emotion. "What you did at Scarsdale was unforgivable. There isn't a sentence long enough to justify your actions."

"Shush, shush, shush," said Magpie, waving a patronizing hand toward them both, "there's no need to be unpleasant. And in any case, let's leave the past behind and concentrate on the matter at hand. I have a transaction to propose."

Magpie walked a little closer to them, toward the white circle on the floor, his feet slapping on the cold stone. His long black coat dragged behind him as he took up a position as close as he could get to the bottom of the giant staircase.

"I," he said forcefully, spreading his hands wide, "have something you want. And you"—he pointed at Flora—"have something I want."

"Come on, then," Flora said assertively, "out with it."

"You have always labored under the delusion that Angel was in my facility at Scarsdale when it exploded. Such youthful exuberance as she had— such a desire to be the one to save the day, that she

293

followed all the grown-up Heroes there to try to help, and perished in the effort. Well . . . here's a plot twist for you . . ."

He dropped his voice to a whisper and looked around mockingly as if to check that nobody else was listening, raising his hand to his mouth like you do when you're whispering a secret . . .

"She wasn't." Magpie widened his eyes, performed a melodramatic gasp, and started smiling. "I had captured her the day before, somewhere very different indeed. She was off on her own secret mission, determined to do her bit for the cause and find out everything she could about me to help you, her darling heroic parents, bring me to justice. And she found out lots of juicy information, you can be sure . . . but then *I* found *her*. She remains safe and well to this day."

Flora's knees buckled and Carl rushed to prop her up. "You're lying!" he shouted.

"He isn't lying," said a shrill voice from behind them.

They spun around to see that a small man, dressed in filthy rags, had appeared from the elevator.

"Ah! Right on time! Blue Phantom, Chauffeur, may I introduce a friend of mine?" said Magpie. "Or perhaps introductions aren't necessary . . ."

"Drench?!" said Flora, peering at the small, stinking creature in disbelief. "What happened to you?"

"Drench? Drench? There's no one of that name here," gloated the little man, capering around. "Drench is the name of a pathetic sidekick. But I am no sidekick. I am the MAIN kick. **I am DoomWeasel! Ahahaha!**"

Carl and Flora looked completely bemused. And rightly so.

"I am DoomWeasel and this is *my* sidekick, Ratsputin," Mr. Drench went on. He gestured to his pocket, where a very sweet, whiskery brown face could be seen darting its head from side to side.

"Squeak?" squeaked Ratsputin.

"Feast upon the sound of pure evil!" cackled his master.

Nobody said anything for a few seconds. Flora and Carl had too much information to take on board to worry about Mr. Drench and how he had come to lose, seemingly, every single one of his marbles. So Flora concentrated on the only thing that Mr. Drench had said that made any sense.

"What do you mean Magpie isn't lying?" she said. "What do you know about it?"

"I've been there," DoomWeasel continued, stroking Ratsputin. "I've seen her."

"You've seen Angel?!" asked Carl.

"I saw her. She's trapped. But she is alive!"

Flora turned on Magpie. "How is this possible?"

"I'll tell you that," Magpie replied, "once you've given me what I want." Turning to DoomWeasel, he said, "Show them the device."

DoomWeasel pulled a metal cube out of his pocket—small enough to fit into the palm of his hand. It was studded with flashing red lights.

"That," Magpie told them, "is an ingenious little gadget of my own invention. I call it a Proximity Detonator. It is linked to a bomb inside the secret laboratory where Angel has been . . . preserved. While it remains nearby, she is safe. But, unfortunately . . ."

"I took it!" squealed DoomWeasel in delight. **"I took it away!"**

Magpie smiled thinly. "Yes—I asked your former colleague here to remove the Proximity Detonator from the bomb several days ago. Unless it is replaced within the next twenty-four hours, I'm very much afraid that the bomb will explode—taking your daughter with it."

Before even Flora, with her lightning-quick reflexes, could react, he held out a pale hand, and DoomWeasel threw the metal cube through the air and down into the base of the stone amphitheater.

Magpie caught it neatly and placed it in the pocket of his coat.

"So," he snarled, "as I said, now I have something you want: the only way of saving your daughter's life. But I can only replace the detonator if you allow me to escape from prison."

"How can we do that?" shouted Carl. "The security system will blow this whole cell up if it sees you try to get out of the circle . . ." He trailed off, suddenly realizing what Magpie was demanding.

Flora let out a small cry.

"Yes, you've finally puzzled it out," said Magpie smugly, folding his arms. "Blue Phantom, I need to take your power of invisibility. In return, I will go back to my laboratory and stop it from self-destructing."

He spread his arms wide, his wrinkled face breaking into a hideous grin of triumph. "Choose, Blue Phantom! What will it be? Your power . . . or your daughter?"

Compared to the cramped interior of the *Banshee*, the inside of Gertie was relatively luxurious. Jasper's wheelchair was clamped into place in front of the semicircular main control panel, but farther back were two full rows of comfortable, leather-upholstered seats. The Super Zeroes flopped into these as the car clattered away from The School, and for a long time they slumped there, panting, regaining their energy after a morning that had seemed like a constant cycle of sprinting, mystery solving, fighting, and getting rescued. Oh, and attempting to play the bassoon.

At no point, Murph realized, had it included any eating, and his stomach rumbled loudly.

"I made sandwiches, if anyone's interested?" called Sir Jasper over his shoulder, pointing to an old-fashioned wicker picnic basket on the floor at the back of the cabin. "Never like to set off to save the world without a bit of lunch handy."

The Super Zeroes fell on the hamper like a group of seagulls who had skipped seagull breakfast, and for a while there was no sound but the clatter of Gertie's rotor blades and the munching of cucumber sandwiches.

Presently, as the flashes of green through the clouds below them gave way to the cream-flecked gray of the ocean, Hilda spoke up. "Right then, Sir Jasper. So how, in fact, did you end up here? Please. My, er, lord."

Jasper looked back over his shoulder. **"I was about to ask you the same question, you bunch of young hooligans!"** He pointed to a large screen in front of him, which was showing the same display as Murph's HALO unit: their five mugshots and the instruction to "apprehend and detain." "I might not be a Hero anymore, but I still like to keep up to speed, you know." He looked a little sheepish. "Carl helped me fit this years ago. Then today it goes mad with activity. First Flora gets declared a Rogue Hero. Well, I know that's got to be a load of old hogwash, so I climb into the old girl and fly over to see what the blazes is up. Next thing I know, your faces pop up on the old HALO screen as well. Then all these scary-looking Cleaner goons arrive in their black helicopter. And lo and behold, you come flying my way like a bunch of blasted balloons. And now that we've run away from the Alliance, I suppose we're all Rogue Heroes together. Rather exciting, eh? Although technically I'm not a Hero, of course," he added, almost to himself. "Not for a long time."

Squinting through the windshield, Murph could just make out the white rows of wind turbines that he'd seen on his first visit, and beyond them a series of black dots that could only be Shivering Sands.

"Let's lose some height, get away from their radar," said Jasper calmly. "Do take a peppermint, everyone! It'll be a steep descent." He passed the brown paper bag back over his shoulder and they all took a candy. "Right, down we go!" he yelled, pushing forward on the joystick. Everyone's stomach did a quick somersault as Gertie plunged toward the sea.

As they got lower, the cabin began to shake.

"Bit windy at this altitude, sorry!" said the pilot.

They were now frighteningly close to the wind turbines, their huge white blades spinning around at dizzying speed. The Super Zeroes looked at one another in alarm, all except for Nellie, who was staring fixedly out of the windshield.

As they approached, the sickening rocking motion lessened. To everyone's amazement, they saw that the wind turbine blades were slowing, until they were finally turning around lazily in a gentle sea breeze.

"Thank jeepers for that," said Jasper, wiping his brow.

"Actually, I think we should thank Nellie for that," corrected Mary, reaching out to give her a grateful squeeze on the knee. Nellie emitted a small noise, tugging Jasper's right sleeve and pointing ahead.

"Right you are," he agreed, pulling the stick to the right. "Thanks, Nell."

As they got closer, everyone strained their eyes out of the windshield. "Look! Over there," said Murph, spotting the familiar bluish gleam of the *Banshee*. It was parked on a narrow platform on the edge of one of the towers. "We were right—they're here." He didn't know whether to be relieved that they'd found their friends or afraid of what might be happening to them inside the prison.

"South landing platform, I see it. But something's not right," said Jasper sharply. "It's too quiet. Why's nobody spotted us?"

As Gertie flew closer to the tower, Murph saw that

its landing lights were flashing. He could hear the faint hooting of a siren.

"Something's definitely going on," Murph agreed. "We've got to get in there."

"Roger and wilco," replied Jasper. He brought them in smoothly, pulling back on the joystick to land Gertie elegantly beside the *Banshee*.

"Off you go, then, Heroes!" he told them as the doors opened. "Time to get saving!" The Zeroes all looked at him, openmouthed.

"You're not coming?" said Billy weakly.

"Good crumbs, no!" said Sir Jasper with a crooked smile. "You'll be far faster without an old codger like me getting in the way." He coughed in an embarrassed fashion. "This is a job for Heroes, not retired oldies. And besides, I need to keep an eye on the *Banshee* and Gertie. Not much point rescuing your friends if you don't have a plan for getting away again, now, is there?"

It sounded like he was keeping something back, and Murph suspected he knew what it was. For all his bluster, Sir Jasper didn't seem to have the confidence to go into action without a Cape. But this wasn't the time for a pep talk. As soon as their feet hit the metal floor of the platform, they realized they were in the middle of something extremely dramatic.

As well as the strobing red lights, there was a loud alarm going off every few seconds while a metallic voice recited the same words over and over again: **EMERGENCY LOCKDOWN. EMERGENCY LOCKDOWN. EMERGENCY LOCKDOWN.**

"That is a VERY annoying noise," shouted Hilda over the very annoying noise.

"I think that's sort of the idea," said Murph.

"Well, I think an emergency situation is stressful enough without having to go and make a really annoying noise all the way through it. It's giving me a headache!"

"Come on, maybe it'll be quieter inside," said Murph unconvincingly.

As yet, they had no actual plan for getting into the prison, but as they reached the entrance door they realized they wouldn't need one. The electronic pad beside the door was glowing an ominous green, with the words **SECURITY SYSTEMS DISABLED** visible. Murph touched it with a nervous finger, and the doors sprang open. *That*, he thought queasily, *is definitely not the way high-security prisons are supposed to work.*

Something was very, very wrong.

The scene inside Shivering Sands is probably best described as absolute chaos with whipped cream on top. When Murph had been there with Miss Flint, the atmosphere had been quiet and businesslike. Today it looked like someone had set fire to a cat and released it into a fireworks factory. (No cats were harmed during the writing of that last sentence.)

The Zeroes were in a room that must have usually served as a dining hall, but today the tables and chairs had been knocked over, and there was food scattered crazily across every surface. Bill Burton would have had a seizure at the sight of it. Slumped against the wall not far away was an unconscious guard, his black uniform splattered with what looked like globs of cream and his face obscured with what could only be a custard pie.

"What's happened to him?" whispered Billy.

"OHHHHHHH! He's just ALL PARTIED OUT!" came a

roaring voice from the doorway opposite him.

Before he'd even looked in the direction the voice was coming from, Murph knew with a nasty certainty exactly what he was about to see. It was the massive, looming, bedraggled form of Party Animal, his eyes wide and staring. It was the first time Murph had caught more than a partial glimpse of the clown through his cell bars. Now, he had the full widescreen view, and it wasn't pretty.

Party Animal was huge and fat. He wore a frilly shirt with wide-striped pants and gargantuan, clomping shoes. His enormous, chalk-white face wore an utterly demented expression underneath a shock of frizzy scarlet hair.

"DO YOU GUYS LIKE TO PARTY TOO?" the villain

screamed at them.

"To tell you the truth," said Murph, deciding to try a dash of honesty, "not really."

"I'm not great at parties either," agreed Mary.

"Oh, you misunderstand me," roared Party Animal, "you don't get to choose. **It's not your party, it's mine. It's my party and you'll DIE if I want you to.**"

Having unleashed the full force of his favorite catchphrase, he proceeded to laugh maniacally for a full minute, which is even longer than it sounds. Then he stopped abruptly and stared at them in silence for another ten full seconds, which, if anything, was weirder.

". . . Okay, so, we're gonna shoot off," said Murph breezily. "Nice to see you again."

"Don't leave," said the eight-foot clown, "I was about to give you some balloons. Would you like that?"

"Um," began Billy, swiftly realizing that it's very difficult to politely refuse the offer of a balloon.

"NO! No, we wouldn't! We hate balloons!" squealed Mary, who had perceptively deciphered the "die" part of the catchphrase, but it was too late.

Party Animal had reached into his top pocket and pulled out a handful of bright red balloons. Holding one between finger and thumb, he blew it up with a single huge breath and then released it. It flew toward them, making a piercing ducklike screech.

"Duck!" screamed Mary.

"It does sound a bit like a duck, yes," mused Billy, before being pulled to the ground.

The Zeroes dived to either side as the balloon flew between them and exploded against the wall behind, blowing a huge hole in the plaster.

"NOW we've got ourselves a party!" laughed Party Animal. "Another

balloon, you say? Coming right up!"

They all dashed for cover under a nearby lunch table, just in time to miss the clown's next projectile. The balloon flew through the hatch into the kitchen next door. It must have landed in a pot of baked beans as it exploded, because a gentle autumn shower of warm bean juice suddenly rained down on the Zeroes. There was no time to worry about it, though, or even grab a spoon. More balloons were already shrieking and banging their way around the room. Party Animal was turning on the spot and firing them in all directions, screeching with

crazed·laughter. As another balloon exploded within an inch of their hiding place, the Zeroes scattered.

Murph and Mary dodged behind another table.

"We've got to take this maniac down," said Murph desperately. "The only way to Magpie's cell is through him."

"Okay. Think," said Mary, half to herself. "What's a clown's weak point?"

"Um, unreliable cars?" suggested Murph.

"What?" snapped Mary.

"You know, clown cars?" Murph replied. "The doors fall off them and stuff. Must be hard to get insurance."

"That is the least helpful answer ever given during a battle," Mary scolded him. "Now try again. What—that could help us beat Party Animal at this exact moment—is a clown's weak point?"

"SHOES! Their really big, clumsy shoes," said Hilda from the other side of the table.

"That's it!" said Murph. "Where's Billy gone? **BILLY!**"

"I'm in here," said a muffled voice. "I don't like this party so I've gone in the kitchen."

Let's just pause here briefly for a useful life lesson. If you're the kind of person who isn't a fan of parties, always head straight for the kitchen. It seems safer and more comfortable, somehow, and everyone else there will be feeling the same as you.

But the kitchen Billy found himself in on this occasion wasn't particularly safe, unfortunately. Just then a balloon flew in and struck a huge pot of custard, which exploded all over him. Billy's ears inflated upward in fright, making him look for a moment like that popular children's character, the **CUSTARD RABBIT.**

The **CUSTARD RABBIT** scampered from the kitchen and took shelter behind Murph's table. Murph folded its ears down to avoid detection.

"What did you say?" asked the **CUSTARD R—** sorry, asked Billy.

"The shoes," Murph instructed him, licking custard off his hand and nodding appreciatively. "They're a clown's weak point. Do the shoes."

Billy wiped a strip of custard off his eyes, thereby transforming himself into that other popular character, the **CUSTARD NINJA,** and threw himself out from behind the table. Party Animal's shoes abruptly ballooned to several times their normal size, and given that their normal size was eight-foot-monster-clown size, that was very big indeed.

Party Animal stopped rotating and tried to lift his legs, but he was stuck fast to the floor. **"WHO'S TRYING TO SPOIL MY PARTY?"** he roared. "It'll take more than that to stop the fun!"

As well as sending out more balloons, he fired a web of brightly colored streamers from his sleeves right at Billy, trapping him in a flamboyant cage.

"Who's next?" he said, looking around the room while still stuck to the spot.

"You are," said Billy. "I've just remembered that clowns have another weakness."

Party Animal's squeaky red nose started inflating. Not to double the size, or even triple, for that matter. Within seconds, he was just an enormous nose on legs. **"Mmmnnnth brrrrth orrrth durrn flirrrm weeern!"** he roared, which was by far his worst catchphrase to date. As he struggled to move on his hugely inflated feet, the weight of his nose caught him off balance and he suddenly pitched backward to lie prone on the floor.

"Party's over." Billy winked, ripping his way out of the streamers and rejoining the other Zeroes.

"So I guess you'll be taking care of Party Animal from now on, Billy?" said Hilda, emerging from her hiding place.

"What do you mean?" he said.

"Well"—she raised an eyebrow at the others—"it looks like you just got custardy!"

There was a silence. Then another one.

Eventually, Murph coughed nervously. "Anyway, on we go. We have to find Flora and Carl before it's too late."

Leaving Hilda's joke hanging in the air above the struggling clown like a cloud of unfunny gas, the Super Zeroes moved deeper into the prison.

20

A Bad Memory

Down on Sublevel One, Flora was smiling gently.

"This is the problem with you supervillains," she said to Magpie calmly. "You don't have your priorities right. My power or my daughter? It's the easiest choice I've ever had to make."

"You are the one with the wrong priorities," scoffed Magpie. "But only because you underestimate the true nature of power."

"What's the use of a power unless you've got a reason to use it? Someone to protect? Something to fight for?" asked Flora.

Carl said nothing. He just squeezed Flora's hand. He had tears in his eyes.

The last Hero of the Golden Age raised her head, shut her eyes, and held out her hands. "Go on, then!" she said from the top of the steps, ready for Magpie's purple lightning to envelop her. "Take it!"

There was a long silence. Nothing happened.

Finally, Magpie coughed apologetically. "Oh, I'm so sorry," he said, a thin smile painting his lips. "I forgot one tiny, insignificant detail. I won't take your power while you're way up there. First, you have to come down here. Inside the circle."

"WHAT?!" Carl bellowed. "But once you take Flora's Cape from her . . . she won't be able to get out again. She'll be trapped down here forever!"

Magpie's smile grew into a sneering grin as his plan finally became clear. "Yes. You and your heroic friends locked me down here. And now, you're about to take my place." His voice grew to a shout. "That, Blue Phantom, is the meaning of true power, not your sickly storybook nonsense! It means being able to do exactly what you like. It means having your enemy totally at your mercy. Now, do as I demand. Or your daughter dies!"

Up in the main prison, the Zeroes marched on. The

flashing red emergency lights illuminated particles of smoke and dust from the chaos that surrounded them.

"I always did hate clowns," said Billy, feeling his ears gingerly. They were slowly shrinking in size but still retained a slight rabbitlike pointiness.

"Come on, let's not worry about him now. We need to hop to it," said Murph. The subtle rabbit reference was lost on everyone except Mary, who managed a brief—and slightly world-weary—thumbs-up.

"You'll make an excellent dad one day, you know, with jokes like that," she told him. Murph raised an eyebrow at her disapprovingly.

The Zeroes were aiming for the elevator to Sublevel One, but it wasn't easygoing. It seemed that every prisoner in the whole place had been released. Beside each cell they read the same message: **SECURITY SYSTEMS DISABLED**. Cells were empty or trashed; smashed furniture littered the corridors.

Occasionally they saw a few figures running down hallways, frantically shouting to one another, but they seemed so preoccupied it wasn't hard to avoid detection.

The Zeroes ducked into a vacant cell as the clatter of more boots approached.

"Corridor secure. Time to move! And where on earth is Flint?" a Cleaner yelled as the group rushed past.

As they disappeared out of sight, the five friends emerged into the smoky corridor. It was quiet: they could only just make out a distant banging and crashing from the floors above. They were suddenly very aware of their own footsteps echoing around the dingy hallway.

Hilda clung on to Billy's hand, which in turn frightened Billy, causing the hand to inflate and making Hilda scream.

"Shhh! Guys, keep calm!" said Murph. "The elevator's not much farth—"

Mary put her hand up to his face to halt him midword.

"What's that noise?" she whispered.

They all stopped in their tracks and adopted the internationally recognized listening face: craning their necks forward a bit, furrowing their brows, and squinting their eyes.

They could hear urgent mumbling voices and an eerie squeaking coming closer.

"Whatever it is, we face it," whispered Murph tensely. "The elevator's only around that next corner—we can't turn back now. We've come too far."

From around the corner a tall silhouette emerged and came slowly toward them. It was pushing what seemed to be a hospital bed. The bed had one wonky wheel that gave off an irritating **cheep, cheep, cheep** as it rolled.

"Not down here, you empty-headed nincompoop," came a raspy voice from the bed. "We've been this way three times already."

"Really, old pal? I don't remember coming down here," replied the second figure, his voice calm and ponderous.

The Zeroes stood their ground watchfully, looking at one another with growing puzzlement.

"Oh, you don't remember anything! *About turn! About turn!*"

But as they started their turn, the bedridden figure spotted the Zeroes in the near distance.

"Stop turn! Continue wheeling!" he bellowed. "Whatever do we have here, then?"

As the squeaky bed drew closer to the Zeroes, the figure in it became clearer. He was swathed head-to-toe in bandages, with his leg in stirrups, but even so he was unmistakable.

"Nektar?!" declared Hilda, for it was indeed the mad wasp-man himself.

"Oh, not again," sighed Murph.

"You!" Nektar glared savagely at Kid Normal. "It's you, isn't it! My . . . picnic! No, not picnic." As a half-wasp, Nektar was obsessed with picnics. It tended to get in the way of sensible conversation. *"Argh! What's the word I want?"*

"'Nemesis'?" suggested Hilda.

"Yes! Nemesis!" screamed Nektar. *"My pic-nemesis!"* You're the peddling mipsqueaks who foiled all my evil plans. Well, now it's time for me to buzz all over your barbecue!"

"What are you going to do?" asked Mary testily. "Run us over with the world's slowest bed?"

Nektar refused to let Mary's scorn put him off

his stride. Nodding toward the figure behind him, he said proudly, "Allow me to introduce you to my good friend, and new partner in crime!"

Nektar's partner in crime was an extraordinary-looking creature. His head was thin and pointed, and his eyes were bulbous and glossy black: one on each side of his face. His broad shoulders were covered by a shimmering orange jacket.

"He has one of the most evil criminal minds in the world," Nektar continued, "and with his help I will wreak terrible picnic on you!"

"'Revenge'?" suggested Hilda.

"That's what I said. Revenge!" Nektar shouted.

"And with the help of this evil genius, it will be a truly, truly terrible picnic. For this . . . is GOLDFISH!" He raised both arms in the air as if to say "Hey presto!" But he was so wrapped in bandages he barely managed enough movement to cover the "Hey" element, if we're being quite honest.

"Goldfish?" said Mary. "What a lame name for a supervillain."

"Excuse me, young lady," said Goldfish in his slow voice, "but as, er, this fellow here rightly said, I am, um, frightfully evil. I just don't seem to be able to quite recall . . . um . . ."

"He forgets everything," Murph realized. "Just like a goldfish. I heard about him when I visited this place the first time. Not that he'll remember that, of course."

Nektar clearly felt that this was enough chitchat.

"SILENCE! Goldfish, let me introduce you to the people we're about to dispose of. These idiotic termites put me in this blasted bed in the first place. We have . . . well, we have the umbrella girl, weird inflating boy, the quiet one, horse machine, and, of course . . . my boy. My dear, dear son, Martin. How are you, my child?"

Murph rolled his eyes. The other Zeroes laughed.

"He's not your son, Nektar! We went through this last time!" said Mary, exasperated.

"Silence! I know the real truth. I AM MARK'S BASKET! Gah! No, not basket. Father! I am Mark's father."

"Wait, so who's Martin's father, in that case?" replied Mary, quick as a wink.

"Enough!" Nektar screamed, incensed. "Goldfish, attack!" he continued, which is one of the least terrifying orders ever given.

The Zeroes readied themselves for whatever a goldfish's attack strategy might be. Which, let's face it, isn't likely to present much of a problem. Unless you're a bit of fish food.

"Right. So, sorry, um . . . why am I attacking these children again, Lord Nektar?" asked Goldfish placidly.

"I just said this literally three seconds ago, you complete waste of tank space! They ruined everything! They came into my lair, just as I was having a really fun day, and kicked me over the balcony with horses!" He waved a bandaged finger in the direction of Hilda, who instantly adopted a combat pose but was unable to suppress a small smile as she remembered her horses' proudest moment to date.

"Rides a horse, does she?" asked Goldfish. "Talented young lady."

"No, she doesn't RIDE a horse, you aquatic loon. She has these pet ones that go big," explained Nektar, badly.

"Oh gosh, how wonderful," gushed Goldfish. "I do love the races. Like a little bet, you know. Trouble is, I can never remember which one I picked."

"Rugs! Sandwiches! Gah! Picnic!" squealed Nektar. He was growing more and more incoherent in his agitation. He had been hoping for an evil henchman, but this guy was more like a benign old uncle. *"Just . . . SEIZE THEM!"* he managed to blurt out finally, jiggling around in his bed like a wasp in a jar.

"All right, old chap. Don't get your bandages in a tangle. Why are you all bandaged up, out of curiosity?"

"SEIZE THEM!"

"Right you are," agreed Goldfish, leaving Nektar and beginning to march toward the Zeroes.

"We can't waste time with this," decided Murph. "Get ready, Billy."

"Yes, boss."

"All set, Hilda?"

"Locked and loaded."

"GO!" yelled Murph.

Hilda held out her hand. Her two tiny white friends appeared on her palm.

"Oh, how charming! Horses, only smaller!" burbled Goldfish, completely forgetting about his task.

"No!" called Nektar, thrashing about in the bed. "Don't get distracted by the horses—repeat, do not get distracted by the horses. They go big."

"What?"

"They GO BIG!"

"Now, Billy!" ordered Murph.

"No! Argh! Sausage rolls! Abort!" shouted a panicking Nektar, but to no avail. Quick as a flash, Billy had used his Cape to inflate Hilda's horses.

Goldfish recoiled in fear from the full-size stallions who were pawing the ground, preparing to thunder toward him. He darted back behind the bed.

"Argh! They've gone big! Why didn't you tell me they go big?!" he quavered.

"I did, you big bald . . . baldy! Napkins! Just . . . get us out of here!"

Hilda's horses reared up and whinnied loudly in the direction of the two cowering supervillains.

Goldfish grabbed the back of Nektar's bed violently, spinning it around and clunking the wasp man's elevated feet on the wall as he did.

"Ouch! Ow! Pork pies! Careful!" screamed Nektar as the wonky wheel buckled, causing the bed to lurch violently from side to side as they bashed, panged, and bumped their way out of sight.

"Great work, Hilda; excellent from you too, Billy," said Murph.

But the smile on his face quickly faded. Nektar being at large once again was the least of their worries right now. Their route down to Sublevel One was clear. The elevator was just around the next corner. He only hoped that they had made it in time to help Flora and Carl.

Beckoning his friends onward, he led them into the elevator itself.

They were
silent as they
packed themselves
in. A brief image
of a bullfighting
poster swam
through Murph's
mind as he fought
down an urge to
panic, and the
elevator door
closed.

Who knew what
they would find
when it opened
again on the seabed?

21

Last Stand of the Blue Phantom

Murph could barely take in the scene that met his eyes as the elevator door slid open and they stepped out onto Sublevel One. Magpie was still trapped at the bottom of his stone amphitheater, but Murph couldn't be relieved about that. Because now there was a second figure inside the white circle with him.

It was Flora.

Not far from the elevator shaft, Carl was standing near the top edge of the stone steps. The old man was staring in disbelief at the scene unfolding below. They rushed over to join him.

He was too distressed to question their arrival. "I couldn't stop her," he said weakly.

"How did she get inside the circle without the cameras seeing her?" Murph asked urgently.

"She used her invisibility," said Carl. Murph registered, with shock, that there were tears in his eyes. "But that doesn't matter now. What matters is that she'll never be able to get out. It's the only chance to save Angel. Our . . . our daughter. And she took it."

There was nothing any of them could do. As they watched on, horrified, Magpie held out his palms toward the Blue Phantom. Jets of crackling purple lightning surrounded her, lifting her into the air.

"NO!" screamed Hilda, but Carl held her back.

"She knows what she's doing," he said sadly.

A bluish glow surrounded Magpie, whose mouth was stretched in a grotesque grin. Abruptly, the lightning disappeared and Flora slammed to the floor.

Without a backward glance, Magpie walked toward the white circle painted on the ground, the cameras above moving to track him.

"For thirty years, I've been watched," he said softly, looking up at them. "Thirty years."

And then he vanished.

"Where's he gone?" yelled Mary urgently, her glance darting around the huge space.

"He could be anywhere! Be on guard! Don't let him steal your Capes!" shouted Murph.

"He's done it! He's free!" squeaked a voice from back near the elevator. "The Alliance is defeated!"

Murph glanced across to see a little man in filthy rags capering around. **"Is that . . . Mr. Drench?"** he murmured wonderingly. This was all too much to take in.

All of a sudden, Magpie reappeared right inside the entrance to the elevator, holding a metal cube dotted with red lights in one hand.

"Don't worry," he called out to Carl, "I'm a man of my word. I'll replace the Proximity Detonator, just as I promised. Angel won't be blown up."

Mr. Drench joined him in the elevator.

"Besides, I've got something far worse planned for her," Magpie concluded as the elevator doors snapped closed and whisked him away.

For a moment, nobody spoke as the clanging of the elevator door reverberated around the undersea prison like the tolling of a bell. But then a faint groan from Flora at the bottom of the amphitheater sent Mary rushing down the stone stairs.

"No!" said Murph. "Don't go near her! Don't cross the white line."

Mary came to an agonizing halt only a couple of steps above the prone figure of Flora.

"Then what do we do?" yelled Mary, looking desperately back up at Murph. "We can't just leave her! She can't be trapped here forever. She can't!"

Murph dithered uncertainly at the top of the steps. It seemed like an impossible dilemma. They had to try and chase after Magpie to have any hope of saving Angel. But to do that, they would have to leave Flora imprisoned at Shivering Sands.

"So, if the cameras see anyone crossing the white line to help her, this place will blow," summarized Hilda, joining him. "And now that Flora has lost her Cape, if she leaves the circle—"

"This place will blow," Murph completed for her.

"Great set of options we've got," added Billy.

"Come on," Murph said, beginning to walk down the stone steps to join Mary and beckoning the others to do the same. "Carl, you too. Flora's in a trap. So what do we do?"

"Spring the trap?" answered Carl uncertainly, as all six of them gathered not far from the white circle.

"We spring the trap," confirmed Kid Normal.

"But . . . this whole place will fill with water," said Hilda in a small voice. "We'll never make it."

"We came here as a team," Murph told her. "And we're leaving together. All of us. Agreed?"

Hilda nodded. As Murph looked around at the faces of his friends, he saw their expressions gradually change from panic to determination.

"All right," said Hilda boldly. "Together, then?"

"Together," confirmed Billy.

"Together," said Mary, patting Murph's shoulder.

"Together," came a soft whisper from behind Nellie's curtain of hair.

Carl's eyes were moist as he looked along the line at his five young friends. He nodded proudly. "Spoken like true Heroes," he told them. "You're on! Together!"

"Now!" yelled Murph, and as one they raced toward the fallen Phantom.

"BOUNDARY ENCROACHMENT. STEP BACK," came the automated warning.

They kept on.

"BOUNDARY ENCROACHMENT. STEP BACK."

Nobody stopped. All six of them stepped over the line and ran to Flora.

"BREACH. DANGER. DETONATE. BREACH. DANGER. DETONATE."

Immediately, there was a series of deafening explosions. The first came from the elevator shaft, which erupted in a curtain of flame, cutting off any possible escape. Then, one by one, the red boxes blew up, punching holes in the thick glass wall. Seawater began pouring in.

Carl was oblivious to this as he raised Flora up and patted her gently on the cheek. He checked the pulse in her neck. The faintest of groans brought a radiant smile to his face. "Hold tight, Flo," he told her. "We'll soon have you out of here."

"Yeah, about that," said Billy nervously, looking over his shoulder. Freezing-cold seawater was sluicing down the stone steps; the base of the amphitheater was already knee deep.

"We've got to gain some height," Murph told Mary. She nodded.

"Hold on," she told everyone, pulling her umbrella from her pocket. "Carl, bring Flora here and grab this."

She pressed the button and unfurled the umbrella as Carl picked Flora up and put her over his shoulder, gasping with the shock of the cold water.

With the weight of two grown adults added to their own, flying wasn't quite as easy as it should have been, and it was hard for everyone to keep a grip. They rose uncertainly above the lapping water, bobbing and dipping alarmingly.

"I'm not sure I can hold it!" Mary screamed. Billy didn't help matters by inflating both his feet in panic.

Mary steered them crazily toward the elevator, swooping so low at one point that Murph's foot hit the stone floor of the top level. It splashed in icy water, and he registered with shock that already the entire lower section of the amphitheater was flooded. To make matters worse, now they could see that the elevator shaft had been totally destroyed.

"How do we get out of this one, then, old girl?" muttered Carl to Flora. Her eyelids fluttered open.

"Oh, I usually find that a solution presents itself," she muttered.

They were all so reassured to hear Flora speak that they were starting to feel slightly better even before they saw a pair of bright headlights cutting through the murky water. With a roar and a splash, a silvery-blue vehicle shot through one of the gaps in the glass wall and bobbed to the surface just below them, like an extremely welcome dolphin.

As Mary guided them down onto the vehicle's roof, they could make out Sir Jasper's grinning face through the cockpit window.

"Jasper!" yelled Carl. "What are you doing here?"

"It's a rescue, old boy," Sir Jasper explained as the door opened. "I heard explosions and thought, that's usually a sign someone requires my help. Need a lift?"

"I've never been so pleased to see you, my friend,"

said Carl shakily as they climbed in. "Now get us out of here. I never want to see this place again."

"So," said Murph gently to Carl once they had all squeezed inside, "the *Banshee* can travel underwater then, can it?"

"Oh yes," replied Carl. "I told you last time, didn't I? I've made a lot of special modifications." A little of the old twinkle reappeared in his eyes.

Leaving a trail of blue bubbles behind it, the *Banshee* turned and plunged out of Sublevel One, back up toward the rusting towers of Shivering Sands.

Fittingly for this point in the story, the weather had just become more dramatic, and the *Banshee* broke the surface of the sea into driving rain and gusty winds. Sir Jasper wrestled with the controls as their craft was buffeted this way and that; sea spray spattered the windows as they lurched upward. But finally, after a nerve-jangling couple of minutes, he managed to steer them around to the landing platform and set the *Banshee* down next to Gertie.

"First things first. Is everyone okay?" asked

Sir Jasper, taking his hands off the joystick and turning around in his seat. The Super Zeroes nodded as they all piled out of the cramped vehicle to lie panting on the landing platform.

Carl was still in the back, cradling Flora's head. "How are you feeling?" he asked her gently.

She didn't open her eyes, but it looked as if she smiled slightly as she replied, "Normal. I'm feeling . . . normal. But there's nothing wrong with that."

Murph felt a stab of sadness. The Blue Phantom had been one of the last Heroes of the Golden Age—and thanks to him she had become Magpie's latest victim.

But this was no time for regret: that would come later. For now, there was work to do. Murph decided to channel every molecule of the pain he was feeling into making sure that Magpie got his comeuppance.

"There's no time to lose," he told his friends. "This is where we have the advantage."

"How do you work that out?" asked Billy, who had taken off his wet shoes and was wringing one of his socks out. "We almost got killed down there."

"Yeah—but we didn't." Murph grinned. "And that's

our advantage. He'll think we're still down there trying to help Flora. He'll never know we're coming."

"Coming where?" asked Hilda blankly.

"Coming to rescue Angel, of course!" replied Kid Normal. "You heard Magpie; he's got something planned for her. **We've got to find her and bring her home."**

Wordlessly, Carl reached a hand out of the *Banshee* and grasped Murph's shoulder. Flora's eyes flickered open, and she said weakly, "You never give up, do you, young Murph?" She looked at him with so much pride that Murph felt it radiating from her like physical warmth, and all at once he felt less chilled in spite of the sea breeze on his wet clothes.

Suddenly, there was a flash of purplish light from overhead. Murph peered into the sky. One of the huge black Alliance helicopters had just taken off, and Murph could make out crazed veins of purple lightning running along its sides.

"It's him!" said Murph quietly. "Look at that light. He's using his tele-tech to take control of the helicopter. Carl, can you track it?"

"I certainly can," replied Carl, leaning over Jasper and tapping some buttons on the *Banshee*'s control panel. A flashing red dot appeared on his display as the helicopter vanished into the murk. "Let's just give them a short while to get clear, and we'll see where he's off to with his little friend."

"Mr. Drench," Mary said. "When we get a minute we simply must have a chat about how weird that was."

"Definitely," agreed Murph, "but now is probably not the moment."

"Time to engage in a delicate bit of vamoosing, then, perhaps?" suggested Sir Jasper. "I'll get the old kite fired up and follow you back to the coast—and you can be off on your rescue." He backed his wheelchair away from the control panel and made for the ramp at the back of the *Banshee*.

"You're not coming?" asked Murph softly.

The wheelchair stopped. "I told you. You don't want a creaky old codger like me getting in your way," said Sir Jasper, with a bravado that sounded distinctly false to Murph's ears. "I'm supposed to be retired, you know.

Time for a cup of tea and a sit-down." He restarted the wheelchair and rolled down the ramp.

"You brought us here on a rescue mission," said Murph, following him. "You piloted the *Banshee* down to an exploding underwater prison without thinking of your own safety. And you saved our lives. That all sounds pretty heroic to me."

Sir Jasper coughed. "Well, thank you very much, young sir. You're too kind to an old man. But without a Cape . . . what use can I really be?"

"I don't have a Cape!" Murph argued. "I never did! And now Flora doesn't either."

Carl broke in kindly. "You've done more than enough, Jasper. We'll take it from here. You get yourself home safe." He took a long look at Murph as Sir Jasper rolled back into Gertie and set about her controls.

"Ta-ta for now!" Sir Jasper cried over his shoulder.

Murph turned back to the *Banshee*. He thought he understood Carl's look. It wasn't fair to try to convince Sir Jasper to pursue the villain who had caused him so much pain. He would have to follow his own path. But Murph couldn't help feeling frustrated.

"Right," Carl was saying, climbing over into the pilot's position his friend had just vacated and folding out a chair. "Let's get airborne. You kids take care of my Flora back there, and Nellie—you come up here and take her place. Will you do that for me?"

Nellie let out a minuscule squeak of excitement and bounded up to the copilot's place. This was the flight she'd been promised.

"Buckle up," Carl told her, "it's looking nasty out there." He flicked a few switches on the control panel, and the jets screamed to life.

As the *Banshee* lifted off into the driving rain, a lone ray of sunlight broke through the clouds, sending a rainbow arcing across the crashing waves.

"Very pretty," said Carl approvingly. Behind him, a clattering sound reverberated off the metal walls of Shivering Sands as Gertie's rotor blades started up.

Gleaming blue and jet black, the two cars hovered beside the metal towers.

Carl turned his attention back to the route ahead. "Good to go, Little Nell?" he asked.

Nellie nodded.

"Rotate engines ninety degrees, and let's fly."

The *Banshee* shot forward as Carl steered them low over the water, kicking up a wake of spray as it zoomed through the rainbow and pierced it with a vapor trail of different shades of blue.

Murph gazed out of the back window to take one last look as the towers of Shivering Sands grew smaller and smaller.

Carl made for a deserted headland and gained height as they came over the coast.

"Let's have a look, then," he said, tapping a few more buttons and inspecting the control panel. "Magpie's headed off to the south. You're right, Murph. He's not expecting to be followed." He grinned savagely for a brief moment before radioing Jasper. "Okay, my friend, this is where we say goodbye!"

"Roger, old scout," replied Sir Jasper. "See you all back at base soon. I'll get the kettle on. Good luck, Zeroes!"

The Super Zeroes all craned around to the back window to give him a little wave, squashing Murph's face against the glass in the process. They saw Sir Jasper salute smartly in Gertie's cockpit before leaning on the joystick and peeling smoothly away.

"Safe home!" added Carl. "And thanks for everything."

"It's been a pleasure, my friend," came Jasper's voice in reply. "As always."

And with that, the *Banshee* flew on alone, following the blinking red dot that would lead them to their unsuspecting enemy.

22

Behind the Waterfall

Carl continued to gain height until the *Banshee* was surrounded by thin wisps of cloud.

"Keep her at this altitude, Nell," he said. "Don't want any prying eyes seeing where we're headed."

Murph squinted at the display in front. "Carl, look! The tracker—it's stopped. I think Magpie must have landed."

Mary pushed forward and looked over Carl's shoulder at the glowing map. "Seems like they're in the middle of hills. No buildings nearby or anything."

"Magpie's secret lair," breathed Hilda.

"Must be. We always suspected Magpie had another base besides Scarsdale," Carl said. "A place where he was carrying out his experiments. He must have captured our Angel there. How she found it by herself I'll never know."

"And now, thanks to Murph, we've just discovered where it is too, thirty years later," said Flora emotionally. Murph turned to look out of the window and did a bit more private blushing.

Carl steered the *Banshee* down through the clouds until they were skimming along at treetop height.

"Looks like he's somewhere along this valley," he said, piloting them into a gorge between steeply sloping hills. A stream wound along the valley floor, and Murph could see a few sheep running away up the hill, startled by the scream of the jet engines.

They carved their way through the narrow valley as Carl and Nellie flew them expertly through its many twists and turns. As they reached a relatively straight section, Carl turned in his seat to address the Super Zeroes.

"We've got the element of surprise, so Magpie won't be listening out for us," he began. "Let's see if we can keep it like that. From here on, silence should be our watchword wherever possible."

"DAAAAAAAAAAAAAAAM!!!!!" shouted Murph suddenly at the top of his lungs.

"No need for that kind of language, Murph," said Carl, affronted. "Especially after I was just saying that—"

"No, not the rude word!" yelled Murph, pointing frantically out of the windshield. **"DAAAAAAAAAAAM! A massive DAAAAAAAAAAM! Right ahead!"**

They had emerged from a bend in the river. There, blocking the entire valley with an expanse of gray concrete, was an enormous dam. Two curtains of water cascaded down it on either side, plunging into a deep pool at the bottom. And the *Banshee* was about to crash straight into it.

"It's not come up on the radar," muttered Carl. "And it's not marked on the map . . ."

"Bwark!" squawked Billy unhelpfully as both feet inflated simultaneously. **"We're gonna CRAAAAAAAAAAAAASH!"**

"There's no time to pull up." Carl fumbled for the joystick.

Nellie reached out one of her hands to stop him. She'd narrowed her eyes and was peering right at the lefthand waterfall through the cockpit window.

"Yes!" breathed Carl. "I see it! Well spotted, Little Nell!"

Nellie moved the joystick to the left, steering them directly toward the sheet of plummeting water. Murph detected a slight flash from behind it—a blink of light reflecting on metal.

"There's something in there!" he shouted, at the same time as Carl cried out, "Grab hold of something and make sure Flora's comfy! We're coming in hot!"

The *Banshee* smacked into the wall of water. Nellie was straining her eyes so intently it looked as if they might actually pop out. Her knuckles were white on the joystick, and just as they passed through the waterfall she slammed it sharply right.

With inches to spare, the flying car slipped into a wide, low hangar built into the side of the dam.

"It's going to be a bumpy landing!" Carl yelled.

The Super Zeroes slipped and slid around as the *Banshee* screamed into the hangar and slammed into the floor. They were only saved by Billy, who ballooned his entire body to prevent them all from being thrown forward into the cockpit window.

"I'm the human airbag!" he exulted as they bounced into him.

The *Banshee* crunched to a halt less than a foot away from a large black helicopter.

"This is it!" whispered Murph after a long pause in which the only sounds were breathless sighs of relief. "We've found Magpie's secret lair! Nellie, you did it!"

Nellie shook her hair back over her face, but it didn't entirely hide her smile.

"Think we might have lost the element of surprise, though," said Carl grimly. "That was a noisy entrance."

"Then there's no time to lose," decided Murph. "Super Zeroes—let's get in there and get Angel back."

Mary gripped her umbrella: "Mary Canary ready for action."

"Hilda?"

"Artax and Epona ready for action, SIR!"

"Billy?"

"We're gonna DIIIIIIIEEEEE. But also, Balloon Boy active."

"Nellie?"

Nellie gave a tiny salute and an equally tiny squeak to accompany it.

"Carl?"

"Always."

"Flora?"

Flora made as if to struggle into a sitting position, but Carl put a gentle hand on her shoulder.

"You stay here, my love. You're still weak," he said. "We'll get her back."

She nodded at him. "I know you will."

Finally, Carl turned to Murph. "And what about you, Kid Normal? Are YOU ready?"

Murph squared his shoulders as Carl flicked the switch that opened the *Banshee*'s side door. "Ready," he confirmed simply.

Together, Carl and the Super Zeroes left the *Banshee* and started out across the floor of the hangar. It was bare gray concrete—the same material as the dam outside—and the space was filled with noise and spray from the waterfall. The huge helicopter had its ramp down and, they quickly confirmed, was silent and deserted.

"There, look," said Murph, pointing to a small metal

door set into one wall. They followed him over. "Seems like the only way in."

"I don't care what happens next," said Billy, "as long as that door doesn't appear to open on its own like one of those creepy ones in a horror film. That never fails to freak me out."

The door appeared to open on its own, like one of those creepy ones in a horror film. A high-budget, high-tech horror film, though, because instead of creaking open and going "eeeeeeeeeee," the door slid smoothly to the side with a barely audible hiss.

Billy freaked out anyway, his whole head ballooning in panic and making a large, trombone-esque noise that reverberated off the walls.

"IF a FWAPP!" he said through his suddenly massive lips.

"It's not a trap, Billy, it's an elevator," said Hilda kindly.

"Fur boors wopened wom wear woam!"

"The doors didn't open on their own," she replied. "I pushed this button."

"How on earth can you understand what he's saying?" Mary wanted to know.

351

"Faff wha WHY wamma mow!"

added Billy, which explained nothing.

They stepped into the elevator, which was large and silver, and the doors closed smoothly.

"Great," said Murph sarcastically. "More elevators."

"I wonder what this place is," pondered Mary. "Some kind of old military bunker or something?"

(As you're our favorite reader, we can tell you exclusively that Mary was absolutely right. It was indeed a former military bunker, built into the hillside behind the dam long ago for a war that never came. Magpie took it over after the army abandoned it. It's not relevant to the story, but you should feel very smug that you alone now have this information. Keep it to yourself, though, okay? This is our little secret. Don't tell all the other readers. We don't like them as much as you. They smell.)

After a minute or so, the elevator lurched to a stop. The Heroes inside steeled themselves. This was it. Whatever secrets Magpie had been keeping all these years were concealed in this place. It was the dark heart of all his plans. The elevator doors slid open.

They were looking out across a huge, poorly lit room with metal control panels and screens set into the walls. There was a constant, buzzing hum from the banks of equipment—and the panel of lights nearest to them was flickering eerily, not to mention irritatingly.

"Why do the places villains hang out always have really substandard lighting?" demanded Mary.

"The quality of the lighting is likely to be the least of our problems," reasoned Murph tensely, peering off into the murk.

High up toward the center of the room was an odd, pulsating reddish glow. Gingerly, they began to edge closer to the source of this unearthly light.

It was coming from a huge glass structure suspended from the ceiling. The glass was bell-shaped, and it was filled with a smoky, purplish-red light that seemed to be swirling around a large, indistinct shape in its very center. Thick electrical wires snaked from the metal panels in the ceiling and were plugged into various points around its outside.

"It looks like a birdcage," marveled Murph, creeping

closer and examining a large control panel that rose out of the floor a few yards from the glass structure.

The panel was covered with complicated screens and dials. One small green dial was marked **STASIS TEMPERATURE**.

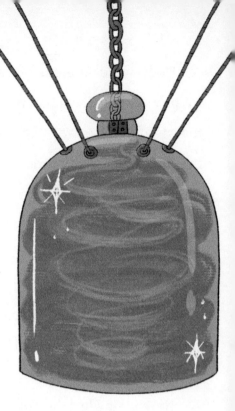

There was a brass plaque at the very top, into which were carved the words **PROJECT WINTER** underneath the neat, stenciled outlines of three black-and-white birds.

"Magpies," breathed Murph. "Three magpies!"

"One for sorrow," began Billy.

"Two for joy," Hilda joined in.

"Three . . . for a girl?" Mary asked tentatively.

She was interrupted by the clatter of footsteps on the metal floor. Carl had rushed past them and was running toward the glass cage.

They all dashed after him.

Carl stopped underneath the cage and craned his neck upward. It was still hard to see through the glowing gas, but now they could just make out the figure of a girl suspended in the center of the glass. She was frozen midjump, with one leg outstretched and her hands clenched in a combat stance. Her long hair flowed out behind her.

"I don't believe it," muttered Carl to himself. "It's her. It's Angel. She's here."

"Goodness me, what a dramatic moment," broke in a cruel, cackling voice from somewhere away in the gloom. "How very touching. And how very tragic it's about to become."

23

Project Winter

They all spun around to try to locate Magpie. He was nowhere to be seen, but Murph thought his voice had come from somewhere near a large metal plinth all the way toward the back of the huge room. As he watched, a small metal cube with red lights suddenly appeared on top of the plinth as if out of nowhere. It slotted into place with a small click.

"Look! Over there!" he cried.

Carl had spotted it too. "That's the Proximity Detonator," he murmured. "He's deactivated the bomb. Thank goodness."

"I told you I would," hissed Magpie's voice, startlingly close to Carl's ear. His approach had been silent and invisible.

The janitor whirled around in alarm. **"Show yourself! Coward!"**

"Keep your ears open," Murph told the other Super Zeroes as they backed into an uneasy circle. "He could be anywhere. Keep your eyes peeled for his lightning."

"Well done on finding my research facility, Chauffeur," Magpie went on, his disembodied voice ping-ponging across the laboratory this time as he taunted Carl, before coming to rest somewhere near Angel's cage. "Like father like daughter, it would seem, eh? Tell me, how does it feel to find out your daughter's still alive, only to realize there's nothing you can do to rescue her, and you have nobody to help you but a gang of useless children?"

"We're not scared of you!" shouted Murph.

"Perhaps. But that's only because you're STUPID!" Magpie was close, too close— whispering right in Murph's ear.

"Now, which power shall I take first?" Magpie mused. "The horses?" he whispered to Hilda. She blanched. "The storms?" An invisible breeze disturbed Nellie's long hair. "Or what about . . . flying? Yes, real flight would be a wonderful thing. I could finally live up to the name you fools gave me all those years ago."

Instinctively, the others moved to surround Mary protectively. "You'll have to come through us first!" shouted Carl.

"With pleasure!" said Magpie, as a huge blast of purple light shot over their heads. A warning volley. They ducked as one to avoid it, but as they began to get back to their feet, Magpie fired another jet from behind them and they hit the floor again.

"Who knew invisibility would be such fun?" Magpie laughed. "I could keep this up all day, watching you bob up and down like the powerless puppets you are. But it's time to get serious. This next one's going to hurt."

Murph might not have been able to see it, but he knew the villain was gazing right at him. He could feel that strange sensation in the air again, like wings of thin metal brushing his skin.

"Zeroes, get ready! He means business this time," he said wildly. "Prepare Capes!"

Billy ballooned a fist experimentally and Nellie shut her eyes as the friends desperately tried to determine where Magpie's next strike would come from. Hilda adopted her usual combat stance. She looked agonized as her two delicate horses began popping and neighing their way into being. Just the thought of them falling into Magpie's hands was unbearable.

But instead of staying near Hilda and awaiting her command, they immediately galloped away to the left, tossing their manes and whinnying.

"What are they doing?" Hilda wondered in panic. "Artax, Epona! To me!" But the horses continued to gallop purposefully across the metal floor before coming to an abrupt stop, rearing up, and snapping at thin air.

"Get away from me!" hissed Magpie's voice.

"They can see him!" Murph realized joyously. "The horses can see him. **You're not so invisible now!"** Murph crowed, as they all turned to face the spot where Hilda's two tiny friends had pinpointed their enemy, and prepared for a fairer fight.

Sure enough, the stooped form of Magpie slowly materialized in front of them. He had his hands clasped behind his back and a mocking smile plastered across his face.

"Impressive," he told them sarcastically. "Most impressive. But utterly pointless, because once again your pathetic reliance on your friends is about to prove your undoing."

Behind him, the elevator doors slid open and DoomWeasel came through. But not alone. He was dragging with him the struggling figure of Flora. Her hands were lashed tightly behind her back and her face was scarlet with fury behind the gag that had been tied around her mouth. Her eyes widened as she saw Angel frozen in the purplish-red light.

"Now," continued Magpie. "I'd like you to line up nicely, one by one, and *give* me your powers. Or I'm afraid the ex-Phantom over there will meet a very nasty end."

TO BE CONTINUED . . .

AFTER THIS STORY ABOUT KITTENS

Interlude:
Alan Rabbit and the
Kitten Kollective

Once upon a time there were three fluffy little kittens, and their names were Meowzla, Yarn Boss, and Fuzz-E Q. They lived beneath a large sycamore tree at the very edge of the forest and loved nothing more than chasing butterflies, lying about in the warm sunshine, and hardcore gangster rap.

One summer's afternoon, Old Mrs. Pollyanna Rabbit had given her son Alan permission to go off for a bike ride all by himself.

"Now then," she told him, "you may go down the lane, or around the copse to gather blackberries, but do not venture into Mr. McDougal's garden. Your father had an accident there."

"What happened to poor dear Papa?" Alan wanted to know.

"He fell into an enormous vat of acid," his mama said, laughing. "Now, fish and fettles, run along. I have packed you a picnic." She handed Alan a basket chock-full of her signature dishes. Kale and hay sandwiches, roast parsnip and beetroot hummus, chocolate-dipped carrot sticks, and three vegan Scotch eggs.

"The Scotch eggs are left over from dinner the other night when Mr. Pobbletoes came over. He has quite the appetite, that one," said Old Mrs. Pollyanna Rabbit. Mr. Pobbletoes, the death metal badger, was an old family friend of the Rabbits and had, like most badgers, a real penchant for Scotch eggs.

And so, Alan Rabbit set off on his adventure, and after an hour of cycling reached the very edge of the forest. He leaned his bicycle up against a very impressive-looking sycamore tree, and decided to rest his fuzzy little thighs. As he was unpacking his delicious picnic, three fluffy kittens appeared.

"Hello!" said Alan Rabbit.

"'Sup, fam?" said one of the kittens. "We're the Kitten Kollective. I'm Meowzla, this is Yarn Boss, and that's Fuzz-E Q. We're very cute kittens, but make no mistake, we don't take no nonsense."

"Oh, I'm sure you don't. Very nice to meet you. I'm Alan Rabbit," replied Alan.

"Do you like music, Alan Rabbit?" asked Yarn Boss.

"Yes. Yes, I do. I love music and I LOVE singing."

"Cool, us too, yeah? We absolutely love sick beats. Would you like to hear some of our stuff?"

"Yes, please," replied Alan Rabbit, tucking into his kale and hay sandwich.

"Right, guys," said Meowzla, "let's drop a sweet verse for Alan."

"Take the bass line out," said Yarn Boss.

"Hold on tight!" added Fuzz-E Q.

Alan Rabbit held on to his picnic basket, just in case this was a vital instruction.

The kittens began rapping the following rap, which you must join in with OUT LOUD, no matter how old you are:

Kitty Rap
by The Kitten Kollective

Here we are, sittin' in the sun,

Rollin' around, havin' lots of fun.

Livin' in a tree coz a tree's rent free,

We call this home coz we're family.

We are cute kittens but we also rap,

We are very small, don't confuse us with cats.

It's the kitty rap,

It's the kitty rap.

Here we go, we're going with the flow,

Welcome to the future,

The kitten rapping show.

Are we cool?

You know the drill.

Of course we are,

We're super chill.

No need to pay us,
Spend an arm or a leg;
Just give us some treats
And the occasional egg.

It's the kitty rap,
It's the kitty rap.

At the end of the second chorus, the Kitten Kollective stopped, folded their arms, and leaned on one another in a freeze-frame.

"That was wonderful," said Alan Rabbit, holding the remains of the sandwich between his big teeth so his hands were free to clap.

"Thanks, brother," replied Meowzla.

"Did I hear you say that you like eggs?" asked Alan.

"That's right," replied Yarn Boss. "Most people associate eggs with badgers, but kittens quite like them too."

"Well, today's your lucky day!" replied Alan, holding aloft the three vegan Scotch eggs in delight. And the four of them sat around for hours, munching and chatting and rapping.

Alan Rabbit had made some new friends.

What a lovely tale. Now, where were we? Ah, yes, Magpie's bunker. You'll like this next chapter; it's extremely dramatic.

24

Ice and Lightning

"**N**ow," continued Magpie. "I'd like you to line up nicely, one by one, and *give* me your powers. Or I'm afraid the ex-Phantom over there will meet a very nasty end."

None of the Super Zeroes moved. DoomWeasel pushed Flora to the floor and placed a foot on her back as she continued to struggle against her bonds.

"Come on." Magpie beckoned them. "This is checkmate. You are trapped. It's time to surrender."

"Never," Murph breathed defiantly. "We might be trapped, but you're alone. Outnumbered."

"Outnumbered. By you?" spat Magpie. "Five children and an old man? Or perhaps you expect your precious Heroes' Alliance to swoop in and save you? I assure you, they're much too busy dealing with the chaos we caused at Shivering Sands."

"We confounded them!" squeaked Mr. Drench. "We released all the prisoners! The Alliance is thwarted!" He began dancing around, releasing his foot from Flora as he cackled: "Victory! Victory! They will all feel the wrath of DoomWeasel!"

While he was distracted, Flora had stopped struggling and begun edging her way closer to Carl and the Super Zeroes.

"Quiet, you pathetic creature!" Magpie bawled at him, finally losing his patience with Mr. Drench's trash can–addled nonsense. "Do your job and pay attention to the prisoner."

Mr. Drench stopped capering. He went after Flora and hauled her back roughly, muttering. He looked hurt.

"See," Murph said, stepping bravely toward Magpie. "You're just like every other villain in history, aren't you? You might be able to force people to help you out because they're scared of you or want something from you, like Mr. Drench. But when it comes to the crunch, you're on your own."

"Why should that concern me?" shrieked Magpie.

"I grow stronger each time I attack. More dangerous than you can imagine! I don't need some pathetic collection of misfits to back me up! I stole two new powers only this week—from your precious Blue Phantom and the head of the Heroes' Alliance! You cannot possibly hope to stop me!"

The other Super Zeroes stepped forward to join their leader, looking at Magpie without fear.

"Murph's right," said Mary. "You're on your own. That's how they defeated you at Scarsdale. You're outnumbered. We're a team."

"TEAM?" screamed Magpie contemptuously. "A pathetic notion. Those who are too weak to stand alone huddle together like frightened insects. Teams are built on fear."

"No," Murph corrected him, "teams are built on trust. These are my friends, and I trust them."

"And we trust him," Mary chimed in, glancing sideways at Murph and waving him a reassuring eyebrow. "So, go on, take our Capes if you want. We'll keep fighting you in any way we can, and in the end we'll beat you. Together."

This show of friendship seemed to hit a nerve.

Magpie was livid. He raised his hands and purple tendrils began crackling around his clenched fists. But before he could strike, a new voice rang out from the side of the room.

"Together."

Magpie spun around.

The elevator doors had opened for a third time, and lined up inside were Sir Jasper Rowntree and the rest of the Ex-Cape Committee. The Gemini Sisters and Lead Head were decked out in their original Hero costumes. Lead Head was spilling out of his slightly.

Sir Jasper lifted his chin in defiance and led his team into the lab.

"Thought you were going home for a cup of tea?" asked Carl wryly.

"Well, I was," Sir Jasper said, a little shamefaced. "But I couldn't shake young Murph's words. He's right. There's room for all kinds of Heroes in this world. It's a lesson I should have learned a long time ago."

"So we're coming out of retirement!" added one of the Gemini Sisters.

"Besides," Lead Head's deep voice chimed in, "who better to have on your side when you're up against this guy than a group of Capeless Heroes?" He indicated Magpie, whose anger at having allowed his old adversaries to sneak up on him seemed to have stayed his hand for now. He had been watching this exchange wordlessly, his face scarlet with rage.

Sir Jasper turned to face his enemy. "So, what do you say, Birdy? Ready for round two? This time we've got nothing to lose!"

Magpie collected himself. "Oh, Tech-Knight. Look

how old you've become," he snarled at Sir Jasper contemptuously.

"Not too old to give you a dry slap in the kisser," yelled Sir Jasper. Without warning, his wheelchair launched into the air and he plunged straight at Magpie. Lead Head and the Gemini Sisters rushed after him. While Magpie's attention was taken up by Sir Jasper menacing him from above, Lead Head managed to get in a solid blow with his walking stick that took Magpie's legs from under him.

"Quick," Murph told the Super Zeroes, "let's take out Drench while Magpie's distracted! Hilda, summon your horses again and stay on lookout. Jasper will need them if Magpie tries to go invisible. Carl, you get Flora as soon as she's clear. Everyone else, with me."

Murph, Mary, Billy, and Nellie led the charge over to the side of the laboratory where Flora was lying on the ground by DoomWeasel. They made to surround their ex-teacher, but were knocked back by the power of an almighty stench.

"You will be defeated!" DoomWeasel screamed at them.

"What on earth is that smell?"

countered Mary, whose eyes were watering. As she peered at DoomWeasel, she could see he was glistening damply. "Are you . . . soaked in garbage juice?"

"Have you been living in the trash cans at Shivering Sands?" Murph added, holding his hands to his face like a makeshift gas mask.

"I have been in hiding, preparing for our greatest triumph," gibbered DoomWeasel, hopping from foot to foot and smelling.

"Hiding . . . in the trash cans," clarified Murph.

"Well . . . yes," admitted DoomWeasel. "But it was worth it, to claim a great reward!"

"The only reward you need to claim is a shower," Mary told him bluntly. "And what reward do you think Magpie's going to give you? He thinks you're an idiot, didn't you hear him? You're just his sidekick."

"I am NOT . . . A SIDEKICK!" Enraged, Mr. Drench ran at them, screaming and flailing his arms around. He might have been a mad, weedy little man, but he barreled into the Zeroes with a ferocity born of the disappointment and

bitterness of decades, and that and his overpowering *Eau de Garbage* was enough to send the four of them flying. It left Flora unguarded, though, and Carl took the opportunity to rush over and ferry her out of harm's reach.

Murph and Nellie found themselves behind the control unit for Angel's glass cage as the Zeroes prepared a counterattack. **Project Winter,** Murph read once again, glancing up at the girl in the mist before turning his attention back to the job at hand.

Away to one side, Billy leaped into action, swinging a huge fist at DoomWeasel, who was skittering this way and that like a rabid shrew as Mary channeled her inner old lady once more and drove him into Billy's path with sharp jabs of her umbrella. Billy's fist connected and laid the little man out cold.

But farther away, the battle wasn't going so well. Magpie had gathered his wits after the surprise attack. He'd used a force field to send the Gemini Sisters shooting across the laboratory. Lead Head he sent sprawling with a flick of his wrist, which brought a huge desk crashing toward the old man, pinning him down. Now he had Sir Jasper in his sights.

Murph could only watch in horror as the control panel of Sir Jasper's wheelchair suddenly stopped responding in midair. Sparking with purplish fire, the chair jerked toward the ground as Magpie's tele-tech took control of it. The chair zoomed away in reverse, slamming into the elevator so hard that the doors buckled and metal ceiling panels rained down on Sir Jasper's head.

Having dispatched his old enemies, Magpie turned to face his new ones in cold fury.

"Watch it!" warned Murph, beckoning the others to join him behind the relative shelter of Angel's control unit. "Sir Jasper's out of action. We're next."

Magpie was concentrating. Bolts of purple fire ran up and down his ragged coat, before a cold, white mist began to flow from him, pooling at his feet.

"Is he . . . growing?" Hilda huffed nervously as she ducked down next to Murph.

"He's getting ready to use a Cape," warned Carl, moving across to join them with Flora. "Hang on—did he say that he'd stolen Miss Flint's?"

"Yeah," said Murph.

"Why, is it a really scary one?" moaned Billy.

"You might say that."

Something very strange was happening to Magpie's hair. As more of the chilly mist poured from him, it changed into a gleaming block of ice. Then the rest of his body began to alter too. Pale crystals formed along his arms and legs as they expanded at an alarming rate.

"She was able to transform," continued Carl, "into a kind of . . . I don't know how best to describe it, really."

The stooped figure of Magpie had by now been replaced with a towering, glittering beast.

"An enormous ice monster!" breathed Mary.

"Yes, a kind of enormous ice monster," confirmed Carl. "That's a good name for it."

"Iiiiice monsterrrrr?" wailed Billy. **"WRAAAAAAAARRRRRRRRRGG GGGGGGGHHHHHHHH!"** the ice monster interrupted, lumbering toward them.

Hilda fearlessly stepped out from behind the control panel and ran to face it with arms outstretched. "Billy!" she shouted as her two horses neighed into existence. "Pop them!"

Billy rushed over to join her, skidding the last part on his knees, which looked cool but was actually quite painful. Heroically, though, he kept quiet about it and concentrated. By the time the cantering horses reached the ice monster they had become two snorting, rearing stallions. They faced it down, battering at it with their powerful front legs.

"BWOOOOOOOAR!" complained the ice monster, flailing its crystalline arms at the horses to deliver a killer blow, but one of its cartwheeling arms connected with a metal control desk. The desk keeled over, and broken glass splintered across the length of the lab floor as a bank of display screens shattered.

"MAARGGGGHHHHH!" added the ice monster, enraged even further by this destruction. It seemed that Magpie hadn't counted on the unpredictability of his latest Cape. He'd sacrificed precision for brute force, and his laboratory was paying the price.

The ice monster pawed the ground like an angry bull—a large bull made of ice that can stand on its hind legs—and charged at the Super Zeroes. One horse managed to get in a kick to its shin, but the monster barely slowed. Billy and Hilda dived to either side as it pounded straight toward Murph and Nellie.

"Grab on!" yelled Mary, zooming in from above as the ice monster bore down on them, roaring and trailing white vapor.

The three friends rose into the air just as the ice monster shot beneath them like an unusually chilly train that wants to kill you. It smashed into the wall, leaving a huge dent in the metal paneling, before backing up and making a wild swipe at them.

"It's got my foot!" shrieked Murph in an embarrassingly high-pitched voice. The ice monster tugged downward sharply, and Mary's umbrella flipped inside out as they shot toward the floor. She managed to slow their landing, but they still hit the ground hard enough.

The impact loosened the monster's grip on Murph, and Murph and Mary scrambled to their feet and began backing away. Hilda and Billy rushed to their aid.

"I don't suppose ice monsters have as many weak points as clowns?" said Murph out of the corner of his mouth as the Super Zeroes regrouped in the center of the lab.

"Not looking very hopeful, is it?" answered Mary seriously.

"FLAAAAAAA AAARRRRRRRR GGGGGGGHHH HHHHH!" agreed the ice monster, crouching and slamming its fists into the ground as it prepared for another charge.

"What about warming things up a bit?" Murph realized suddenly. "Fire beats ice, right?"

"It's risky," Mary wavered. "But it's worth a try."

"Nellie, can you short out some of these electronics?" Murph urged. "If we can just get some flames going . . ."

Nellie nodded and screwed up her face in concentration. The air seemed to thicken with static, and thunder rolled, so loud that it sounded like it was actually inside the room.

Murph's eyes widened as the ice monster looked

for the source of the noise and roared. **"C'mon, c'mon,"** he murmured. Drawing lightning down from the air was one thing, but summoning it all the way down into a secret bunker was quite another. Nellie was shaking with the effort.

As the monster refocused and prepared to charge again, the storm finally broke. Nellie's lightning came crackling into the

382

lab in forks of blinding white. It fizzed up and down the metal walls, which sparked and popped. It flowed around the ceiling and the elevator, and at last it flew to Nellie's outstretched hand, where it gathered in a ball of dancing blue fire.

Nellie slammed her hand into the electrical system closest to her—the Project Winter control panel. It exploded in a shower of bright white sparks.

The control panel was in flames, and small electrical fires had broken out across the lab, but the heat wasn't enough to stop the ice monster. With a horrible nerve-smashing screech like splintering ice, it launched itself into the air toward them, arms outstretched and crystal fists clenched.

The Super Zeroes prepared for impact.

Murph braced himself, determined to fight back in any way he could.

Mary gripped her umbrella.

Hilda bent her knees in her trademark combat pose.

Nellie balled her fists, still bright with white energy.

Billy did the rabbit thing with his ears again.

But the impact never came. As the ice monster

smashed down into their midst, two dazzling bolts of light shot over their heads. They hit the creature full in the chest with such force that it somersaulted backward in the air, spinning around and around and, as it did, transforming back into the ragged shape of Magpie.

He hit the floor with a pleasing smack and lay still, surrounded by a ring of frost.

There were four seconds of complete silence. Count 'em.

The Super Zeroes slowly turned around.

Crouched in a combat stance, on top of the shattered remains of the glass cage that had held her prisoner for the last thirty years, was a teenage girl with long, silvery hair. Her eyes were wide and her hands outstretched. Clearly she had been the source of the beams of bright light.

"Winter's not for me," the girl exclaimed in a satisfied tone of voice. She dusted her hands together and regarded the fallen ice monster coolly. "I've always preferred springtime."

"Angel!" breathed Murph.

"Close your mouth, Cooper," Mary told him.

There was a sudden crunching of feet on the broken glass. Carl and Flora were racing toward Angel as fast as they could, limping but determined. They reached her at the same time and enfolded her in an enormous bear hug.

"Mom! Dad! You found me!" cried Angel. "All right, all right. Relax, dudes," she went on as the hug showed no signs of stopping. "It's only been a couple of days. Anyone would think you hadn't seen me in years!"

Flora sobbed.

Angel stopped and touched a hand gently to her mother's face. "Mom, what's the matter? And . . . why do you look so old?"

Any minute now, thought Murph, *Angel is going to completely and utterly freak out.*

"Magpie! He's up!" warned Sir Jasper sharply, rolling toward them. His wheelchair was operational once more, and he and the Ex-Cape Committee were regrouping as best they could.

The Super Zeroes turned as one to face the spot where Magpie had fallen. He had gotten to his feet and was staring at Angel with a strange expression on his face. He caught Murph looking at him, and his lip curled in contempt, before his gaze was drawn back to Angel once again, as if by a magnet.

He's frightened, thought Murph with a thrill. *He's frightened of her.*

Abruptly, Magpie turned and ran.

"Stop him!" shouted Murph, but it was too late. Grabbing the still-unconscious DoomWeasel, Magpie rushed across the lab toward the gloom in the far corner. As he went, one hand reached out and plucked the Proximity Detonator from its plinth. Then there was a metallic clanging and the pair of them vanished.

"Escape hatch!" shouted Lead Head, who had picked himself up off the floor not far away. "He's made a run for it, the great big coward!" He reached the hatch and banged on it urgently with his fists. "It's sealed shut!"

"He won't get the jump on us," cried Sir Jasper. "Back to the vehicles."

The Gemini Sisters were over by the elevator. "We can't go out the way we came," one of them said, jabbing its control button and gesturing toward its buckled doors. The combination of Jasper's crash and Nellie's electrical antics had proved too much. It was completely dead. "He's slipped through our fingers, the snake."

"Don't be downhearted!" exulted Hilda. "We beat him! He's left, tail between his legs! And we rescued Angel!" She began a little jig of triumph, but it petered out after a few seconds when she realized nobody else was joining in. "Not joining me in the jigging?" she asked in a small voice. "What's the problem?"

Everybody else was looking at the plinth that had held the Proximity Detonator. It had lit up with pulsing red lights.

"Does that mean what I think it means?" said Hilda, all thoughts of triumph dancing out of her head like fleeing ballerinas of the mind.

"He's activated the bomb," Carl confirmed grimly, striding over to the pillar and inspecting a screen. "Three minutes till self-destruct."

"Would it be too much to ask," moaned Billy, "to go into just ONE building today that isn't wired to explode?"

"Well, it's kind of Magpie's thing," reasoned Murph. "So," he said, facing the group, "everyone ready to find a way out of this bunker before it self-destructs?"

"No objections here!" said Sir Jasper.

"Right then, Ex-Capes, try those elevator doors again! Quick! Zeroes, look for alternative escape routes."

Angel joined the Super Zeroes as they desperately searched the walls for a way out. "So, what's the 411 here?" she asked. "Who are all of you? Your outfits are, like, totally tubular."

"I'm Mar— . . . Murph," said Murph, clearing his throat slightly and blushing. "I mean, Murph. Just Murph. Haha."

"Shall we save the introductions for later?" asked Mary a little tartly, as she used a handy fire extinguisher to try to bash in the escape hatch through which Magpie had vanished. But it wouldn't budge.

"Two minutes!" shouted Carl.

The Ex-Cape Committee was puffing and panting with the effort of trying to dislodge the elevator doors.

"We're gonna diiiiiieeeee," moaned Billy. **"The bunker's gonna exploooooooooode."**

"Not . . . helping . . . ," said Mary.

"One minute twenty!" yelled Carl, his arm around Flora protectively.

"And it's really drafty as well," Billy complained. "We're gonna diiiiieeeee in a really chilly, drafty bunker."

Murph stopped: "Wait! What did you say?"

"We're gonna diiiii—"

"No, the other bit . . ."

"It's really drafty?"

"That's it! Billy," said Murph, rushing over to him and looking up, "I think you just saved everyone's lives."

"Oh, cool," said Billy brightly.

"Everyone here—NOW!" Murph bellowed. He pointed up at the large circular air vent way above Billy's head. It was in the center of the ceiling, exactly where Angel's glass prison had been. "That's our way out. Mary, give me your umbrella!

Billy, stand by. Everyone else, grab on to Jasper's chair. Sir Jasper—get ready to take us up . . . fast!"

Whipping off his belt, Murph lashed Mary's umbrella to the back of the wheelchair and unfurled it.

"Hold on and get ready to help us fly!" Murph told Mary. "We'll need all the lift we can muster."

Eventually everyone managed to find a part of the wheelchair to hold on to. Lead Head was balancing on the back, and there was a Gemini Sister perched on each arm. Carl, Flora, and Angel were all draped uncomfortably across Sir Jasper's lap. The Zeroes were gripping whatever part of the umbrella handle they could reach. It was a physics-defying squash and far from dignified, but it worked.

"Right, Billy," Murph ordered. **"POP THE UMBRELLA!"**

Billy concentrated. With a loud **crack,** Mary's umbrella ballooned to many times its usual size.

"SIR JASPER! NOW!" yelled Murph. Sir Jasper's chair lifted slowly into the air, the fans underneath it creaking and groaning with the weight. It began gathering steam as Mary added the strength of her own flying Cape to the mix, rising faster and faster still.

They all managed to hang on as the chair finally smashed through the grating covering the air duct and shot up the shaft like a champagne cork.

"This is going to be close!" said Jasper grimly.

"Wouldn't have it any other way," answered Carl, grinning wolfishly up at his old friend from where he was wedged by Flora's elbow.

The giant umbrella smashed through another metal grating at the top of the ventilation shaft, and they spilled out onto the floor of the hangar where Magpie's Alliance helicopter was parked—alongside the *Banshee* and Gertie.

"Let's move! Go go go!" screamed Murph as they all scrambled for the vehicles. There were mere seconds to spare.

At that moment, there was a huge roar from beneath them and the entire floor shook. A lick of flame spouted from the top of the shaft.

The Super Zeroes made for the *Banshee*, but it was agonizingly slow going with Flora still so weak. Once inside, she collapsed to the floor. Carl was already at the controls, and Nellie joined him as copilot. Through the windows Murph could see huge flames pouring out of the air duct.

"Come on, slowpokes!" crackled Sir Jasper's voice out of the radio. Murph caught a flash of black as Gertie cleared the entrance, then splashed through the waterfall and out of view. The *Banshee*'s jets screamed as it rose ponderously into the air, turning to face the exit, which was almost totally obscured by flames and choking black smoke.

"We'll never make it!" squealed Hilda, looking out of the windshield in horror. The hangar was disintegrating. As they watched, the huge black helicopter was crushed by falling debris and burst into flames.

"We have literally a one in a billion chance of making it out of this alive," muttered Billy.

"Never tell me the odds," replied Carl.

Bouncing from one side to another like a pinball, the *Banshee* made for the entrance, dodging explosions and falling concrete. A metal support fell from the roof, knocking into one of the jet engines and sending them spinning.

"Keep her steady, Little Nell." Carl's teeth were clenched. "Maximum thrust!" He pushed a lever and the car leaped into the inferno.

A huge explosion filled the hangar, turning the waterfall to steam as the silvery-blue car shot through the mouth of the fire and away into the outside world, like a bread roll being spat out by a gluten-intolerant dragon.

Murph smooshed his face against the back window in time to see part of the dam collapsing in on itself. Water spilled over the top as it fell, quenching the fire that was still blazing from the hangar entrance. Before the entire structure was lost to view as the *Banshee* rounded a bend in the river, Murph saw it buried in a heap of rubble and smoke.

"That was righteous!" Angel exclaimed beside him.

All Murph could do in response was breathe a huge sigh of relief.

25

The Pilot

ONE WEEK LATER

"**O**n a ship full of garbage?" asked Flora for the third time, suppressing a smile.

"Yes," answered Murph. "They found Miss Flint stuffed in a trash can, quite a long way out to sea, apparently. She wasn't very impressed."

"But she's back in charge again?" asked Carl, taking a sip of his tea.

"As much as it's possible to be," said Murph. "The HALO system has been useless since Magpie hacked it. But Miss Flint's called all the Cleaners back to Shivering Sands to decide on their next move."

"Most of the prisoners were able to get away after the breakout," Mary continued. "Some made for the remaining helicopters; others managed to commandeer boats. They think Goldfish just swam for it. Assuming he could remember *how*, of course. So now the Alliance really has its work cut out."

"And so do we," added Murph determinedly. "All of us. Every Hero has been told to be on standby. Oh, and by the way, Miss Flint asked us to tell you that your status as a Rogue Hero has been officially revoked, Flora."

"Well, that's nice." The Blue Phantom smiled.

The Super Zeroes were sitting on striped deck chairs in the garden of Flora and Carl's cottage a mile or so from the outskirts of the town. It was surrounded by fields of golden wheat, and not far away Murph could see the silver ribbon of the canal sparkling as it ran between banks of tall rushes. It was the last sunny Sunday of the year, with a low sun bringing out the colors of the trees and reflecting blue glints from the *Banshee*, which was parked on the lawn not far away.

"How's Angel getting on?" Murph asked Carl, glancing at the cottage windows.

"She's doing okay," said Carl. "Whatever that

technology was that Magpie had developed, it seems to have kind of frozen her in time. She has no memory of the years passing. When she broke out of her cage, she thought she'd been trapped by Magpie only moments before. She's glad to be home—but it's just a lot to get used to."

"So, she's suddenly, like, traveled thirty years into the future?" marveled Billy. "Cool! Was she expecting everyone to have flying cars and stuff?"

"Angel's had a flying car since she was a baby," Mary pointed out, slightly sniffily. "And she's the least of our worries. Magpie's still out there. And thanks to him, just about every supervillain going is back at large."

"Sounds like the world needs Heroes more than ever," Hilda said proudly.

"Well," said Flora, "we're ready to fight beside you in the battles ahead. As Mary says, there are dangerous times coming. The Blue Phantom stands with you."

"Really?" asked Murph, his heart beating faster. "But I thought you were retired?"

"I was. I retired the day I lost Angel. I blamed myself,

you know. But that was the wrong decision. I want to make up for lost time. The Ex-Cape Committee came out of retirement to help us, despite having no Capes. It looks like Miss Flint intends to carry on without hers. Well, I'll do the same. Because if you've taught me one thing, Kid Normal,"—she ruffled Murph's hair—"it's that you don't need superpowers to be a Hero."

There was an interval of feet-shuffling as everyone realized they weren't sure what to say next.

Angel appeared at the back door of the cottage. "'Sup?" she asked, seeing the Super Zeroes. "Ooh, tea and cakes, is it? Bad!"

"What's bad about them?" Hilda queried.

"No, I mean 'they're bad.' You know, like, they're really good?"

Hilda looked blank.

"We're going to have to update her slang," said Mary acidly, looking a bit miffed as Murph got up to offer Angel his deck chair.

"Oh, I know!" said Carl, breaking the tension. "Talking of the battles ahead, there's something that I wanted to give you all. Something I think you'll find helpful." Eyes twinkling under his checked cap, he raised his eyebrows and inclined his head toward the flying car behind the Super Zeroes.

"Is it . . . something in the *Banshee*?" asked Murph.

Carl opened his eyes wide, waiting for the penny to drop.

"You're . . . you're giving her to us?" said Mary, completely awestruck. **"You're giving us the *Banshee*?"**

"Well, you said you're on constant standby for missions now. The Super Zeroes will need a way of getting places fast," said Carl. He sounded light-hearted enough, but his eyes were glistening. "I know you'll take care of my old girl for me, won't you?"

"Of course!" said Murph. "But who's going to fly her?"

"I would have thought that was the one question you didn't have to ask," said Carl, pointing to Nellie. "You've got a very promising pilot right there."

Nellie looked up at him as if there were fifty million things she wanted to say. But she only nodded, and Carl did the same, ending with a wink.

"Off you go, then," he told them. "Haven't you got homes to go to? Take her back to my workshop, and make sure you lock the garage door after you." He took a set of keys from his pocket and threw them to Nellie, who received them with a neat overarm catch.

The Super Zeroes climbed into the *Banshee*. Murph looked around the cockpit as if seeing it for the first time, breathing in the smell of oil and warm metal, and running his fingers over the well-worn rows of switches along the dashboard. He couldn't quite believe that this incredible vehicle was theirs.

Nellie climbed into the pilot's chair, pushing his hand out of the way and confidently flicking some of the switches down. The engines began to hum and the cabin lights flashed on.

At the doorway of the little cottage, Carl, Flora, and Angel turned and waved.

"Everybody ready?" Nellie asked softly.

Murph looked around at his friends. **"Kid Normal ready,"** he confirmed.

"Mary Canary ready."

"Balloon Boy ready, but please don't go too fast."

"Equana ready, pilot."

Nellie met their eyes one by one, her face set and serious. **"Rain Shadow ready,"** she said. Then, like the sun bursting from behind a cloud, her face broke into the biggest grin imaginable. "Hold on!" she told her friends, narrowing her eyes and pulling a lever.

The *Banshee* whirred to life and rose into the air. For a second it hovered over the sunlit garden. Then, leaving a delicate vapor trail of different shades of blue in its wake, it shot up over the roof of the cottage and away.

THANKS . . .

First of all, thanks to **YOU** for reading our story.
Now go and write your own!

We'd also like to send a massive huzzah to the
matchless Stephanie Thwaites, and an entire cask
full of awe to the peerless Hannah Sandford.
Love and lamingtons to all our other friends at
Bloomsbury, especially Rebecca, Ian, Emma,
Charlotte, Andrea, and that bloke at reception.

Abrazos muy fuertes to Erica and her magic pencils.
You brought Murph's world to life and
you're truly amazing.

We of course also send peace and love to the
Podcast family.

And thanks to Michael Palin for being Michael Palin.

GREG WOULD ALSO LIKE TO SAY:

Hello! Thank you to my friends and family for your
support and excitement. Having you alongside
me on this extraordinary adventure is the best.
To my incredibly talented and creative Radio 1
team, thank you for always encouraging me to
be as silly as possible.
And finally to Bella—thank you for making every
day at least 100 times better. I love you.

AND FROM CHRIS:

First and foremost, thanks to Jenny and LJ. Without
you it's a waste of time. Thanks to all my brilliant
friends, to the British Library, Primrose Hill
Community Library, and indeed all libraries ever.

© Jenny Smith

CHRIS SMITH is an award-winning author, broadcaster, and parent (a mug saying "World's Greatest Dad" counts as an award, right?). He grew up in leafy Northamptonshire, England, and now lives in not-as-leafy North London with his wife, son, and a cat named Mabel, who can talk. If you listen very carefully to the George Michael song "Outside," you can hear a sample of Chris reading the news. He makes excellent tea.

GREG JAMES is also an award-winning author and broadcaster, best known for hosting BBC Radio 1's *Breakfast Show*, but he hasn't won any awards for being a parent because he isn't one. He circumnavigated the M25 motorway in London during his childhood and is now living with his wife, Bella, and their dog, Bonnie, in North London. Greg and Chris's houses are connected by a secret tunnel they use for exchanging ideas via an elaborate pulley system. He makes terrible tea.

FIND OUT HOW
IT ALL BEGAN . . .

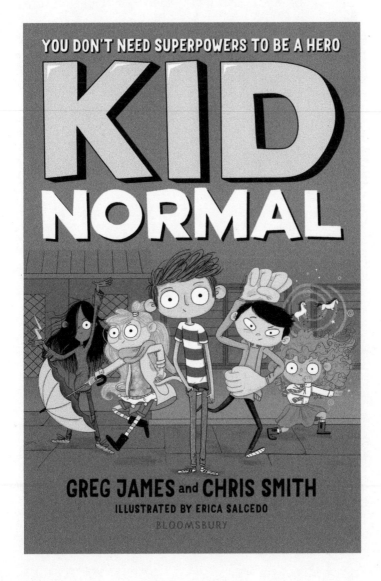

YOU DON'T NEED SUPERPOWERS TO BE A HERO

KID
NORMAL

GREG JAMES and **CHRIS SMITH**

ILLUSTRATED BY ERICA SALCEDO

BLOOMSBURY